The Hidden Queen of Alphas

To my beautiful baby boy, JDogg

It is my greatest privilege to be your mama.

You have brought us all so much joy and taught us all more than we could ever teach you.

You are our little warrior and we all love you so much.

Contents

	Map	IX
	Blurb and Trigger Warnings	XI
1.	Chapter One	1
2.	Chapter Two	15
3.	Chapter Three	29
4.	Chapter Four	43
5.	Chapter Five	53
6.	Chapter Six	67
7.	Chapter Seven	79
8.	Chapter Eight	89
9.	Chapter Nine	99
10.	Chapter Ten	105
11.	Chapter Eleven	117
12.	Chapter Twelve	129
13.	Chapter Thirteen	141
14.	Chapter Fourteen	153
15.	Chapter Fifteen	163
16.	Chapter Sixteen	175
17.	Chapter Seventeen	185

18.	Chapter Eighteen	195
19.	Chapter Nineteen	203
20.	Chapter Twenty	215
21.	Chapter Twenty-One	227
22.	Chapter Twenty Two	237
23.	Chapter Twenty Three	249
24.	Epilogue	257
Acknowledgments		271
About the Author		273
Also By		275

The Reverent Moon Territory

This map is not to scale and is only a basic visual of the territory

Blurb and Trigger Warnings

Synopsis:

Deep in the werewolf kingdom, one devout and pious pack continues to live by the ancient teachings and scriptures of the Moon Goddess, but not everyone is happy about it.

Sweet and innocent Soraya wants more from life than her mother and sisters have settled for. As an unmated female, she must live a pure and chaste life until she finds her mate or face being shunned as a Scarlet Woman. She dreams of being free, but her life is thrown into uncertainty when she finds her mate on her eighteenth birthday. Which path should she choose?

Her best friend, the feisty and determined Fallon, is the daughter of the strict and unyielding Alpha. She has no idea how much danger her life is in until she starts to search for the truth behind her older sister's disappearance. Will Fallon's curiosity and concern lead her to the same fate of the sister whose name is no longer spoken?

Full of intrigue, mystery, passion and love... are you ready for The Hidden Queen of Alphas?

Author Notes:

Dear readers,

Just a short note to thank you for choosing my story. I hope it lives up to your expectations. I wanted to take the time to address a couple of issues that may upset some so that if they so wish, they do not continue to read. I know hard hitting issues are not for everyone and that some readers may find it disturbing and upsetting.

This book exists in a realm that is a part of my imagination. No parts are reflective of real life, and the opinions expressed are not mine or ones I want to impress on anyone to have. The pious element is completely fictional and again is no reflection on any religion or the followers of those faiths.

Please bear in mind that this book contains material of an adult nature, including but not limited to: mistreatment and oppression of women; sexual abuse, including incest; and some violent/graphic scenes. There are also explicit and graphic consensual sexual scenes. If this is an issue, this probably isn't the book for you.

Thank you,
Love, Emma

Chapter One

~ Brandon ~

My eyes roll to the back of my head as the woman on her knees in front of me hollows out her cheeks, taking my cock deep down into her throat. Willing females are always hard to come by when you are a member of the most devout pack in the kingdom. Fortunately for me, I am the Future Alpha, my father's heir, and therefore have a pick of the disgraced ladies who are not only willing to partake in sins of the flesh but are eager and honoured to please me.

When the woman, who is offering her services to me, first approached me, I almost declined. However, the desire to be somewhere else, with anyone else, won out. And at this exact moment in time, as I watch my cock disappear into her welcoming mouth, I believe I made the right choice. The day has been long and hard, and from my past experience, I know it is only going to get worse.

"That's it. Take all of me in," I murmur to her as she wraps her lips around the head of my cock, swirling her tongue around it. She remains a nameless entity; however, I know she is a Scarlet Woman because, unlike the proper ladies in our pack, she doesn't wear a veil and she lacks a mate's mark. With her skilled tongue and accommodating mouth, she blows me like a trumpet.

We are just getting into the swing of things, her lips wrapped around my cock, when my bedroom door blasts open and the sweet smell of cinnamon wafts across the room to me, leaving me entranced. My wolf, Maverick, purrs in deep satisfaction: *Mate!*

In every vision I have ever had about meeting my fated mate, this version of events has never once occurred to me. This is not the way I want it to happen.

I scramble to get up, trying to pull up my pants, but in my haste, I fall over, and the Scarlet Woman face plants into my lap. However, my mate, the one I will spend eternity with, takes one glance at the scene in front of her and bolts out of my room, shouting an apology that is muffled by the compulsory veil the unmated females of our pack are obliged to wear.

Although it only takes me a few seconds to right myself, by the time I get downstairs, there is no sign of my mate. Doesn't she feel the pull? Why isn't her wolf howling to come back to me?

She's not old enough; she doesn't feel it yet, Maverick tells me. I can tell from his tone that he is annoyed at me for jeopardising the mate's bond. How was I supposed to know my mate would finally present herself today, and what was she doing in my bedroom? *She won't want to feel it now after seeing you being deepthroated by a whore.*

My stomach turns, as I search the main hall, looking for her. The thought of being mated to a child is too much for me to comprehend. How long will I have to wait for her? When can I claim what is mine? I wish the first time we met was not in such a crude and sinful manner. What will she think of me? How can I show her that she will be the only one for me from now until the end of time?

My search is cut short when my father, Alpha of the Reverent Moon pack, storms into the main hall. With his face ruddy in anger and his intimidating form standing almost seven feet tall, a sense of foreboding washes over me. This is bad. This is really, really bad. The problem of my runaway mate unfortunately will have to wait. Guiltily, I also think of the willing woman, waiting patiently for me in my bedchamber. My father will kill me if he even has a sniff of a clue of what I have been up to. "Bran, quickly, I need your help. Alessia is missing, again, and we need to find her as soon as possible. She needs to be punished for what she has caused. I cannot turn a blind eye for a second time."

My older sister, Alessia, has a bad habit of getting into trouble, but this time, she has really done it. Our father, the unyielding and sadistic tyrant, will not let his eldest child disgrace him in such a way. In other packs she would be considered the rightful heir, but our pack denies females positions of power. So, even though I am younger than Sia, by less than a year, it is my job, as his heir, to exact my sister's punishment.

The rumours of Sia's sexual exploits have spread fast throughout the pack, and although everyone turns a blind eye when I take the occasional lover, Sia will be dragged over hot coals for even thinking of removing her veil, never mind her dress and cloak. The last time this happened, she was punished, but this time, that punishment, no matter how severe, will not be enough.

It has become public knowledge that she has been lying with wolves and none of them are her fated mate. Her actions have brought the whole foundation of our pack into disrepute. The Shaman and the Holy Circle are up in arms about Sia's insulting behaviour and are now calling for my father's titles. Father has already decided Alessia must go for the greater good. She is a female and therefore disposable to him.

"Don't worry, Father, I know where she will be. I will ensure she knows her behaviour is unacceptable," I assure my father and assemble my team by mindlink, ready to track down my sister.

"You know what must happen, Brandon. You have no choice. Do not let me down." My stomach turns when I hear my father's stark instructions. I know what needs to be done, but *he* looks practically delighted. How can he relish what he knows his son will do to his daughter for her crimes? How can that inevitable prospect cause such excitement in his eyes?

"Yes. I'll take care of it. You can rely on me." My father's cold stare all but chases me from the hall. I quickly return to my room and send the Scarlet Woman away with two gold coins. My hands tremble in fear, for the task I have been chosen to perform is gruesome, but if I don't complete it, my father will oust me. He won't think twice about wiping out his two oldest children if it means he gets to keep his prominent and revered position.

"Are you ready to leave, Bran? I will keep a watch here while you are gone and ensure no one asks too many questions." My brother Clayton, two years younger and nearly as tall as me, stands slouched against the window. I nod to him but don't meet his eye. After today, how will I ever look any of my other four siblings in the eye? "Deacon has gone to collect his regalia for his Shaman training, but Euan is still around to keep an eye on Fallon."

Assured my siblings are all taken care of, I set out to complete my task. After tonight, if my mission goes well, there will be no further threat to our pack because of Alessia's wrongdoings.

From now on, the memory of Alessia will fade like a whisper in the wind.

~ Soraya ~

After I finish school for the day, I head out to help my sister and visit my best friend, Fallon, who is the Alpha's youngest daughter. She finished class early today as her mother, Luna Beverly, was taking her to get measured for her shifting veil. Once Fallon gets her wolf on her 18th birthday, she will get to change to a more sophisticated veil until she finds her mate.

I won't receive a new veil; I will have to wear the same one my two older sisters wore until they found their mates. Since my father died, money has been extremely tight, and therefore, we have to make do. Both my older sisters found their mates within a couple of months of gaining their wolves, so their hand-me-down veil still has plenty of wear left in it.

As a Daughter of the Veil, I am required by Reverentarian law to wear a full headdress. Every female in our pack is given a veil on their eighth birthday and is required to wear it at all times. No one is allowed to see her face, shoulders and especially her hair again until she is unveiled by her fated mate. The only exception is one family member for annual hair grooming, in my case my mother, and then in extreme situations, the healers are permitted to see but not look.

Fallon lives in the Alpha Quarters. This was once the packhouse; however, over time less and less members of the pack were permitted to live there and eventually, it became the home of the Alpha, his family and a few of his close team, such as his Beta and Gamma wolves. The large stone building stands intimidatingly in the centre of our territory. There are rumoured to be over one hundred rooms across the two floors. The windows are numerous, and all light up at night, showing that the Alpha is wealthy and is able to light up the whole house without a concern. The building is surrounded by grassy planes that are sometimes used by the warriors to train. There are lots of pretty flowers and lanterns all around the building, giving it an opulent and grand appearance. As a little girl, I used to dream of living in a stone house like the Alpha Quarters, where it always seems to be warm and safe.

When I arrive at Fallon's home, my sister is here cleaning the bedrooms. Her tummy is swollen to capacity as she reaches the end of her pregnancy. My concern for her is mounting; she looks ready to drop and she should be resting. "Come on, Savana. Sit down, and I'll finish for you." I take the cloth and duster from her hands and instruct her to sit down.

My sister, usually so proud, looks at me with gratitude, as she leans against a chair that is placed outside one of the bedrooms. "Thank the Goddess you're here, Raya. I still have two bedrooms to clean. I'm so slow now that the pups have gotten so big!" I look at my sister; it's true she is about the size of a house and unable to do her work as fast as usual. Her twins are due in another couple of weeks, and she is still working as she can't afford not to.

I know times are hard and Savana's mate can be very strict. I need to try harder to help her at least for the next month or so. "Your ankles are all swollen. Sit there and rest your feet while I clean the next room," I tell her, and unable to deny the need to rest, she sits down in the chair with very little argument.

As I walk towards the room that Savana points out to me, she calls out, "Thank you, Raya, you're an angel. I'll do the same for you when your time comes." Her automatic assumption that 'my time will come' annoys me. Both Savana and our older sister, Sirah, assume I hope for the same fate as them. They found their mates within a couple of months of their 18th birthdays, mated, marked and bore pups. They both followed the expected path set out for she-wolves in our pack. Now, they obviously believe I will do the same. In a few months' time, I will celebrate coming of age, and I will get my wolf. And, from that point, I will be able to sense my mate. I am a ticking time bomb of honour and duty.

There is so much more that I want from life. Having a family is nice and decent, but it isn't all I dream of. I want to really live my life, through the realms of learning, training and travelling.

Training to be a teacher is a dream I'll never be allowed to fulfil unless my fated mate dies and I dedicate myself to the Edors of our pack. However, my destiny is not mine. It is dependent on so many other outside factors. If only I had been born a male, things would be infinitely better.

My deepest heart's desire to travel the great Kingdom of Veridonia, perhaps over to the Edge and down to Aquaport, will always go unmet unless by some miracle, my future mate decides to travel *and* also take me along. If I must have a mate, I want a mate who loves me for being me and not just because we have some bond that dictates we must be together. For as long as I can remember, I have dreamt of being free and independent, but the laws of my pack will forever prevent me having any semblance of what others take for granted.

After cleaning the first bedroom, I double check with Savana which room is left to clean. She points to the one furthest down the hall, but as I walk towards it, a sense of foreboding washes over me. For a moment, I stop, my senses on edge, but I cannot find a single reason why.

I push open the heavy door to the darkened room, and despite the lack of visibility, I can clearly see two semi-naked bodies as they move against one another.

The scene before me shocks me to the core. The Alpha's son… cavorting with a Scarlet Woman, right here in the pack house. His dark, chiselled body is illuminated by the sun that streams through the window that is only partially concealed by white voiles.

My compulsory veil obscures the finer details, and I thank the Moon Goddess for this small grace. However, I can still see his large erection as it sinks repeatedly into the mouth of the woman on her knees in front of him. I shout an apology as I flee from the room.

"Raya? RAYA! Where are you going?" my sister shouts under her breath as I leave.

"The Alpha's son was in there; I'm leaving before he punishes me. He'll know it wasn't you; you don't have a veil and you're massive." My sister huffs in indignation at my assessment of her appearance, but my fear is real; everyone knows that Fallon's oldest brother is mean.

"Well, go on then. Get going!" she instructs me, quickly getting back to her feet and resuming her duties.

I run away until my lungs sting. Running through the village and into the forest, I keep running until I reach the border of our land. Leaving the territory is forbidden because it is unsafe.

Ensuring no one else is around, I sit at the base of a tree and remove my veil, letting my long, golden hair blow in the wind. It's been years since I last allowed the wind to flow through my hair. Emotion battles inside of me. Fear mingles with disappointment, and despite my best efforts, I can't hold my tears any longer. No matter how hard I try, I can't think of a single logical reason for feeling the way I do. Why am I upset? And why does my heart ache?

Before long the pounding of paws breaks my peaceful interlude. Returning my veil to my head, whilst running to hide in the prickly bramble bush, I reach cover just in time.

The Alpha's oldest son, my best friend's scary older brother, who I just witnessed cavorting with a Scarlet Woman, leads a group over the boundary, all of them in wolf form. However, before he leaves, I take the time to watch him from a distance. His nose twitches, and he turns to the direction where I am hiding. I hold my breath until he continues across the border with the rest of his friends, exhaling in relief when he is finally out of my sight.

Unable to resist the luscious berries on the prickly bushes, I pick as many as I can carry home with me. Mother will make fruit crumble and jam with my haul. We can't afford to let decent food pass by, every bit of sustenance is needed in my community.

As I reach the door to my family hut, my best friend, Fallon, runs towards me. I know it is her from her fine clothes, and because her beautiful dark skin glistens under the lace of her trailing veil.

"Raya, can we go somewhere and talk. Something is wrong. Something is really, really wrong."

~ Fallon ~

** Three Months Later **

My mother and father stand proud at the front of the pack's Ceremonial Hall as my brother Deacon takes his oath as a Shaman. The last time this Hall held a ceremony was almost twenty-five years ago when Mother took her vows as Luna to the pack. Despite the time that has passed, the room remains impressive with its rich mahogany panelled walls and floors, the gilded decorations, and the columns and statues of pure brilliant jade, the clearest, most magnificent of greens worth more than any other building in our territory. This is an area of celebration, a room to witness all important occasions. A space that defies the impact of time.

The monotonous voice breaks through my daydreaming. Goddess above, the Shaman are incredibly dull! "By the power that is invested in me, I pronounce you, Deacon Ward of the Reverent Moon pack, a Shaman of the Bastion of Worship. Congratulations, Shaman Deacon." I applaud my brother along with the small congregation that are here by invitation of my father to bear witness. However, I only do it because it is required of me. Inside, I am shocked he is actually going through with it.

Deacon made the decision to become a Shaman after his fated mate died, shortly after they mated and marked each other late last year. Once he had worked through his grief, he had a choice of what he would do with his life. Of course, as a male, he could have taken another mate, a mate of choice, if it pleased him, but no, my idiotic brother is throwing away the freedom he has and is chaining himself to the faith instead. Though at first my father protested his son throwing away one line of our family tree, he relented when the Holy Shaman from the Bastion of Worship made it clear it would be unholy and insulting to the Moon Goddess to deny Deacon his calling. And Deacon made it clear that with his mate gone, the only thing left for him was to dedicate himself to supporting his fellow werewolves on the path to redemption.

What an idiot! I would give everything I own to have a smidgeon of his liberty.

Only certain people are allowed into the Pack Ceremony Hall. Today it is my family and our pack's higher ranked wolves and their families. The rest of the pack will be notified outside in the courtyard, where we begin to make our precession to.

As the Alpha's youngest daughter, I am flanked by my three other brothers and obscured mostly from view. When Alessia, my older sister, was still here, we would hide together and make a game out of the suffocating situation, which made it more bearable. However, Alessia isn't here, not anymore. Although, where she actually is remains a painful, inexplicable mystery.

Three long months have passed by since I last saw my sister. Three whole months of torment of not knowing where she is and if she is safe. In the weeks following Sia's disappearance, her name has been made forbidden. An unspoken rule, and yet a rule all the same. We can not ask where she is. Not that I would dare to ask questions. I might be the youngest, but I have learnt at the heel of my siblings what is good for me, and angering my father and being caught not abiding by the draconian rules of our pack is a death sentence. If the rumours about my sister are to be believed, her disobedience led to her demise. I hope against hope that this is not true, but as time continues to tick away, my hope in Alessia returning to the bosom of our family wavers. Where my sister was once the epicentre of my life is now a vacant space and radio silence.

My concerns about my sister are genuine. Her disappearance into thin air has me worried about myself too. Whatever trouble Alessia had gotten herself into more than likely cost her her freedom, if not her life. What if the same thing happens to me too?

The disregard of my other family members puzzles me. They act as though Alessia was a passing fad that fell out of fashion. Don't they miss her and want to know what happened to her, like I do? How can they act like our circle isn't broken? A piece of our puzzle has gone astray. Their lack of concern infuriates me. I want to hate them for not caring, firstly about Alessia, but also about me for being upset that she has gone without a trace.

In my inattention, I walk straight into the back of one of my brothers, not realising that they have stopped walking. "Fix your veil and stand up straight, Fallon," my oldest brother, Brandon, chastises me under his breath. If Clayton or Euan had told me off, I would have hissed and retorted, but Brandon has changed since Alessia vanished. As the Future Alpha, he has always been stricter than my other brothers when it comes to me, his baby sister, but now he is downright mean and cold.

Swallowing my pride, I know I must answer the Future Alpha, or I will be punished for my insubordination. "Yes, sir," I reply, using the correct title as required in public. I don't want to rile him even more, not today. Not on the first formal occasion since Sia vanished, which raises all the old questions once again. Where exactly is the Alpha's oldest child and why has she been gone all this time?

"Keep walking, Fallon! You're stalling the procession." I yelp when Clayton elbows me in the ribs as he warns me. I will get him back for that later.

Once we reach the courtyard, I quickly scan the crowd looking for my best friend, Raya. There are roughly two thousand wolves in our pack. The square, cobbled courtyard is full to bursting, and the crowds continue to flow down the eight narrow side streets that come off the courtyard. The bunting sways in the wind, and music can be heard even from a distance.

Despite how busy the courtyard is, it doesn't take long to locate Raya. She stands to the left side with her family. Her mother still wears black, irrespective of the fact that Raya's father died over two years ago, but it is the sight of Raya's sisters and their children that catches my attention. Sirah, the oldest, carries one child on her hip, another strapped to her back, and her mate carries a sleeping child too. Savana, who is the same age as Alessia, looks frazzled with twins crying out at her, while her mate stands a short distance away, scowling in indignation. Raya holds hands with a little girl, Savana's oldest child, who is still young enough to not require a veil yet.

I don't notice Brandon watching me until he moves closer to me. Even through my veil, I can see the desire and determination in his eyes.

"Who is she?" Brandon whispers harshly into my ear whilst gripping my upper arm. "Who is that girl you're looking at?"

"Ouch, Brandon, you're hurting me!" I whisper to him as I try fruitlessly to pull away from his painful grasp.

"Just tell me her name. Who is she, Fallon?" I look into my brother's brown eyes, eyes that burn with a passion I have never seen there before. "The one with the pale blue veil. Who is she?"

Anger and worry engulfs me when I realise it's Raya. He wants to know who Raya is. "Why? What did she do? She's my friend; leave her alone, Brandon!" He shakes his head at me, genuine hurt crossing his face at my assumption.

"I'm not going to hurt her! She's mine. My mate. I just want to talk to her, little sister. I do not want to harm her." My mouth falls open in shock and surprise. Raya is Brandon's mate? Why hasn't she told me?

"No! She can't be. She would have said." I furiously refute his claim. Raya is my friend, and I don't trust Brandon anymore. I want him to stay away from me and my best friend. I will never give him another opportunity to hurt someone I love, not after Sia. "I don't know what you *think* she might be, Brandon, just stay away from her." My brother, normally so solemn and contained, stares at me in annoyance.

"She doesn't know we're mates. She isn't of age yet," he whispers back at me, reminding me that although I have recently celebrated my eighteenth birthday and got my wolf, Raya hasn't yet. "I thought she was your friend? Do not deny me, Fallon. What is her name?" I feel his Alpha aura, his right as the Future Alpha to command me, and I have no choice. "She is mine to claim, Fallon. Just tell me!"

"Soraya. Her name is Soraya Burke. Don't hurt her, please, Brandon. She's my best friend." My eyes fill with tears. Thankfully, my veil prevents anyone else from seeing it.

"Why would I harm her? She is mine. She is my blessing sent from the Goddess of the Moon." He scowls at me and my rigid opinion of him, and I frown back, unyielding and unafraid. I still don't trust him; I will never trust him ever again. "I want to get to know her until her wolf presents and she can feel the bond for herself."

Although he can't fully see my face, I still pout in frustration. I have already lost Alessia; I will not stand by while Brandon or anyone else takes Raya away from me, too.

I know I cannot interfere any more than I already have, but before I step aside, I give my brother one last stark warning. "I've got my eye on you, Brandon Ward. Remember, you might be the Future Alpha, but the same blood flows through my veins regardless of our age and gender. I will hurt you if you hurt Raya. That is my solemn promise."

Brandon's eyes widen at the strength of my conviction, but I am annoyed to see he actually looks impressed. "You cannot tell her. I forbid it."

His fear makes me smile. Why is he so scared of Raya finding out? "I won't need to tell her; you're going to, right after the announcement for Deacon."

Shaking his head at me, Brandon reminds me of the pack rules. "You know I can't, not until she is of age and can feel the bond for herself."

Curiously, I watch for his reaction as he looks back over to Raya and see both longing and desperation in his eyes. Will he truly look after her and keep her safe? The Moon Goddess believes so, and without any further reason to deny my brother, I give him one last drop of information.

"Well, you don't have long to wait. It's her birthday next week."

Chapter Two

~ Soraya ~

Standing in the courtyard with my family, while we wait to welcome our new Shaman, amplifies how stressful I am finding the day. This feeling is only compounded when Fallon comes out of the Ceremonial Hall surrounded by her older brothers as part of the procession for the new Shaman, who happens to be their brother, Deacon.

Accidentally catching the attention of Fallon's oldest brother, Brandon, my whole-body flushes with shame and embarrassment as I recall the day I walked into the Future Alpha's bedroom. The thought of him and his naked body has continually caused a mixture of feelings to course throughout my own body. Feelings that are both inappropriate and dangerous.

Not for the first time, I remember the contours of his body, and the now familiar ache begins in my tummy, occupying my thoughts and distracting me. The almost constant impure thoughts trouble me. Imagine if I confessed to our new Shaman what depraved acts I have been dreaming of. He would probably punish me and then run back and tell his brother.

Well, there is no way in the whole kingdom of Veridonia I will confess a thing to Shaman Deacon. No way. Not even on my mother's life will Brandon Ward *ever* know what sinful imaginings I have had as a result of seeing him in a compromising situation! No way at all.

"Ray-Ray, look, look at the shiny!" My niece Anais giggles giddily with excitement as she clings to my hand. She points to the Circle of Shaman and one of the elaborately adorned staff and goblet, opulence of like we very rarely see, if at all.

Following Anais' little finger, I watch in awe at all the splendour. The Moon Goddess alone knows when we will see this kind of event again, and I intend on savouring the festivities.

That is until I feel Brandon Ward's eyes on me, burning through my veil, exposing me and my misdemeanour. He must know. He has somehow worked out it was me who walked in on him that day. My insides turn to jelly, and underneath my veil, sweat beads on my brow. I am going to be punished for sure.

I haven't seen Brandon since the day I walked in on him with his Scarlet Woman. I avoid going to Fallon's house unless I know for sure that he is away. Naively, I hoped that enough time had passed to let him forget about the indecent incident and the person who witnessed it. However, from the way he glowers at me, I know he hasn't forgotten and he isn't about to either.

If only it had been Clayton, Fallon's next oldest brother. He is so kind and understanding that I think we could have actually talked it through. However, I don't think Clayton would do something like that to begin with. He is a good and decent wolf, unlike the Future Alpha.

Looking back to the raised stage area as they introduce Deacon as our new Shaman, I'm distracted by Brandon once again. He glares across the courtyard at me until Fallon distracts him. My heart pounds in my chest, and I struggle to catch my breath. The midday heat beats down onto my covered head and face, only adding to my deep discomfort.

Feeling unsteady, I sway on my feet. Little Anais lets go of my hand and returns to her parents while my mother fusses over me.

"Soraya, are you okay, sweetie?" my mother asks me, her voice full of concern.

Using my dizzy spell as a way to get out of Brandon's eye line, I indulge my mother. "I need to sit down; I feel hot and dizzy," I tell her, and she immediately takes me by the arm and directs me to a small hill that I now sit upon.

However, my reprieve is short lived. "Is everything okay?" I recognise the voice instantly. Brandon Ward is standing right in front of me. "Are you sick?" he asks in a cold, clipped voice.

"I'm fine. Thank you for your concern, sir," I tell him as I look at my feet, not feeling brave enough to meet his eyes despite wearing my veil.

"I will walk you home so you can rest. You may return to the celebration, Mrs. Burke; Soraya is safe with me." My mother nods at him willingly, happy that the Future Alpha has noticed us and wants to help us. Whereas, I am in shock that he knows my name. I don't think we have ever been introduced and I am wearing a veil... how does he know it's me? My hope is that it's through my friendship with Fallon, though how this can be so is a mystery to me. Brandon has never paid any notice to me before.

My mother looks pleased that such a high-ranking wolf is offering his assistance. She practically gushes when she talks to Brandon. "Thank you, sir. Soraya, there is fresh lemonade at home; be sure to offer the Future Alpha some for his trouble." I nod to my mother, as I accept Brandon's hand, while I stand up. If he looks closely enough at me, he will see flashes of my face through the lace of my veil, and so I refuse to look directly at him, keeping my veiled face downcast.

Once we are alone, Brandon talks to me. His voice is deep and soothing. "You're trembling. Are you sure you're okay to walk? I could carry you." I shake my head stiffly. He knows as well as I do that he is pushing a hard boundary. This type of intimate contact is forbidden, and Brandon knows full well it is.

I continue to walk, even though inside I still feel weak and unsteady; anything to put a tiny amount of distance between myself and this dangerously magnetic man. "I'm fine. Honestly. I can make my own way from here if you want to go back to your family."

Brandon smiles back at me. He has beautiful, straight, pearly white teeth that seem to glow in contrast to his dark skin. He doesn't look too intimidating when he smiles; it's just that he doesn't smile all too often.

"Are you trying to get rid of me?" he asks me with the hint of a chuckle in his voice. "I thought we could talk. I have been meaning to say something for a while, but you are one hard person to track down." He continues to hold my hand tight, restricting my ability to move away from him.

My stomach drops in nervous anticipation. I know what he wants to talk about; I just don't want to talk about that. "Do we have to talk, sir?" He frowns at my question, and again, I worry about the consequences of my rudeness.

However, I don't have to wait long for him to reply. "Is talking to me such a bad thing?" he asks me plainly, looking wounded and even slightly angry.

Taking a deep breath, I bite the bullet and answer my Future Alpha. "Talking to you isn't a bad thing, sir. It's what you want to talk about that I find... uncomfortable." I answer as honestly as I can, although the reason my words have obviously hurt him still confuses me.

"I would like to talk, Soraya. I want to apologise. I'm sorry you saw what you did." He looks at me sincerely, and for just a moment, I feel a genuine connection to him. Relief floods me; he didn't want to punish me for intruding. He doesn't blame me for walking in on him that day.

Realising my rudeness towards him is based on my fear of punishment, I quickly attempt to make amends by explaining my actions. "I never told anyone, and I never will, I promise. My sister was about to have her pups, and I just wanted to help her. I never meant to interrupt you."

He smiles at me again, but this time it doesn't reach his eyes. His peculiar reactions to me and my responses draws me closer to him, like a moth to the flame.

"I know you didn't tell anyone, and I want you to know that I appreciate your discretion. I haven't done anything like that since that day and I'll never do it again." Perplexed at the reason my Future Alpha is promising me good behaviour, I stop walking, forcing him to either stop too or let go of my hand.

"What you do is none of my business, sir. Your secret is safe with me. I will never breathe a word to another soul." He not only stops but pulls me towards him too, causing me to crash into his hard chest. My hands are raised to protect myself, and they land with a thud on his broad shoulders, causing them to tingle from the contact.

"What about your mate? Will you tell him?" he whispers into my veil, while gently holding me close to him, and my whole-body flames in reaction to his touch. If anyone sees this interaction between us, I will be whipped and then stripped of my veil, and yet I cannot move away from him.

Mustering all the courage I have, I answer him. "If he commands me to, I have no choice. But there is little chance of him commanding me if he doesn't know to begin with. Besides, I don't have a mate yet." Using all my strength, I push Brandon away from me and quickly take the final few steps towards my hut.

"What can I do to make it up to you? To make things even between us," he shouts out at me once I reach my front door. What a strange thing to say. I am his subject. He has no reason to make things even between us!

There is one thing I would like from him, though, and I waste no time in telling him. "Stay away from me. That's all the payment I need." I don't want or need anything from Brandon Ward, nothing except my own peace of mind and safety.

"Please, I will give you anything you ask for," he pleads, looking so genuine, so eager to please me, and yet, I shake my head and tell him no, but seeing my reaction, he moves towards me.

"I want to never see you again, sir," I tell him plainly, and he laughs at my request.

"Oh, sweet, sweet Soraya. If only it was that simple."

My annoyance grows even more when I hear his words, and I slam the door shut.

~ Fallon ~

All I can do is watch in horror as my brother runs off into the crowd. I am helpless to do anything but pray to the Goddess that Raya will be safe with him. Brandon taking off like this in front of an audience is an unnecessary risk. Presenting himself to Raya in such a forward and public manner puts her under scrutiny, not that he will understand this. Let's face it, Brandon and my other brothers have never had to worry about shit like this, unlike me and Soraya. And Alessia.

Mrs. Burke leaves Brandon to walk Raya home, and my heart sinks, especially when the others near the back turn and openly gawp at my brother, walking alone with a veiled woman. It's fortunate he is the Future Alpha; every other woman would have been dragged to the stocks to be flogged by now if any other man did the same as what Brandon just did. Not that Brandon has any idea how lucky he is. Freedom has always been given to him, and therefore, he doesn't know the value of it.

In my opinion, Brandon is the biggest piece of crap, and I have no qualms telling him so when he finally returns home, looking all happy and smug with himself.

Ensuring no one else is around to overhear our conversation, I pounce on him. Unable to keep the venom from my voice, my wolf, Rogue, is on the surface ready to emerge too. "What did you do? If you scared her, Goddess above help me!" I tell him, which makes him laugh all the more. He doesn't even resist me, allowing me, for the first time ever, to pin him to the ground.

"Don't worry so much, Fallon. Sweet Soraya is more than capable of handling herself," he whispers to me, grinning to himself. I can't recall ever seeing my brother grin before.

Why Raya has to handle herself in the first place is what worries me. Brandon may think he is a big hot shot, but I know how callous he can be, and if my wildest suspicions about his involvement in Alessia's disappearance are true, it makes him a cold-blooded murderer. This means Raya is anything but safe until I find definitive evidence that suggests otherwise.

Although I can easily recall the wistful look Deacon had when he found his mate, it is strange to see Brandon replicating it. We had all poked fun at Deacon for the way he pined and instantly fell for a girl he hardly knew. Is this genuine? Does Brandon really feel this way about Raya?

"Will you invite her here? I need to spend more time with her," he asks me, still distracted.

I stand my ground; he is not using my connection to Raya for his own gain. "No. Go away, Brandon. Do your own dirty work. She's *my* friend." He scowls at me in an attempt to intimidate me. He might be the Future Alpha, but he is not the boss of me *yet!* I may fear what Brandon can do, but I will not wilt away from him. He will get nothing from me unless it is a direct command that I cannot deny.

"I don't know why you are so stern with me, sister. Surely you want your friend to have her mate? You seen what happened to Deacon when–"

"STOP!" I shout. I don't want to even think about the suffering Deacon went through. It was devastating to watch the first time around. I roll off Brandon and walk away from him. The further away from him I stay, the safer Raya will be.

⁕⁕⁕

After our nightly prayers, my mother sends me to bed. As always, I remove my veil, but instead of going straight to sleep, tonight I pretend to settle. After waiting for a little while, I get dressed again, but this time I cover my hair with a hooded cloak before I climb out my bedroom window to freedom.

Landing on the ground in front of my window, I look around to see if any guards are nearby before allowing the mindlink to open between myself and my team.

Miss Fallon, are you there? Usual meeting place in ten minutes.

Running at my full speed, I head to the west of the territory to an old, abandoned compound. Inside the barbed-wire fence is a collection of broken and neglected items. Things that are ignored because they are apparently of no use or value to anyone anymore.

Under the cover of darkness, I quickly locate the hole in the fence and crouch low so I can climb through it.

"You took your time!" The voice of an older male carries over to me, causing me to smile. I expected him to have an opinion on the length of time he has waited for me to get here.

I smile at my comrade. Despite being old enough to be my grandfather, he didn't hesitate to come to my aid when I began a secret investigation of my sister's disappearance. "I couldn't shift in case I got caught. Are the others here yet, Ernest?" As if on cue, the four other men come into view.

"Hey, little bird! You're finally here. So, did you find out why Brandon ran away during the ceremony? What's he up to?" Ernest's son, Elton, asks after bowing to me.

For the first time since I brought this band of misfits together, I withhold the information I have. I downright lie to the men who pledge their loyalty to me. In the back of my guilty mind, I tell myself I have to do this, for Raya's sake. I must lie to protect her. I lie without any remorse as it is for the good of my best friend.

"My father instructed him to help the widow Burke when Raya was ill." Their faces all fall in abject disappointment. "Sorry, guys. But what information do you have for me? Do you have sightings or reports of my sister?"

They all look back bashfully, and my heart begins to sink again.

"Don't tell me that you still have no news about Alessia? It's been over twelve weeks and there is no trace of her." My voice rises as my anguish grows inside me. I don't want to let go of my hope, for to do so would be to admit what everyone else believes. Until I see it with my own eyes, I will never believe the rumour, which is that Alessia is dead.

"We heard whispers of a new Scarlet Woman working the docks, so we are going to check that out after our meeting, but there is no trail. There is nothing leading us anywhere, little bird. We might have to accept that–"

"NO. Don't say it. Don't even think it. I will never give up…" Ernest stands beside me and awkwardly pats my shoulder in an attempt to comfort me.

"We won't give up either, little bird. I promise you that we are at your disposal until we find your sister and uncover the truth about her disappearance. Come on, boys, let's head over to the docks. Good night, little bird. Sweet dreams."

On the verge of tears, I run back home. The wind pelts me in the face and the rain begins to pour, as I scale the wall to my bedroom window. The hand and foot holes are slick and harder to grip because of the rain, and I am relieved when I finally reach my window, which I scramble through ungracefully.

The light flicks on once I stand back up, and dread floods me. Who has caught me out of bed and, worst of all, without my veil?

My mother, Luna Beverly, sits rigidly in my high-backed chair, with my veil in her hands.

"Mother, I can explain." My voice trembles with utter fear. What will my punishment be? Will I vanish in thin air just like Alessia did?

My mother stands up and paces across the room to me before she raises her hand and slaps me across the face. My cheek flames and stings, but her whimper stops me from reacting.

"What were you thinking, Fallon? What if it had been your father or your brothers checking on you?" The murmured ranting continues, and I listen intently to every word, absorbing the information she inadvertently gives me. "Do you want to vanish like Alessia did?"

Horrified by her question, I shake my head at her. "No. I'm sorry. I miss her too."

My mother's large, brown eyes assess me, annoyance mingled with love and fear pouring from them. "Then learn from her mistakes. Keep your veil on and your head down until you are mated. Do as I say, Fallon, or I will lock you in this room. I will do whatever it takes to keep you safe."

She pulls me tight to her in a desperate embrace. "Please, Fallon. Do not make the same mistakes as your sister. Do not be so careless and do not trust your father or brothers."

Reeling at her bleak alert, I quickly reassure her so she knows I understand. "I promise I will do as you ask me. But, please, tell me: where is Alessia? Do you know?" Shaking her head back at me sadly, she confirms she doesn't know anything.

"I don't know, Fallon. I really, really have no idea what happened." Her anguish is so apparent that I have no doubt that she is telling me the truth. "All I know is that I have a horrible feeling deep inside that I will never see her again, and I can't bear the thought of losing you too."

~ Soraya ~

After running away from Brandon, and shutting the door firmly closed behind me, guilt flows through me until I fall to my knees and pray to the Goddess for forgiveness. How can I hate and fear someone but also feel attracted to them at the same time? Keeping busy should help curb the forbidden thoughts that continue to trouble me. Relief fills me when a much-needed distraction presents itself. A few grains of sugar on the ground that mother must have spilt when she made her lemonade are my saviour. I scrub the cold stone floor in the kitchen with the small, stiff brush and the soda crystals. We don't want or need ants in the kitchen to add to our worries.

Along with my shame and embarrassment is a lingering confusion that refuses to go away. How had Brandon identified me? Why is he so insistent about making things up to me? He is the Future Alpha, and I am the daughter of a dead omega and his pauper widow. I am merely vapour to the likes of Brandon Ward. Full of the same compounds but not really relevant.

Full of concern, I ruminate so much that the whole house is gleaming by the time my mother returns to our hut, but my mind is still no clearer on the motives of Brandon Ward.

My mother fusses over me when she sees me. "Are you feeling better, sweetie? Did the Future Alpha get you home safely?" Her questioning eyes burn into mine, giving me a fleeting thought that my mother may have read my mind.

"Yes, he walked me to the road sign and watched me until I was safely in the hut. He didn't have time for lemonade." She looks back at me, crestfallen. Her disappointment is so obvious to see, but I struggle to understand why.

This evening we have just about enough to make a meagre nettle soup, mixed with the herbs we grow in our window pot, and the cool lemonade chases off our sweet cravings. We have no bread or vegetables left, and despite taking my fill, my stomach growls and rumbles all evening.

My hope that my mother will accept my explanation and therefore end the discussion regarding Brandon is all but shattered when she continues to probe me about why Brandon came to my aid. She questions and muses about it right up until our nightly prayers, until I finally ask her to stop.

"Mother, I do not know what goes on in his mind. Quite frankly, he scares me, and so I would prefer to forget about the whole incident and move on."

"As you wish," she mutters under her breath, and we spend the rest of the evening in silence.

My mother no longer rambles on about Brandon, but he still takes up most of the space in my thoughts, and it begins to worry me. Thoughts of that day when I walked in on him continue to intrude at the most inopportune moments. A couple of times, during my dreams, I am the woman with him and the yearning inside me is ferocious. I am frightened I have been corrupted; that his impure behaviour has tainted me. I dare not tell anyone because of the consequences I will surely face. Plus, I don't even know how I could explain what is happening to me, when I'm having difficulty understanding it myself.

Since Brandon held me the way he did, I know now how it feels to be in his arms, and the thoughts of him and of us have simply multiplied exponentially. I toss and turn all night, my peace of mind abandoning me, and in the short reprieves when I am able to actually sleep, Brandon visits me in my dreams too.

The following morning, an early morning knock at the door disturbs us from our scripture study.

My mother answers the door and then calls for me to join her too. In the Huts where we live, this usually means someone is about to be born or someone is about to die. But not today.

The grocer's son stands at the door with two large wicker hampers: one in his hands and the other at his feet. His exertion is evident by the flush to his face and the patches of sweat that stain his shirt.

"Soraya, he says it's for you."

Thinking this must be some sort of early birthday present, I thank the young boy, but he shakes his head. "I'm sorry, miss, but he told me I have to take it inside for you."

My heart sinks in trepidation, and I question him even though I already know the answer, and probably will not like the answer. "Who did?"

"Future Alpha Brandon. He left a note and told me to bring you whatever else you need." Any hope of squashing my mother's questions is completely and utterly ruined. She raises her eyebrows at me, as the young boy carries both hampers to the kitchen table. "My father said just pop in and tell him what else you want and need, and we would be honoured to get it for you."

After he takes his leave, my mother says to me, "Don't tell me there is nothing more to this, Soraya. Whether you want to see this or not, that boy has his eye on you, and I beg you to be careful. Your own mate could present himself in six days' time; do not throw away your life because Brandon Ward has turned your head."

Unable to explain why Brandon feels indebted to me, I assure my mother that I will continue to be a model Daughter of the Veil and that I will not do anything to jeopardise my future.

As we unpack the hampers, I think about Brandon and his reasons for sending such a generous gift. Is this his repayment for my discretion? Has he turned my head? My mother's relief and squeals of delight stop me from finding Brandon and pelting him with the luscious plump, red tomatoes that still grow on a vine. An abundance of fruits and vegetables, of all shapes, sizes and colours, fill one basket. My mother, so desperate to keep us fed, practically swoons when she sees the potatoes and root vegetables that will fill our stomachs much better than the nettle soup we have left over for tonight's supper.

When I open the second hamper, my mother begins to cry. Since my father's untimely death, we have lived off pennies. I will sometimes get work to help, but my mother wants me to finish my studies. My sisters will spare us a bowl of broth or some potatoes whenever they are able, and then whatever we can forage is ours to eat or trade. Now, in front of our very eyes are the ingredients we need to keep us not only well fed but satisfied too. Spices we can't grow, eggs, cheese, fat, flour, milk and cream. Beans and barley, sugar and sausage. Luxury items cram every part of the second hamper. Items I have never seen or haven't laid eyes on for a long time.

"We will have a feast tonight, Soraya. You must invite Brandon too. I'll bake him a cake." I haven't seen my mother with such a spring in her step since before my father died. She pulls the huge pan from the back of the cupboard, the one rendered useless for so long because there has been nothing to fill it with.

I'm happy that my mother has a reason to feel hopeful, but I'm conflicted too. I don't want to be in Brandon's debt, especially if he intends on recalling this debt. I don't trust him, and I still fear him. Fallon has her suspicions about his involvement in their sister's disappearance, and if they are correct, Brandon is a very dangerous man. A man I do not want to cross.

This afternoon, my mother opens the door of our hut, and we place an old table outside and bring out the big pan, the cakes and the breads, and the whole hut community comes out for a bowl of my mother's thick stew. This community has helped us through our toughest time, and we will never forget that. Our bounty is theirs too, and we will not see another family go hungry while we have a feast.

The children come back for another slice of bread that I spread with my mother's jam. The day has turned into a jovial party with the children all playing together and the women gossiping while the men smoke and talk about work. Pride fills me that I am a part of this area, and I am grateful to be in a position to repay them today, even if it does put me in debt to Brandon Ward.

My head sweats under my veil. I will be glad to get my new veil for my birthday. It is lighter, and it shouldn't be as hot as this one. I sit down, and when I look up, Brandon is at the road sign again. This time he leans against it casually, while he watches me from afar, but once he knows I have seen him, he comes over to me.

"That food was for you and your family," he says bluntly, without greeting me. His rudeness infuriates me, and I therefore refuse to stand and bow to my Future Alpha.

"This *is* my family; we look after one another here." I expect him to argue with me, but after opening and closing his mouth a couple of times, he grunts and then shrugs.

"Whatever. If that is what makes you happy." This puzzling remark riles me further, and I can't hold back my questioning any longer.

"What do you want, sir?" Unable to keep the force of my annoyance out of my voice, I am pushing the boundary here, but the whole situation is confusing me, and I just want it all to stop. With Brandon being the Future Alpha, I know better than to disrespect him, and sassing him definitely counts as disrespecting him.

Brandon surprises me by smiling at my retort. "I was checking on you after yesterday. I also wanted to ensure that my gift arrived... and I can see it did." My face flames in embarrassment. I am being rude and inhospitable to the man who has filled not only my belly, but the tummy of my whole community.

"Thank you for your thoughtful gift. It was very kind of you." He looks down at me with a massive smile on his face. He looks so handsome: tall and strong, and the tight knot in the pit of my stomach begins to twist again.

For a moment, I notice that Brandon's eyes flash black. I watch curiously as he closes his eyes and clicks his neck. He has a tic on his jawline that twitches when he sets his lips into a firm line. "See, sweet Soraya, that wasn't so hard. I hope we can be friends. Enjoy your night with your family."

As he walks away from me, I frown in bewilderment. If I don't want anything to do with Brandon Ward, then why on earth do I feel so disappointed that he is leaving so abruptly?

Chapter Three

~ Brandon ~

Since I found out that Soraya is indeed my elusive mate, she has constantly been on my mind. Being honest, I have thought of little else for the past three months but the petite, veiled beauty that will await my claim once she comes of age. When I noticed Fallon looking in her direction, my heart leaped with joy; Fallon was the key to my mate's identity.

Now, I know who she is, where she lives and we have spoken, but it's not enough. My mate is a good, devout girl, and as such, she is aloof and distant with me. How I crave to take her into my arms and unveil her, to kiss her lips, and whisper sweet nothings in her ear in my attempt to woo her. I will give her, my Future Luna, the whole world and more. I just have to be patient while we both wait for the time to be right. We must do this correctly, in accordance with our laws as a pack. I must unveil my mate during our mating ceremony. Everyone else will see my fate before I do, but it doesn't matter to me; I know deep in my gut that she is the most beautiful she-wolf.

My new favourite hobby is spending time musing over my sweet Soraya. The way she resists me leaves me spellbound. No one has ever denied me before. It makes me want her all the more, but I will not ruin or spoil this. My sweet girl deserves to be unveiled in the correct way, and I am more than happy to be the wolf to give that to her.

I have pulled her into my arms just once, to sate my curiosity, and even though I instigated the moment, I was bowled over by how good and complete I felt with her in my arms. Since that moment, all I want is more. I want to claim my mate, and knowing her birthday is a few days away fills me equally with jubilation and impatience.

When I held her in my arms, I also could not help but notice how frail she is. She is petite, but there is no muscle or fat on her bones at all. I know that the community in the Huts tends to be poorer, but Soraya felt like a bag of bones. Who has been looking after her? With her father gone there won't be a natural breadwinner in her home, so how are both her and her mother surviving? Their hut, although clean and well kept, screams of deprivation and poverty. The canvas that is held taut by the beams of wood is worn, and I could easily see a few areas that need repairing as soon as possible.

The situation brings to light the dire conditions some of the most vulnerable members of our pack are living in. While they starve to death, we stand by and do nothing. As the Future Alpha, it is my responsibility to look after my whole pack. I am failing in my most basic duty.

The baskets from the greengrocer are just the start, I will ensure that my sweet wants for nothing, I will build her up, making her strong and ready to bear the future of this pack.

I can't believe my eyes when I check if she received my gift. Standing next to her mother, with her heavy, blue veil covering her almost entirely, they both happily distribute the food to the other residents.

Maverick demands that I go and talk to her immediately, but I resist the urge to take charge and within a few minutes I am glad that I did. Watching as Soraya distributes the food to her neighbours shows me how she is born to be a Luna. Who else could be so selfless and good hearted? As she plays and converses with the adults and children alike, I know for certain the Moon Goddess has blessed me above and beyond what I deserve because my Sweet Soraya is perfect in every way.

Returning home brings the same overwhelming sense of foreboding that hangs over me like a large, black cloud. Just as I thought, Alessia's name and memory is fading with every passing day. The only thing keeping her alive is Fallon's incessant fussing about her. My ability to ensure Fallon is safe depends vastly on her giving up on finding our sister. I often wonder who is the more stubborn, me or her? Her fight to find our sister makes me believe she has more determination than anyone I have ever met, and I am proud of her for that. But at the same time, that determination will land her in exactly the predicament that made Alessia disappear in the first place.

My father continues to lead the pack like a tyrant, favouring the rich and well-placed members over the unfortunate. His callous attitude towards Alessia's demise sickens me to the core. Was this wolf always so cold, or did being Alpha change him over time? I do not want to face the same fate.

Even his mate's pain and desperation at her child being missing doesn't soften his attitude. In fact, I think he enjoys seeing my mother suffer. My mother continues to suspect me and my brothers for Alessia's disappearance, and she is becoming hypervigilant around Fallon now too. My mother's distress pains me, but I have to remind myself that I did what was needed to protect the rest of us.

Now that I have found Soraya, it puzzles me even more why my father can allow my mother to live in such discomfort. I want Soraya to have the best of everything. Her safety and happiness will be paramount to me. For her to look at me the way my mother now looks at my father would shatter my soul.

As I walk through our family residence, I realise how cold and clinical it is. The halls are adorned with thick carpets and rich tapestries. There are glittering chandeliers and fresh flowers. The smell of fresh bread or the lavish dishes that fill our stomachs every evening waft around, creating what should be an ambience of a happy home. But my home is devoid of love. Soraya and her family hardly have two beans to rub together, but they have each other; they have a community and a mutual respect and togetherness. My home to the naked eye looks idyllic, but the saying that looks can be deceiving has never been truer.

The heavy wooden doors to the main hall are uncharacteristically closed, and after pushing one open a smidge, I catch the tail end of the whispered conversation between my father and Clayton.

"Does it mean she is still alive, though? Brandon didn't bring a body back, but I believed him when he told me he had killed her." My father's voice has an edge of worry to it. I have never heard him use this tone before.

"I don't know. Are you one hundred percent certain she was the one? Could The Promised Queen still be out there, undetected?" Clayton adds.

I make an attention-grabbing entrance, so they won't suspect me of eavesdropping. "Why are these doors closed?"

The reactions of my father and brother are very telling. They both shift their bodies and change the conversation, pretending that they never discussed what I overheard.

That suits me fine. This way, I know they are suspicious and that I need to be on my guard. For now, it's not just my safety I have to be concerned with.

~ Fallon ~

After catching me out of my bed, and outside the house, without my veil on, my mother refuses to leave my side for even a moment. My brothers eye us suspiciously, and my mother re-directs them, telling them she is giving me instructions from the Scriptures of the Moon Goddess, and they quickly scamper away. Brandon is the only one who hovers about. He tries to mindlink with me a few times, but I block all his attempts.

As the day rolls into evening, my mother insists on staying with me until I fall asleep. I begin to feel suffocated by her and her constant and imposing presence. "This is what I will do day-in, day-out if I must, Fallon. If this is what it takes to keep my baby girl safe, then I will do it."

The lesson is clear, and having had my mother overwhelm me all day, I am sure I won't do anything to impose this treatment full time. "Okay, I promise I won't do anything stupid. You can trust me to stay in my bed. I'm sorry for worrying you." My mother nods solemnly and finally returns to her own bedroom.

How will I ever find Alessia now? It's beginning to feel like an impossible task, but if I think of it as such, a gorge opens up inside me. I can't let go. I need to find my sister. Maybe it won't be tomorrow or even this year. Maybe I will have to take on this task alone, but I have to keep trying. Alessia is my sister, my blood, and I have to believe she is still out there.

As usual, I sit with Raya for our study group. Our task is to analyse the Legend of the Moon Goddess, an ancient fable passed down through the generations. The text we have to concentrate on is called 'The Promised Queen'.

The old scriptures are sacred to our pack. The leather-bound parchment book is heavy and old, though never dusty or moth-eaten thanks to our constant study of the words written by our ancestors. The scriptures form the basis of the Reverent Moon ethos and the lore we follow as a pack.

I hoped I would get to talk to Raya about Alessia and my mother and ask her advice of what to do, but the chances are few and far between today, and I am distracted by a part of the scripture we are reading.

The segment of the Legend that has caught my attention is the fallout between the two Moon Goddess sisters. Up until this point, I have never really taken much notice, thinking it all to be nonsense, a story told to young girls to keep them in line.

The scripture says:

The Goddesses of the Moon, twin sisters, Diana and Celina, blessed the werewolves of Veridonia with the gift of a mate, the most treasured bond a wolf can have. Two halves of one soul bound together for all eternity once a mark of love is mutually made.

Most of the werewolves graciously accepted their fate and recognised the bond for the cherished gift it was. Others abused the power it gave them, and the sisters quarrelled about what should be done to those who exploited their gift.

Diana believed the gift should remain unchanged; the suffering of a couple of wolves was outweighed by the happiness and contentment of the majority. Celina objected, sure that there was another way to even the power between mates.

Eventually, Celina became overly concerned about the power it gave one mate over the other and began to doubt the integrity of the bond. She introduced the clause of Rejection and the added benefit of a Second Chance.

These changes angered Diana, who declared it a blasphemy against the sacred bond they had created as a gift, and the sisters, once so close, grew into mortal enemies.

The war began as the twin sisters clashed over the adage for a decade until Celina, enraged at Diana's stubbornness, sent an assassin to poison her sister.

Forewarned, Diana took this opportunity to attack her sister, but instead of admitting defeat, Celina pierced her own heart with a dagger and died in her weeping sister's arms.

In order to bring balance to the generations to come, the Moon Goddess, Diana, promised the werewolves that a Queen shall be born into the most loyal pack in the Kingdom. The Queen would be the reincarnation of her sister, holding all otherworldly powers, and she would be a living demonstration to the whole werewolf kingdom that there is power in love, that war is not the answer and that the bonds that tie us can also set us free.

As a final pledge to her twin, Diana changed her mind and kept the added clause she had fought her sister over, finally appreciating that Celina had been right all along.

I re-read the text twice, completely immersed in the words. Alessia and I are five years apart in age, but we had been so close. I can never imagine going to war with her. Parts of the other lessons in this book start to come back to me, but it is all jumbled up, and I struggle to recall it properly.

"There is a copy of the scriptures in the library. I'm sure your mother would give you permission to borrow them," Raya whispers to me when the teacher turns her back.

Our teachers are all female, all dedicated to the faith, but unlike my brother who got to become a Shaman, females have to renounce everything in their life and become an Edor, a teacher of the faith. They wear dirty grey and blue smocks and instead of veils, they shave their heads as a sign of their status. To me they are utter weirdos. I hope my mate is from another pack so I can get out of here. There is no equality, no future and no hope for the female species here.

"I need your help. You know I wouldn't ask if I wasn't desperate. I need you to meet my team tomorrow tonight. My mother caught me out of bed and not wearing my veil; I cannot take another risk yet." Raya raises her head, and although I can't see her face properly through the veil, I notice her eyes widen.

"You want me to go and meet your team? What if I get caught? I can't even mindlink yet!" she mutters under her breath. She has every right to be afraid, and I would have asked the same questions myself.

"Please, Raya, please help me. You know I wouldn't ask, but how am I ever going to find Alessia?" Raya hushes me, before agreeing to do it, and overcome with relief, my eyes fill with tears.

The Edor, sensing our distraction, warns us to carry on working or we will be moved away from each other. Not wanting to write this down, in case it is intercepted, I will have to wait until after class to talk to Raya again.

"Okay, I will do it just this once, Fallon. You best hope to the Goddess I don't get caught too." I thank her profusely for helping me. "What are best friends for? We need to find out where your sister is. There may be one small complication, though." She looks around to ensure no one else is listening in.

"What complication?" I ask her; however, I have a growing suspicion of what it might be.

"Your brother Brandon has been sniffing around me. I think he might have suspicions about you and, therefore, me." Unable to break the solemn oath of revealing a mate to another, I allow her to believe this may be the reason because I don't have another lie or explanation prepared.

"Don't worry, I have the perfect way to distract Brandon. You don't have to worry about him." I truly believe I have the ultimate way to take advantage of Bran. He has repeatedly asked for more information about Raya, and so tomorrow night I will distract him with everything I know that he might find useful.

"Okay, Fallon. If you think you have this under control, I will help you. But just this once. You know the consequences if I am caught. I don't think my mother would be as understanding as yours"

As if on cue, Brandon appears in the garden. His eyes burn as he watches Raya from afar. I mindlink him. *She thinks you are acting weird, so stop acting weird. What are you doing here?*

Brandon scowls before retreating slightly. *As crazy as it might seem, Fallon, I am ensuring my mate is safe.*

Under my veil, I roll my eyes. His obsession is going to get either him or me caught.

~ Soraya ~

Watching Fallon studying the scripture so intensely confirms how seriously she feels about her sister's disappearance. I know these scriptures like the back of my hand, but Fallon has never taken any notice during our studies, declaring it all 'a waste of time'. But now, she clings to the words like they are salvation, like the convoluted words have become hidden clues that hold the secrets of her sister's disappearance.

Having two sisters of my own, I know I would be as devastated as Fallon is if anything happened to them. And so, I do have a lot of empathy for Fallon and her family and want to help in any way I can so that they find out what happened to her.

As we are leaving for the day, Brandon shows up at the ladies' Edor complex, looking as surly and unhappy as ever, and I don't miss the exchange between Fallon and him. When I ask Fallon what he wants, she calls him a douchebag.

"Did he tell you about the hampers he sent me?" From the gasp she makes, I guess he hasn't. "He sent half the harvest to me and my family. I'm worried about what repayment he is going to expect from me."

"I will tell him to stay away from you. Do you have any idea why he would be interested in you?"

The image of Brandon's hot, hard body, dark and glistening and completely naked, fills my mind, and I almost yelp at the almost instantaneous reaction of my body. "No, I have no idea other than me being friends with you," I reply, my voice sounding strange.

Thankfully, Fallon is also distracted and therefore doesn't notice any change in me or question me about my reactions.

"Fallon, I need a word, before you leave, about your research paper." Our Edor chases after us, waving papers in her hand. The sun bounces off her shaven head, and the smock she wears hangs like a tent around her frail body.

"Just give me a minute and I'll walk back to the courtyard with you," Fallon calls behind her as she follows the Edor back to her office. Fallon's veil flows all the way past her waist, completely covering her head and most of her upper body.

It bellows out in the wind behind her as she races to catch up to the Edor. If it wasn't for the clips and combs holding her veil in place, it would completely blow off her head.

I sit down on the grassy plain while I wait for Fallon to return. The sun is shining, and although my whole body is covered from head to toe, it still feels nice to have the sun warming me. A large shadow blocks the sun that has been beating down on me. I open my eyes and through the mesh of my veil, I can see Brandon standing over me.

"What were you talking about just now?" My heart begins to beat frantically. His voice has become familiar to me because we have spoken so many times in the past few days. "Soraya? What were you and Fallon discussing?"

Finally, I look up into his eyes, although I know he can barely make mine out because of the obstructive veil. "Why are you so interested, Brandon? Surely you have more important issues to deal with as Future Alpha than the musings of two girls?" Brandon shifts uncomfortably in front of me. I wonder if any other girl has ever questioned him and why he is allowing me to do so. "As Future Alpha, it is my duty to ensure that the females in my pack do not bring its reputation into disrepute by acting inappropriately." He pauses before continuing lecturing me. "As a brother, it is my duty to instruct my sister on the behaviour I expect from her and her friends. I will punish those who act inappropriately. Tell Fallon our mother wants her to go straight home." His answer not only reminds me of why I should be more respectful, but of the power he holds if I don't comply.

Without so much as a farewell, he stomps away from me. His polo shirt stretched tight across his broad and firm back rippling with his muscular movements, showing me how well built and strong he is. I never realised how tall and manly he is before. I have no business realising it at all.

"What did he want? Is he bothering you again?" Fallon asks as she returns to me. Her face looks like thunder; Brandon is really starting to annoy her.

Shaking my head to her, I reply, "He asked me to remind you that your mother wants you to go straight home." From her moan of disgust, it is evident she is feeling frustrated.

"So, will you meet my team tomorrow? As you can see, I'm being watched." I nod quickly to her. "You're the best, thanks. Now, we best run before my mother gets her tail in a twist!"

This evening, as I burn cheese onto the bread that the greengrocer delivered today, I am unable to stop thinking about my exchange with Brandon. He told me he will punish those who act inappropriately, and yet I have been openly disobedient towards him on several occasions now, and he hasn't reprimanded me.

The table is already set up outside the door, and I begin dishing out the cheese and bread to the children. They are unused to having such fine food twice in a row, so I have to ration their portions. I don't want them to overindulge and get sick. The children, however, have other ideas. "Please, Raya, just one more piece!" they shout to me, and I can't resist their cute little faces.

"You're a natural with them." Brandon Ward is at the Huts once more… I don't think he has ever been here before he walked me home, and now he seems to always be here.

"Future Alpha Brandon, what a pleasure to see you here. Are you hungry?" His eyes flash black once more, and I can sense a fire burning within him, something deeper and more meaningful than anything I have ever experienced before. I want to see that look in his eyes, but I know better than to provoke a beast.

"That food is for you and your community. I have spoken to the greengrocer, and he will bring fresh supplies each day for you to distribute." I am stunned by his generosity and kindness. He has left me feeling speechless

"I- I don't know what to say. Thank you, Brandon. From the bottom of my heart, from my whole community, thank you." Nodding at me curtly, acknowledging my gratitude, it is clear to see in his eyes that he is happy that I appreciate what he has done.

"Future Alpha, what a pleasant surprise. What brings you to the Huts again." My mother's voice is cool and to an outsider transpires as friendly and helpful. To me, I recognise that suspicious, guarded tone.

"Mrs Burke, thank you so much. Soraya is actually helping me with a wellness project I am undertaking as part of my Alpha training." My mother's eyebrows shoot into her hairline. Attempting to hide my laughter is hard, as her reaction is comical. "I hope you don't mind her helping to distribute the food from the project evenly amongst your community?"

"No, not at all. That is very kind of you, sir. Soraya, you're happy to continue helping the Future Alpha, right?" I nod my head, as my mother and Brandon both look at me. When they see my agreement, they both have matching smiles.

"Soraya, is it okay if I just have a few minutes of your time, please? Are you able to continue serving, Mrs Burke?" Brandon asks my mother, who is now very eager to help.

"Yes, of course. Soraya, there is a pitcher of iced tea, offer our guest a glass."

I walk back inside our hut with Brandon right behind me. My heart pounds, and the sweat begins to bead under my veil once again. My hands shake as I pour the iced tea into a glass for Brandon.

"Are you nervous around me?" he asks bluntly. I nod to him. "Why is that?" He looks genuinely interested in my reply, and that empowers me to be honest with him too.

"Well- you're very powerful and important, and I'm worried about how I have to repay you for your generosity." His eyes grow wider with my confession, but I can see sincerity there too.

"This is *my* repayment to you, sweet Soraya. There is one thing you could do for me. To appease my curiosity." Although his skin is dark, I can still see the start of a blush on his cheeks. I like that. It makes him appear more normal, and so I agree to hear his request. "Tell me, Soraya, because I cannot get the thought out of my mind: what colour is your hair?"

Chapter Four

~ Fallon ~

When I arrive back home, my mother sits at the table in the dining room with my brother Deacon.

"I've asked Shaman Deacon to join us for some guidance, but I would like for us to sit down and talk." I roll my eyes, safe in the knowledge that neither of them can see my eyes and, therefore, my disrespectful gesture.

"Mother tells me you are confused about what happened to our sister and that you may need some support. Is there anything you want to talk about?" Deacon asks me, looking solemn in his black and white regalia. This is the same boy who used to threaten me with frog spawn and chase the bogeyman away from under my bed. Now, he is a stranger to me.

"Knock it off, Deacon, for the Goddess' sake!" I shout out before I can stop myself.

"Fallon Ward, your brother is a man of the faith now, and you will respect him and address him appropriately. Shaman Deacon, please accept my apologies for my daughter's insolence." My mother and brother share a small smile, and the raw rage bubbles up inside me.

"No, I don't want to listen or talk. This is all crazy," I screech at them both. My wolf, Rogue, is so close to the surface right now that I know I have to get away before I lose all composure.

"FALLON! Come back!" both of them call as I retreat, and I can clearly hear my brother running to catch me before I leave the house.

However, he has no chance of catching me. I have a head start and have already bolted from the house. Deacon will have a hard job finding me. Running as fast as my legs can carry me, I head straight through the courtyard, down the meandering streets, and into the forest, the only place left in the world I can ever be myself.

Trying to yank off my veil so I can shift only results in hurting myself even more because the combs and clips that hold it in place are tangled in my braids. Defeated, I end up sitting down on a toppled tree trunk so I can separate the two without causing myself any further pain. My eyes cloud with bitter tears. Alessia is missing and presumed dead, Brandon can't be trusted, and now, I don't even recognise Deacon any longer.

Soon, I will lose Raya too, because once she turns eighteen years old and gets her wolf, she will feel the mate bond with Brandon and she will simply become his mate - a mere extension of him, all thanks to the backward customs of our pack.

"What are you doing out here without your veil on, Fallon?" I snap my head around toward the sound of the voice so fast that the muscles in my neck sting in resistance. One of my other brothers, Clayton, stands by another tree.

"I was about to shift but my veil got caught in my braids. It's fixed now, so turn around so I can shift." Clayton shakes his head at me.

"Let's sit down and talk for a couple of minutes about what is troubling you, and then we'll run." He walks over to me and sits beside me on the tree trunk. "You've grown up, little sister. It's been such a long time since I saw your face that I forgot what you looked like."

My tears fall at his words. I can't hold in all the hurt, confusion and frustration any longer. "Don't you find that strange, Clayton. You are my brother, but because I am female, you haven't seen my face or hair in years. Yet, I can look openly at yours."

Clayton chuckles a little but places a comforting arm around me before he answers. "Well, yes, of course it is strange. In the other packs, the girls don't have to wear veils. I suppose that is what sets us apart, what sets you apart." He rubs my back, as I weep against his shoulder. "The Promised Queen is to be born of our pack. We have to guard and protect every female until we are given our Queen. Recite the words with me. You know the words." Having heard the lessons and read the texts myself, I have heard this explanation a million times. Almost automatically, I chant the words of worship that are ingrained in us.

"To the most devout, the blessing of the divine will bestow. Learn. Protect. Reap and Grow," we say together, and I laugh a little when we finish at the same time.

"But what if it's not real, Clayton? What if it's just a story someone wrote?" My brother stiffens beside me, and the comforting arm around my shoulders suddenly becomes suffocating. The hand that had gently stroked my back and arm now grips the tender skin, his nails biting into the sensitive skin. "You're hurting me, Clayton. Get off me!"

"Of course, it's real! Stop being such a spoiled brat, Fallon. I never want to hear you say those words again. Unless you want to end up dead just like Alessia, the whore."

As his words filter through my mind, my stomach turns, and I vomit on both him and myself in reaction. "What did you do to her? Where is my sister, you monster?" I scream at him, chunks of vomit spraying from my mouth, hitting his shoulder.

Clayton grabs me by the chin, pressing hard until I squeal in pain. "You are disgusting, Fallon. Go home. Keep your mouth shut or you will end up like the sister you love and miss so much. *I* will make sure of it."

I kick him full force in the shin, and with my veil in my hands, I run as fast as I can. I hear the familiar sounds of my brother shifting behind me as I run away from him. Zagan, his wolf, is of Alpha lineage and is therefore large and fast and has no trouble catching me.

I fall to the ground when Zagan's large paws connect with my shoulders. Horrifyingly, even when I submit, Zagan shows me no mercy. My blood curdling screams reverberate around the forest when his jaw snaps around my neck. I have never ever seen Clayton so angry or aggressive. I mindlink my plea to my brother. *I promise, I will never question the scriptures or the legend ever again. I promise. Please let me go home.*

The pressure on my neck recedes ever so slightly, but then agony shoots through me. Clayton shifts back and looks deep into my eyes as he breaks both my legs. The world swirls around me, the smell of damp peat on the ground fills my nostrils, and bile burns my throat.

My tormentor isn't finished. While using one hand to press my face into the dirt, he forces one of my broken legs to bend while he threatens me. "If you EVER try anything like this again, Fallon. I won't just break your legs. I will chop the fuckers off and feed them to the hounds. Remember your place. You aren't a child any longer, and I will punish you as an adult."

Through my ragged breathing and tears, I agree to never again question the stance of the pack.

Clayton walks away, leaving me exactly the way I am. The agony renders me motionless, and all I can do is lie on the ground until my body manages to heal enough that I can sit. As a werewolf, I am able to heal faster than a human, but two broken legs will still take a couple of weeks to fully heal.

The pain in my legs is nothing in comparison to the anguish that twists my broken heart until it is no longer whole. Clayton has never so much as raised his voice to me before. This assault is completely out of the blue, and it shakes the foundations of who I am as a person. It changes the tapestry of my life, of my past, present and future. I can't help but question: *Are all my brothers cruel and dangerous?*

It takes almost an hour before I am able to move, my body trying its best to heal this damage.

Where are you, Fallon? Everyone is worried. Please, talk to me, I want to help.

I weep once again when I hear the voice of my final brother, Euan, echoing in my head. Can I trust him? Out of all my brothers, I would have trusted Clayton the most until now, but Euan and I have always been closer. I suppose us being a year apart in age helps with that.

Don't tell anyone. I'm in the forest and I'm hurt. Will you help me please?

Within minutes Euan is next to me. "Fallon? Where is your veil?" Unlike Clayton, Euan averts his eyes, knowing he is not meant to see my face or hair before my fated mate does.

"I think I dropped it; it'll be that way." I point him in the direction that Clayton hunted me down from. He quickly finds my veil, and I cover my hair and face as fast as I can. Euan examines the back of my neck where Clayton mauled me.

"Fallon, I recognise these marks. I know who did this. What did you do to anger him?" How did he recognise them? Does that mean that Clayton has done this before? To whom? Euan's voice is whisper-soft, gentle, there is no trace of anger, and he has complete control.

"I asked if it was fair that I have to wear a veil and he doesn't and I questioned if the scriptures are more than just a story." Euan sits beside me and holds my hand. His large, calloused hands are already double the size of mine, and yet he is incredibly gentle.

"You were always far too astute for your own good, little sister. We have a monster in our house. Keep those thoughts in your head for now; it's too dangerous, Fallon." I nod my agreement to him, relieved that he is at least who I remembered him to be. "Alessia was asking similar questions when she disappeared, do you understand?"

Furiously, I nod at him. "Good. Come on, let's get you home so I can help you with your wounds. I have some witch hazel left from last time."

"Did he do this to you too?" My heart pounds erratically, and my mouth alternates from being too wet to dry. Relief floods my senses when Euan shakes his head, indicating no.

"No, he didn't do it to me. I tried to save the last person he did it to. I'm glad I got to you in time. Now, no more questions. I have told you it's dangerous."

As Euan carries me home, I can't help but wonder who he tried and failed to save.

~ Euan ~

Fury flows through me as I carry my little sister home. No matter her crimes, I will always protect her. The marks on her neck and the way her legs are broken instantly brought flashbacks to Heidi and how I couldn't save her. Her harrowing screams and gurgling as she passed away will haunt me until I die. It is a lesson I will never forget, nor will I ever forget the person who did it and why.

Brandon has his hands full. I know that, and I respect that. Deacon has his head buried in the sand as always, and so it falls to me to protect Fallon and equip her with the knowledge she needs to move forward so she can protect herself. It sickens me that I have to protect her against our own brother, but I will never fail again. Another defenceless female's life cannot be lost because I took my eyes off the ball.

I refuse to lose another sister, because my father and a bunch of old warlocks are frightened to hand over a smidgeon of power to a woman.

Fallon is trying her best not to cry out, but even I can see how her legs have set wrong. She must be in absolute agony, and I fear that she may never use her legs again. "We need to get our story straight. Mother will be terrified, and Brandon will lose his shit if he knows someone hurt you."

My little sister simply nods her head in agreement, a sure sign of the terror and agony she must be experiencing. Fallon is not a follower; she is a trailblazer. Inquisitive, brave and smart. She is of Alpha blood just as much as me.

"Is this how Sia died? Euan? Did he kill Sia?" Fallon questions as her head begins to droop. We cannot go down this path tonight. I know she is desperate for answers, but my overwhelming need to protect her takes paramount.

"I don't know, Fallon. Listen to me, you fell over while running. Mother mustn't know the truth, okay?" She nods her head, and I feel her body relaxing into me. Her consciousness is fading quickly, but I have to got her to understand first. "Tell me what happened, Fallon, and then I'll let you sleep."

"I fell in the forest," she murmurs to me. I kiss her through her veil to where I expect her temple to be, and when I detect her body loosening, I know she has definitely lost consciousness.

I've found her, but she's hurt badly and unconscious. I send out the alert to my family, and Clayton is the first to respond.

Did she tell you what happened to her? His question is very telling. He wants to know what I know. Fortunately, I can play the ignorance card.

No, I just told you she isn't conscious. The family all gather in the courtyard and then rush towards me when I come into view.

"Thank the Goddess you found her, Euan. The healers are on their way." The relief is evident in my mother's face as she gathers both Fallon and I in her arms.

The only members of the family not here are our father and Brandon. Although I know Clayton is around somewhere, he doesn't come over to check on our baby sister and her injuries. His indifference sickens me. Brandon not being here is problematic, and I'm intrigued to know what has him distracted.

The smells of the healers haunt me once more, and when unwelcomed flashes of Heidi play through my mind, I retreat. Fallon is with our mother now. Clayton will not be able to hurt her any further this evening.

Deacon's ashen face stops me in my tracks; however, he quickly looks away when I try to make eye contact, inserting his head firmly back into the proverbial sand. I will get no help from him today. No matter how much he tries to hide behind his Shaman regalia and his stance as a man of faith, I know my brother still mourns his lost love.

When the healers see my sister and assess her injuries, there is much murmuring and muttering before they whisper in my mother's ear.

"Is that really necessary?" my mother answers with panic evident in her voice. "You will have to get permission from the Alpha; he will have to consent first."

However, the healers are insistent. "I'm so sorry, Luna Beverly, but we have to act now, or Miss Fallon will lose her legs; the blood supply has been cut off for a long time and she already has a large clot forming."

Fallon cries out in pain as she drifts in and out of consciousness, and I chastise myself for not finding her earlier.

"Where is Brandon? He is the only one who can give consent while the Alpha is away."

Everyone shifts uncomfortably until finally Deacon tells us what he knows. "Brandon has gone down to the Huts. He says he is helping to set up a Food Initiative as part of his Alpha training. I'll go and see if I can find him." He reluctantly leaves to summon our brother, and as I watch his retreating back, I wonder at Brandon's sudden fascination with the Huts. I cannot recall him ever visiting that part of our territory despite being the Future Alpha.

The head healer returns to us, and although he directs his concerns to my mother, it is Deacon and I that he is imploring for permission from. "I'm sorry, we can't wait any longer for The Alpha or Future Alpha to give permission. If we don't do this now, she could die. The blood is pooling and clotting in her legs." Panic and anxiety flood my senses. I can't lose another. Not like this.

"What is going on here?" my father's voice booms out across the hall. "Why the hell is Fallon sprawled across my dining table and my hall filled with healers?" Everyone immediately submits to our tyrannical leader, terrified of the consequences if we don't.

My mother steps towards my father, her mate and partner, but he pushes her out of the way, and she falls in a heap on the floor.

"Alpha, Miss Fallon has been seriously hurt in an accident. We need to reset her legs and operate as soon as possible." My fathers eyes involuntarily move from side to side, assessing the healer who speaks to him.

"Then what are you waiting for? Save her fucking life, but not on my dining table; I'm hungry and I want my dinner. Beverly? Where is my food?" Everyone scatters around, stumbling to save Fallon, but also to leave the room so my father's meal is not interrupted. "Euan, where is Brandon? Why wasn't he watching your sister?"

As my mother leaves the hall with Fallon and the healers, I try to prepare for one of my father's questionings. I can't help but wonder who is really facing death right now: Fallon or me.

Chapter Five

~ Soraya ~

My hands tremble at Brandon's question. "I think you should leave, and I don't think you should come back. You know what you are asking for is forbidden, and I will not throw away my life and my fated mate because the Future Alpha thinks he can turn my head." Brandon's face changes from curious to horror in the matter of a second.

He steps towards me, but I step back, ensuring there is a dignified distance between us. "Soraya, I'm sorry. I pushed too far. I don't want you to do anything you don't want to. I am sorry." He sounds so sincere, but I can't risk being seen as an immoral woman. I would be unveiled, shamed, and shunned by society. Brandon needs to go and find some other Scarlet Woman to fulfil his curiosity, because I won't. That is not the kind of person I want to be.

"I still think you should leave. My reputation is already tarnished by associating with you. I will not allow you to ruin me. My mate deserves someone pure and untainted. Please leave me in peace." I desperately plead with him because I want to tell him my hair is yellow. A part of me would like to let him have a peek at a lock and touch it with his huge, rough hands, perhaps even smell it. I want Brandon to enjoy it too, and that frightens me. I shouldn't want that with anyone other than the man I am destined to be with unless I am an immoral woman.

"Soraya, we haven't done anything wrong. You haven't tarnished or tainted anything. You are perfect. You are so perfect to me." My heart thumps so loudly that I am sure my mother will come in and demand to know what is causing all the racket. I can feel the heat emanating from Brandon as he edges ever so slightly against me, and the draw towards him is overpowering. I want to be close to him. I want *him*.

This is the knife's edge, the treacherous balance between what is good and what is right. It has to stop; I must stop this right now.

"Brandon. Please. I want to give myself to my mate when the time is right. I need you to leave. If you feel anything for me, anything at all, then you'll do what I ask and not come back here. Please." I choke out the final word, and although I feel his hand gently cup my cheek through my veil before he steps away from me, he is gone all too fast.

"I would give you anything you asked for. I hope you know that." He takes one more glance back at me, his handsome face full of hurt. "Until our paths cross again, sweet Soraya, take care."

The silence of his departure fills the whole hut.

My mother returns inside once she has finished sharing the food we have.

"Future Alpha Brandon told me you were feeling unwell. Is it that time of the month, sweetie?" I shake my head at my mother. I want nothing more than to cry into her arms, but I can't tell her what Brandon asked of me. I know the rules as well as the next person, and there is no way I will be able to justify my feelings.

"No, I think it was the heat again. I'm looking forward to changing this veil." She seems to accept this explanation without much difficulty.

"Well, he has arranged for us to have daily deliveries of fresh food. He said he or one of his brothers will be back to review it next month. I don't know how you managed to do this, Soraya, but the whole community will be in your debt." And now I am very much in Brandon's debt. How did I let this happen?

This evening I go as promised to meet Fallon's team; however, they still have no news for her. Worried about being caught, I don't linger. Instead, I agree to meet them again on the night of my birthday.

The next few days go by quickly. Every night we distribute the food that Brandon has generously arranged. Every day, I attend lessons with the Edors, but Fallon doesn't come. I am too afraid to bump into Brandon to go and check on her, and so, I ask my sister when she is visiting us to get some food for her family.

"Miss Fallon fell and hurt herself badly in the woods. She had to have her legs reset and so she is on strict bedrest." I guiltily think about my best friend in agony, scared and alone. I haven't been to see her because I am too cowardly to face her brother. Well screw that.

Straight after class I walk to the Alpha Quarters to see my friend. I take some currant buns we have left over and a small bunch of grapes that arrived this morning before I left for school.

Warily, I knock on the door and wait to be granted entrance. I am relieved to see Clayton opening the door and not Brandon. "Hello, you're a friend of Fallon's, right? What's your name?"

I bow to him before answering. "My name is Soraya, sir. And yes, I'm Fallon's friend. I heard she had an accident and I just stopped by to see if she wanted some company."

"Well, isn't that thoughtful of you, Sayara. Tell me, are you the young woman my brother has set up a program with, from down in the Huts?" I nod to him, noticing he got my name wrong and that he knows Brandon had at least helped my community. Clayton smiles, and I notice he has a lovely smile, not unlike Brandon's actually. "Brandon will be sad to have missed you then. He has left the territory to deal with a conflict to the east. He should be gone for three weeks or more. Come on, I'll take you to Fallon's room."

It comes as a shock that Brandon isn't here, and my own reaction to the news deeply worries me. Why does Brandon being away cause me so much disappointment? I asked him to leave me alone, and he has done exactly what I have asked of him. And yet, I am sad he has gone so far away and for such a long time. My emotions and irrational reactions confuse me even further, and I am sure I am beginning to lose my mind.

"So, Brandon never said why he chose you as his mascot? Do you know why?" Clayton asks as I climb the grand staircase behind him.

"No, sir. I believe he felt a duty towards me and my community after I almost collapsed at your brother Deacon's ordination ceremony." He nods back pensively.

"So, you're not his mate then?" he further prods. This unanticipated question stuns me. Clayton stops abruptly, right in front of me, causing me to bump into him.

"What? No, sir. I don't have my wolf yet. I am a dedicated Daughter of the Veil. I haven't met my mate. I can't until I am eighteen years old." Flustered, I reply as quickly as I can. I no longer feel safe or reassured. I wish for Brandon to be here instead of Clayton.

"And you wouldn't lie to me? Has Brandon told you to lie?" He grips my arms, and terror sparks through every nerve in my body. Clayton is not what he appears. He isn't kind, not like Brandon. I fear what will happen to me.

I continue to answer Clayton, crying out when he grabs my arms harder and pinches the delicate skin. "Lie about what? He sends vegetables to my mother, and she makes soup for the community. There is nothing else to tell." Clayton releases my arms, tapping them gently before removing them completely.

"My dear girl, of course that's all, I'm just playing with you. Wait until you hear about how clumsy Fallon has been. Two broken legs, can you believe it? She needs to be more careful. She is a Lady of the Veil and needs to be more... graceful, don't you think?"

Clayton is giving me the creeps. I had always thought of him as the fun, easy-going brother. I am starting to see how wrong my presumptions have been.

However, his enquiry about Brandon being my mate leaves me fretting. I'm eighteen years old tomorrow. I will get my wolf and will be able to find my mate. If Brandon is my mate, why has he gone away? Have I really pushed him away for good? Or is Clayton just fishing for information?

The only way I'll know for sure is when I see Brandon again, and the Goddess herself knows when that will be.

~ Fallon ~

Euan brought me home, where, as he had already told me, my whole family gathered together after they frantically searched for me for over an hour.

"What happened?" our mother asked us both when she reached us. Euan placed me gently on the table, and I heard Deacon summoning the healers.

"Fallon was shifting in the forest and had an accident. I think her bones have reset funny; she had already started healing when I found her," Euan told the room, and my mother stepped aside so the healers could check me over. Then I don't remember anything beyond the pain that torments every inch of my body.

My mother cries as she holds my hand. I can tell I'm back in my own bedroom. My legs burn with pain. I wake up, and it must be several hours since Clayton broke my legs. "Tell me what happened, Fallon. I know this was no accident." However, Euan and I had already agreed, before we arrived home, to stick to the story that I fell over.

"It was an accident, mother. I was running too fast, tripped and banged my head, and when I woke up, I couldn't walk. Euan found me and carried me back here." My mother's eyes narrow into thin slits, giving her a cat-like appearance. She looks unconvinced and mean.

"We'll discuss this later. The healer needs to check your legs again."

I'm told my legs had to be rebroken and reset straight into splints. My mother holds my hand when I howl in agony as the healer checks my dressings. The healers say I have to stay in bed for two weeks and they will reassess me.

Later this evening, Brandon returns home in a foul mood. When he is informed of my condition, he rages all the more.

"Who did this to you, Fallon? Give me the name of the bastard who hurt you and I will sort this out. Who had the AUDACITY to touch you?" he roars at me, and I can see Maverick, his wolf, just waiting to burst out.

"Please don't shout at me, Bran. I've had enough for today. Please." Brandon's face clouds over, his torment is evident, but I have a suspicion it is more than just my injuries that bothers him.

What happened? Is it Raya? I enquire through our mindlink so the others don't know what we are discussing.

"Everyone, get out. I want to talk to Fallon, alone. NOW." No one dares to ignore Brandon when he is in this kind of mood. By rights, my father remains the only person who has the power to refuse Brandon's authority, but my father isn't here, and therefore, everyone else files out of my room with no rebukes or complaints.

She sent me away. Told me to stay away. She doesn't know she's my mate and therefore thinks I'm trying to ruin her.

My brother looks devastated. Is he genuine? Or is he doing all this to break down Raya's walls only to hurt her in the end?

Are you going to do as she asks? He nods back sadly to my questions.

I have to. The only way to show I will stick to my word is by sticking to it. It already hurts so much to be away from her.

The mate bond is notorious for both the joy and pain it enables between the fated pair. Having yet to meet my mate, I have not experienced the sparks and tingles that are said to run between the flesh of a mated pair, confirming and reiterating they are destined to each other.

The downside of the thrilling benefits of the bond is that it can kill a wolf to be apart from their fated mate; it is said to be the worst pain in the world. After the amount of agony I have had to endure today, I want to protest that it couldn't possibly be, but from the way Bran hunches over and grimaces, I know it must be really painful.

As much as I am weary of my brother, I am also not cruel, and it hurts me to see him suffering.

It's her birthday in a few more days. You don't have to wait much longer. Brandon, promise me you won't hurt her, will you?

His topaz eyes are aflame with annoyance, and the tick in his jaw jumps as he struggles to control his anger almost makes me smile.

She is mine. I want her and I will never hurt her, or let anyone else hurt her either. This has to stop, Fallon. You need to trust me.

However, my trust in Brandon remains on shaky ground, especially when he leaves the quarters that evening and only returns the following day to announce that he will be attending a diplomatic meeting in the east and won't return for at least three weeks. He will miss Raya's birthday and that rattles me somewhat. If he is so interested in her and wants her so badly, why won't he be here to claim her? It doesn't make sense.

I spend the following few days feeling sorry for myself, whilst being confined to my bedroom. Euan and Deacon come and visit, and my mother sits for hours reciting scriptures to me.

Three whole nights after my so-called accident, my father and Clayton come to visit. I now look at Clayton through new eyes; once he had been cheeky and brooding, but now he is sly, calculating, and evil. My father, as disinterested as usual, makes the correct sounds a doting father should, but there is no sincerity to his actions. I might be his baby girl, but he probably cares more about the fish in the pond than me.

Four days after my injury, my stomach turns when Clayton opens my door and stands in my doorway, until I see Raya in the background. I know she will be avoiding Brandon, but I hoped she would have come sooner. I miss her and I need a friend to talk to.

"Your friend is here to visit you, Fallon. Isn't that thoughtful of her?" I gulp, only realising now how Clayton can use Raya to hurt me and ensure I behave. "She tells me she is a dedicated Daughter of the Veil."

"I'm so sorry I have not visited until now, Fallon. You must think me a terrible friend." She rushes in and bows to me, all the while the tears that filled my eyes threaten to spill and never stop. "What happened?"

Before I can answer Raya, Clayton walks over and sits at the bottom of my bed. "Didn't you hear? Fallon had a terrible accident while shifting and broke both her legs."

Raya looks really uncomfortable, as she stands near my bed. I hope Clayton hasn't said something to make her feel this way, but I have a sneaking suspicion that he has.

"I can't stay long, I just wanted to check on you and bring you some fruit and currant buns." I nod to her, because I want her to leave for her own sake. "I missed you in class and so did the other ladies. They have no news to pass on just yet, but I have another lesson tomorrow, and I'll drop back in then, if that's okay?"

I nod again and smile to myself. To Clayton it sounds like idle chit chat, but I know Raya. There are no other ladies who we chat to during Edor. Raya has just passed me a message about meeting my team.

For the first time since Clayton smashed my legs up, an ember of hope reignites in the pit of my tummy. Yes, this has been exceptionally difficult, but if I ever want to find out what happened to Alessia, I have to keep going.

"Thank you for visiting, Raya. I hope your first shift goes well tomorrow. Don't overdo it, though; you can see what happened to me." I giggle falsely and note the panic in Clayton's eyes when I do. Maybe he is frightened of being caught by someone... But who?

We make small talk, but Clayton obviously isn't going to give us any privacy, so I am glad Raya doesn't linger. I wave goodbye to her and begin to plot my next moves in my head. At least in my head, they are safe from Clayton.

~ Soraya ~

Clayton follows me out of Fallon's bedroom, and the back of my neck prickles anxiously. As my tummy turns nervously, I wonder what changed in Clayton's life. He is usually charming and is considered the nicest of all Fallon's brothers by many.

My thoughts quickly return to Brandon. Am I wrong about him? Fallon has always been pretty vocal to me about her mistrust of him regarding Alessia's disappearance, but she used to tell me stories that depicted Clayton as a gentle giant too. Both assessments are now at odds with my own interactions with her brothers. Clayton makes me feel on edge and scared. Brandon, although he made me nervous, has only ever tried to reassure me and care for me.

"I'll let the rest of the family know that you came to visit, Fallon. I know my father and Brandon will be particularly interested." His voice sends waves of terror throughout my body, and as his lips curl, my hands begin to shake. I have to admit, if only to myself, Clayton Ward frightens me.

For the first time, I begin to wish that Brandon would come back from his mission sooner rather than later. My soul senses his absence and I fear I will not feel safe until he returns to the territory. Fleetingly, I regret sending him away, which does nothing but cause fresh confusion to trouble me as I make my way back to the Huts.

When I arrive home, I can hear crying coming from our hut. Not wanting to interrupt, I wait outside for a couple of minutes, but I can still clearly hear my sister, Sirah, crying to our mother.

Her voice thick with emotion, she wails unceremoniously. "We're already struggling and now we'll have another mouth to feed. He's so mad, mother. He will punish me again tonight; I know he will. What should I do?" I am unable to hear my mother's reaction, but my anger spikes and threatens to spill over.

Pretending I have just reached home, I open the door, and find my sister wrapped in my mothers arms. Her children play on the stone floor, with mothers jam still glistening around their mouths. The fact that their mother's distress does not affect them concerns me.

"Hello, everyone." I shout, announcing my arrival. My mother and sister quickly spring apart.

"Raya! Look, we found some building blocks." The children shout to me, beckoning me over, but I wink at them and tell them I'll be over soon.

"What's going on? Why are you crying?" I ask directly. I don't have time to mess about, the previous few days have taught me that.

"Sirah is expecting again, and Nero hasn't taken the news well." My brother-in-law, Nero, is an overbearing asshole. He regularly hits both my sister and their children for insubordination. He stands double the size of my sister and uses his strength to its full ability.

"I suppose you got pregnant all on your own?" My mother's eyes widen at my brazen comment. "How is this her fault? They are mates, who mate, which results in pups. It's ridiculous of him to be mad at her," I continue, biting my tongue but still spilling some of the contempt I feel rising up inside me.

Sirah stands up, and as she usually does, she defends her piece-of-shit mate. "What would you know, Soraya? You're just a stupid kid who has no idea how hard life can be."

"I know you don't deserve to be beaten, Sirah. This is a blessing from the Moon Goddess, the same Goddess who sent your mate." As my voice reaches a fever pitch, Sirah shakes her head at me angrily. Undeterred, I try to reason with my big sister. "You did your duty, Sirah. You should not be punished for that."

"We're leaving, come on children." The children groan, and my mother fusses and panders to Sirah and her outburst.

"You can't sit there and tell us he's going to punish you for getting pregnant and expect us to be happy about that. You're my sister and I love you. I hate him for hurting you," I tell her passionately, as I fight back my tears of frustration.

"When you get your own mate, you'll understand. We don't have the privilege of the upper hand or the moral high ground. We get what we get." Sirah is calm and controlled, all evidence of her earlier anguish has vanished.

As she walks away with her three children in tow, shame and remorse courses through me. How could I have made her feel worse? Not only have I upset my sister, but I have turned her away from a place of comfort with my own pig-headedness. What do I seriously know about the mate bond and my role as a female in my pack?

With my birthday only a day away, I don't have long to wait to find out.

My mother sits quietly, and when I mention what happened, my mother tells me she finds my behaviour insensitive and doesn't want to discuss it any further, and so I don't push the issue.

My mother wakes me up as dawn kisses the ground. Its orange and yellow rays glow around her like a halo, as she sings happy birthday to me. The tradition in our family has always been the same. Simple pancakes made from flour and milk and a hens egg if one is spare, topped with lemon juice and sugar, in bed, with a mug of hot tea.

"Happy Birthday, Soraya. May the Goddess of the Moon bless you, keep you safe and lead you on the path to your fate." My mother sings to me, as she serves me breakfast in bed. "I cannot believe my baby girl is all grown up. Soon you'll find your mate and be having your own pups just like your sisters."

As sweet as her sentiment is, I can't help but feel deflated. I have spent my whole childhood looking forward to and training for becoming an adult, and the moment arrives without fuss or fanfare. The only point of interest is the reminder of my duty as a Daughter of the Veil: find my mate and procreate. Like many other ladies before me, a feeling of futility flows throughout me as I think about a life that I face. A life that has been paved for me by someone else.

Of course, the biggest perk of the day will be finally shifting and meeting my wolf for the first time. I can't wait for that, but first I have some gifts from my mother and sisters.

My mother's gift, wrapped beautifully in material that forms the first present, is small and compact. "For your eighteenth, something you want, something you need and something to read. Happy birthday, Soraya. Your father would have been proud of the young woman you have become."

Thoughts of my father catch me off guard. He had been ill before he passed over to the Promised Lands and we welcomed his death, as it freed him from the prison of pain he had been locked in. Death did not come easy for him, and my memories of him are distorted; all I can recall of him is the desperate breath-taking cough that plagued him right up to his dying moments. I wish for one last dance with my papa, but I know he has gone on.

"I wish he could see me today. I miss him," I tell my mother truthfully, but I don't expand on why, because it is evident to see how much it hurts her. The pain of losing a mate can kill the survivor. Losing a mate to death is less painful than the pain of rejection, but even now, my mother still mourns my father, and I believe, perhaps she always will.

Preserving the material carefully, I open the small box inside, which reveals a book and a tiny, thin, golden chain with a heart pendant.

"It's to keep for your mating ceremony; I thought it would give you something special for the occasion. I know it's not Jade, like Fallon's, but it's small and delicate and pretty, just like you." I thank her for her thoughtfulness, blushing at her compliment. It isn't like my mother to be overly complimentary, and so it comes as a surprise when she does offer one.

My mothers eyes well up with tears, but I know there is happiness tinged with her sadness. "No matter what happens, you will always be my baby girl and I am so proud of you, Soraya. Are you ready to do your first shift?"

I nod to her nervously, as anticipation and excitement threatens to overcome me. "Yes. Will you come with me?" My mother nods, as she passes me my new veil, the one that demonstrates to everyone that I am now an adult.

We walk to the forest in companionable silence, and I desperately hope and pray that my first shift happens without any issues.

Turning my back to my mother, I remove my blue veil for the final time; it has been on my head the past five years. When a girl in our pack gets her moon blood, she transitions from the white veil of childhood to a colour of her choosing. I however did not get to choose mine; it was Sirah's. After slipping off my cloak, I concentrate as I have been instructed by the Edors. I focus on my inner wolf and my changing body, and just as they told me, my shift begins.

My spine snaps first, breaking, and elongating and arching, and then my hind quarters follow suit. My hands and feet become paws with pads and claws, and then fur sprouts out all over my body. Light golden-brown fur that covers everywhere, including my face.

Finally, I drop to all four paws and howl once my snout has finished forming.

Hi, my name is Pandora, and I am your wolf.

Letting out a sigh of relief, I reply to the new half of myself. *Hello, Pandora, I'm so glad to finally have my wolf.* However, before I can finish the sentence, Pandora sniffs and looks searchingly amongst the trees.

MATE! She declares strongly in my head before surging forward in search of what she can smell. It is weird sharing this vessel with another entity. I know Pandora can sense our mate, and I overwhelmingly want to find him too. Her need to be as one with this unknown wolf drives my own need too. I cannot recall ever feeling need like I do right now. How stupid I must have been to think I could just deny the mate bond. This person completes my soul, and I need to be with them. I want to be with them.

After half an hour of frantically searching, I am exhausted. I forcibly take control back from Pandora and shift back into my human state, which she whines about.

Mate was here. Why didn't mate stay?

I don't know why, but at least now I know that Brandon Ward can not be my mate; he is hundreds of miles away and my mate had been right there in the forest at the same time as me.

Two things now consume my thoughts. The first problem is: why didn't my mate present themselves and claim me? Didn't they like me? Were they shy? Am I not what they expected or wanted? What is wrong with me?

The second problem, I will have more trouble coming to terms with, because it confuses me and makes me feel shame and doubt. However, no matter how much I try to make sense of how I am feeling, I still have to ask myself: why am I so disappointed to confirm that Brandon Ward could not be my mate after all?

Chapter Six

~ Brandon ~

My week has presented a tornado of emotions. I found my mate, but she isn't old enough to recognise me yet. Then my attempts to get to know her better are rebuffed by her, as she wants to preserve her innocence for her mate. It both elates and exasperates me to no end.

Fallon was attacked, and I know who did it and the probable reason why he attacked her, but to stand up to him right now will jeopardise everything I have been working towards. However, I am far from happy about the whole situation. I thought Fallon had more common sense than what she is showing, and it hurts me to see her frightened, just like Alessia had been.

Fear that my father has his suspicions about me now plagues my waking hours. Fantasies about my mate and our future together overwhelm my sleep. Soraya is never far from my mind, and my body quickly responds every time my sweet mate crosses my thoughts. It is becoming harder and harder to control my urges for her. I want nothing more than to unveil my fate and present her to the pack.

However, it will have to wait. I will have to wait. There is unrest in the east, and although Clayton's behaviour fuels my reluctance to leave the territory, I have no choice when my father commands it.

Before heading east, I have to attend to my duties elsewhere too. I, of course, want her counsel and her approval, but mostly, I miss her, and I want to ensure she is safe and happy.

I enter the cold, decrepit crypts that hold her safe and drop to my knees in her presence, bowing my head low. The gold and jade ruins that are slowly being unearthed glow against the debris. The kingdom we were promised is within the mountains. It is our job to restore it.

"You may stand, Lieutenant Brandon Ward. You look well... you've met your fated mate, Diana tells me," the ethereal voice sings out to me.

In awe at her magnificence, I nod as I explain, "Yes, Your Majesty. I found her, but she isn't of age yet."

"You cannot claim her. You mustn't claim her yet. Or she will be in peril too," my Queen informs me, and I shake my head involuntarily, in denial and distress.

"No, you're wrong. I must claim her. I want her. I have never felt this way about anyone or anything ever before. Please, my Queen. Do not take away my fate." I plead with her even though I know it is forbidden.

"I wish I had the power to make this happen for you. You have been a loyal comrade. You deserve your blessing. However, if you claim her, she will suffer like many before her, as you've already seen." She pauses, with large tears brimming her blank, pearlescent eyes in recollection. "You remember what happened to poor Heidi. I never want another woman to suffer like she did. Your mate is now your weakness, and you are hers."

They will hurt Soraya to get to me; they will use her to bend me at will. As my anguish wars with my longing, I accept my Queen's counsel, for I know she desires the same as me. I am struggling to align what I must do with what my body and soul tells me is the right course of action. I know my Queen's advice to be sound, I just don't want it to be, not this time, not about my mate.

I want Soraya like my lungs need air. But my want and desire pales into insignificance when compared to Soraya's safety. Visions of Heidi the night she died flash through my memory, causing me to recoil. I would die if my Soraya was harmed like that. With a resolution that feels like failure, I concede, my Queen is right. My duty is to protect my mate at all costs.

"It's not forever, Lieutenant. It's just for now. You will of course have to think of a reason to not be around her, so she doesn't realise you are her destiny." I nod to my Queen, but my zest for the conversation has all but dispersed.

"I will tell father my trip will take longer than usual and use the opportunity to spy."

My Queen gives her consent and blessing, and so once I finish my diplomatic mission in the east, I come back home, but stay in wolf form on the outskirts of our territory. I use my time wisely, documenting all our defences and the weaknesses that exist. I watch out for wolves that fail to do their job correctly. In the evening, I sit and watch my sweet Soraya from afar, as she serves food to her community. Although I can't see her face, I sense her joy. The way the others flock around her confirms she would indeed make a fine Luna when my time comes to lead the pack.

How I wish to touch her hair, to feel the soft skin on her face, to kiss her lips. The aching in my heart only seems to further fuel my desire for her, and I therefore double my efforts to serve my Queen, because once she is safe to lead us, as intended by the Moon Goddesses, it will also be safe for me to finally claim my mate.

Having already discovered the date of Soraya's birthday, I hang about the forest near to her hut so that I can see her wolf once she shifts. Excitement bubbles up inside me. I have already decided that she has light brown hair, like her sisters. Her pale skin, like milk, will be a stark contrast to my own. I have spent hours fantasising about how our contrasting limbs will look entwined around each other. Her eyes are probably green or blue, like her mother and sisters. I know she is gorgeous no matter what, but I will have to wait to see that side properly until she is officially 'unveiled' by me.

Her decision to remain veiled shows my mate has integrity and morality, and I will therefore do what I can to respect the custom of our pack. It goes without saying that I look forward to the day she is ready for me to see her. I have no desire to break her trust; all I want right now is to see her shift successfully.

I close my eyes, allowing her time to take off her veil unseen, until I hear the familiar cracking that accompanies the shift from human to wolf. When I open my eyes again, a golden wolf glances around, bewildered.

Mine. Maverick chants in my head, *go to our mate now and claim her.* Reasoning with him to calm him is quickly revealed as futile because all Maverick can do is act on his basal instincts. He wants his mate. *MINE!*

Soraya's wolf responds enthusiastically to his call. *Mate.* And when she bounds towards me, I do everything in my power to get Maverick to run away.

We have to keep her safe, Maverick. However, he is set against my argument.

Safe is with us; we can protect her. She is ours to protect. Part of me wants nothing more than to relent and agree with him, but the flashes of Heidi's fate and then the thought of Soraya being in danger too stop my impending recklessness.

We cannot keep her safe every second of every hour of every day... Do you want her to be hunted down and killed? Maverick, having caught the scent of her now too, is lost in his animalistic instinct to claim what is ours.

In the end, I have to shift back to human form and hide away from Soraya's wolf. There is no other way to get Maverick to cooperate with me. He refuses to acknowledge me for the rest of the day and his anger spontaneously flares up inside me for no reason at all. He doesn't understand this isn't what I want either, but we have to do what we can to keep our mate safe.

Later this evening, while patrolling the forest once again, Maverick chants for Soraya. His disobedience will get us all killed. Soraya is nearby, I can feel it and Maverick can too. This time he isn't giving up. Even while in human form, he is fighting for control. Clawing to claim his destiny. I wonder where she is?

Sensing three or four other wolves in the forest, it comes as a shock when I finally realise one of them is Soraya. What is she doing here after dark with three strange wolves?

Maverick growls and hisses; he wants to kill them all for being close to our mate. Luckily for me, he is distracted by a group of five other wolves also approaching from the other side of the clearing. Not knowing what they want, I hold back with Soraya in my sight just in case. My heart pounds as scenarios run though my thoughts: what if they touch her or hurt her? I will kill them if they do.

As I try to rationalise that Soraya doesn't appear to be in any immediate danger, their conversation filters through.

"There is no news about Alessia, there are still no sightings, but please tell Fallon that the whispers about the Promised Queen are getting louder: some are saying she's already been discovered, others believe it could be Fallon herself." There is a chuckle around the group.

"I will pass on the message. Thank you for all you are doing for Fallon. It gives her some hope that one day she will find out what happened to her sister."

FALLON! That little bitch is the one responsible for putting my sweet Soraya in danger. I will be giving her a stern telling off when I return home. What the fuck must she be thinking getting Soraya mixed up in this crap? And why is she after information about The Promised Queen? It's talk like this that will put her in mortal danger.

"There is a group approaching. Goddess' speed my friends, until next time." Soraya must not be familiar with the group dynamics because as the others scatter and run in different directions, she remains still, on the spot. I quickly call for my own back-up team, but as they don't yet realise that I am back on the territory, it will take them a while to respond. My heart races as my mind screams at her to run, but within the blink of an eye, she is surrounded by the opposing group.

"Grab the woman. She will be unveiled and shamed for her involvement in this plot against my father and our family." As Clayton's cruel voice reaches my ears, I can no longer hold back.

Pouncing from the shadows, I shift in mid air. Maverick, emerging like an avenging gargoyle, tramples over the group, but I'm too late. They have already struck Soraya and she is sprawled on the ground like a broken doll. Completely overcome with anguish, I roar into the night as I fight and defeat every wolf that stands between me and my mate. Until finally, Clayton's wolf, Zagan, is the only one left. His wolf form is as dark as my own but not as thick nor strong.

MINE! I claim my mate in front of the others despite the warnings of my Queen and my resolve to keep Soraya safe by disassociation.

Big brother, what are you doing here? I thought you were in the east, Zagan questions me through our mindlink.

I was and now I'm home. Leave her alone. Go home. Now. Or you'll personally answer for harming her.

However, Zagan's lips curl, revealing sharp fangs, and I wait with bated breath for Clayton to challenge me.

She was here with a group of others. They plot against our family. She is my prisoner, and I mean to question her.

Without thinking, I pin Zagan to the ground, gripping his throat within my teeth. *She was answering my call; that is why she is here. She has nothing to do with the other group. She turned eighteen today, and once she did, I had to come and claim her. I couldn't stop the need to do it.*

So, you abandoned your diplomatic mission to claim a girl. Future Alpha Brandon, what will our father say? Pressing my teeth slightly further into his windpipe and exuding my Alpha aura, I force Zagan and, therefore, Clayton, by default, to yield to me.

He finally replies to me and my authority. I let him go and he limps towards home, but I know deep in my bones that I don't and can't trust my brother. I was supposed to keep Soraya safe by staying away, but now I have claimed her to keep her safe. I didn't see any other way.

I shift back into human form and dress quickly, using clothes from a strategically placed chest in the forest for situations like mine, hoping to cover myself before my mate wakes again. However, my back up team arrives as I am doing so. One of my delta wolves leans down to scoop Soraya up off the ground, and jealousy fires inside me.

"Get your hands off her. She is MINE!"

"We're mates?" Soraya replies, giving me the shock of my life. "You're my mate?"

~ Soraya ~

My whole-body shakes as I meet with Fallon's team for the second time. The first time I met them had been nerve wracking enough, but this time, my nerve endings are on edge for what I hope will be my final meeting with them. Something feels off, but I simply put it down to my earlier shift and unsuccessful attempt to meet my mate.

The pull of my mate took me by surprise. I have never in all my life felt anything remotely like it. Before having that feeling, I used to believe that I could resist the bond if I didn't like my mate or if I had other plans for what to do with my life, I would just walk away.

However, now I know what the bond feels like, I want my mate, and my desire for him to want me back both thrills me and sickens me at the same time. I just don't understand why he evaded me in the forest earlier today. Surely, he felt the pull too. Why doesn't he want me?

All my senses seem off, and my preoccupation with my mate is more than likely the issue. Even now, Pandora whines in my head about our mate being near and my reflexes and responses are delayed and slow as a result.

Despite my hypervigilance, I only become aware of another group of wolves just as they arrive at the clearing. My stomach lurches with nerves when I realise Clayton's wolf leads my captors. This is not good. The only positive thing I can take solace in is that at least I still have my veil and therefore, my identity remains obscured to the new group.

Once the new group of wolves surrounds me, I desperately try with all my might to concoct an excuse as to why I am here, alone, in the middle of the night. My mother will be so disappointed in me for this. I don't think she will ever forgive me for the shame this will bring to my family.

My time to explain is cut short, however, when one of the warriors smacks me on the head, causing me to lose consciousness.

What feels like a couple of minutes later, with my head pounding and spinning, someone lifts me up, and I hear an almighty growl.

"Get your hands off her! She's MINE," commands the meanest voice I have ever heard, and in response, the person holding me allows my body to slip down to the ground so he can obey the order.

Through my veil, my eyes dart open to see who is shouting. I look into the familiar cool, dark eyes of Brandon Ward, my stomach lurching and fluttering at the same time.

"We're mates? You're my mate?" My strained voice squeezes out

"Yes, my sweet Soraya. I am yours and you are most certainly all mine." I faint dead away, as he lifts me from the ground.

When I rouse again, I am in Brandon's arms as he carries me in the direction of the Huts. "It is you. You're my mate? Why didn't you tell me?"

He nods back at me stiffly but doesn't say a word. His disappointment is obvious at finding that I am his mate. As my shame grows, I allow the darkness to take me once more. I can't bear to see the disgust in Brandon's eyes or feel the dread that fills me when faced with the consequences of my actions. He didn't tell me we were mates because he's embarrassed to be mated to me. A scrawny Omega from the Huts. He probably expected someone higher ranked, someone better. A she-wolf who is worthy of him, the Future Alpha. As my tears silently choke me, I surrender to the haze that deadens my awareness.

When I wake up, the scent of pine needles and orange assault my senses. The distinguished and alluring scent of my mate, who has the audacity to sit beside my bed in my hut. Why does he torture me by staying here when he obviously doesn't want me. The quiet despair and embarrassment that bothered me last night now gives way to my anger and hurt. I didn't choose to be Brandon Ward's mate. How dare he be disappointed in me!

"What are you doing here?" I ask him with a croaky voice, while opening my eyes. Despite my sight being encumbered by my veil, my stomach jolts when

Brandon looks at me. Concern lines his face and there is a tenderness in his intense dark brown eyes that I have never noticed before.

"I was worried when you blacked out, Soraya; you took quite a knock to the head. Your mother's hut is nearer than the Alpha Quarters, so I brought you here first." As he explains, I try to cover myself more with the blanket. I hope it was my mother and not Brandon who changed my clothes. He's not supposed to see me until I am unveiled. My pack's traditions and customs are important to me, and I want to abide by them. Plus, it's embarrassing having my pale legs on show. No one apart from my mother has seen me undressed or without my veil. My sisters haven't seen my face or hair since I took the veil at eight years old. It's horrifying to think of Brandon seeing me, especially while I was unaware.

"Please excuse my attire. Did my mother undress me?" He closes his eyes, as though it pains him to think about it, and nods yes, and the relief I feel from this tiny gesture is refreshing. However, I still want to cover my legs, but the blanket is stuck under Brandon's foot.

Leaning forward in the chair, he places his hand over mine. "Stop, I am the Future Alpha, and you don't need to hide from me," he says, raising his voice to make himself heard. Brandon then takes his hand away from mine and sits back in his chair, leaving me none the wiser of his intentions.

"Is that why you are here? Because you're the Future Alpha?" I ask him bluntly, secretly hiding my blush from him as I remain behind my veil for now.

"You know why I'm here," he tells me, as he looks away from me again. I have no idea what he is thinking, and it doesn't look like Brandon will ever voluntarily share his thoughts with me. If I want to know where I stand, I will have to push the matter for myself.

"I wouldn't have asked your reasons if I knew them, Brandon. I don't play games and flirting isn't something the Edors teach us. I'm genuinely asking you, why?"

"What were you doing in the forest last night, Soraya? Do you have any idea how much danger you put yourself in?" My disappointment at his deflection grows and then yields, as my heart begins to race and the sense of foreboding that had swallowed me whole until Brandon arrived at the clearing overcomes me with a vengeance. I did know the danger, but I did it anyway. I did what I could to help my friend. I know now that my fate lay in the balance last night, and maybe it still does.

Sensing my panic, Brandon rushes to my side and holds onto my hand. The overwhelming sensations and tingles of our mate bond start where his fingertips make contact with my skin and travel throughout my whole body. Desire, longing, and a want for fulfilment flood my senses, overwhelming me until tears spring from my eyes. "You're safe, I'm here, I'm here," he tenderly murmurs against my brow.

"But why are you here, Brandon?" I continue to probe him, despite the evidence of our bond still affecting me and regardless of the fact that he holds me like I am his most treasured possession. I need to hear him say the words. I need to know if Brandon Ward is going to claim his mate or reject her.

"Because you are MINE, Soraya. I am yours and you are mine. Now and always. I will keep you safe and I will never let anyone ever hurt you ever again." With our foreheads touching and only my veil hindering us, he gazes upon me as he makes his promises. "Goddess above, you are so perfect. I have wanted this for so long, Soraya. I have been dreaming about this moment."

His words, so simple but honest and impassioned, are more than I have ever wished for. I have my mate, and he is clearly claiming me.

Something still niggles at the back of my mind though. "So, then why did you run away? You were in the forest for my first shift, but when Pandora called out to your wolf, you didn't come. You ran away." I pull away from his embrace, our moment broken by my unanswered queries.

Brandon surprises me by gently taking my hands back into his, stroking my palms with his thumbs. "I wasn't going to claim you right away. You see, I wanted to keep you safe because it's too dangerous right now. But I was never going to reject you. I desired only to keep you out of harm's way."

What danger? Keep me safe from what exactly? And if it's dangerous, why is he claiming me now anyway?

"I know this is confusing at the moment, but I promise I will keep you safe. Despite my want to keep my distance, I couldn't do it, and tonight when that other wolf struck you, I claimed you in front of all my brother's team." He gives a rueful half smile, and although I can see he is worried, I can also detect his joy. He's happy about our pairing; my earlier concerns had been wrong. "Now, keeping my distance and delaying our mating is not an option."

Blushing profusely when he mentions mating, I pull back from him, and he chuckles. Knowing he is my mate is one thing, but I'm not ready for mating. I'm only just eighteen years old. I know Brandon is experienced sexually; the Goddess knows that I have repented for thinking incessantly about the things he was doing with that woman on the day when I walked in on him. What if I can't do the stuff he likes? "Brandon, I can't do this. I don't know what to do. I'm scared."

He continues to smile at me, and his presence alone is comforting to me. "Of course, you don't know what to do. That's okay. There is no rush, my sweetheart. We have eternity together now." My breathing returns to normal and my heart stops beating erratically. "I do have to present you to my father today, though, and I am asking to unveil you tonight before the whole pack."

TONIGHT! "But, Brandon, that's so fast, I-I..." I'm at a loss for words.

There is so much to arrange: I don't have a gown, my sisters will need to organise time off work. As my panic rises in my chest, accelerating my heart rate once more, Brandon gently places his hands on either side of my face. Even though the veil covers my entire head, he pretty accurately finds my cheeks.

"Soraya, calm down. I need to claim you straight away. It's the only way to keep you safe." I nod my agreement to his impassioned plea, knowing from his actions that this is important to him. "I'm the Alpha's son, whatever you want or need for this evening will be catered for. But I need this to happen tonight, in full view of the whole pack."

My mother is going to freak out. "Good luck gaining my mother's permission!" I whisper to him as I acquiesce, which at least gains a chuckle from him.

"We will tell her together; I will go and tell her you are awake." He kisses my hands before letting go, and when he gets to the door, he turns back to me. "Soraya, I meant every word I said. I'm so glad you are mine."

Regardless of the danger he has warned me of, I'm so glad he is mine too.

Chapter Seven

~ Euan ~

The news of Brandon finding his mate spreads like wildfire. Although the initial disclosure came from Clayton, Bran quickly linked me and Fallon to inform us of his happy news.

The whole house is buzzing, and although I want to go and celebrate with them, Brandon gave me strict orders to stay with Fallon and ensure no one else attempts to harm her. I have no intentions of disobeying him, not when the consequences are so dire.

Fallon is quiet. Too quiet really, but she will not talk to me or confide in me about what is bothering her. I thought her friend being mated to our brother would make her happy, but if anything, she seems miserable about the recent news that is causing such merriment in our home.

"It'll be nice for you to have your friend living here in the house with us, won't it, Fallon?" I ask her, but she replies with a grunt. "Brandon will be able to secure our line now with an heir of his own, and we will be here to be a part of it. This is joyful news for the whole family."

She turns her back to me as she retorts, "Oh, yes, this is fucking fabulous news. We have a lunatic living here who gets off on harming young girls; let's bring another one here for him to maul and mutilate."

Her disdain for our brother only seems to manifest further each day, not that I blame her, but I thought the news of Brandon's mate being her best friend would have cheered her up somewhat. Instead, it serves only to escalate her downward spiral of depression.

"Brandon will not let anyone hurt her; you know this, sister. Your friend will be safe under his protection." She laughs and snorts in a very unladylike manner, and honestly, I'm starting to tire of her sour mood. "Would you rather he rejected her?"

She sits up quickly, wincing as she does. "No! I don't know. I just know I don't want Raya anywhere near Clayton. I want her to stay far away from all this."

"Well, there is nothing we can do about that now. Brandon and Soraya are mates, they have their unveiling this evening, and the least we can do is share their joy and support them. You know they need our blessing now." She nods her head reluctantly. I remind her of why Brandon needs our support more than ever. "This will be upsetting for Deacon. It's been less than a year since his own ceremony. Brandon will have this at the forefront of his mind too; I know I will when I find my mate."

It's the cold hard truth. I don't think I will ever forget the day Deacon unveiled his mate or the fact that she died less than six months later. No matter how much he loved her and tried to protect her, it wasn't enough. She died anyway, leaving him heartbroken and alone with nothing but the memories of their short time together.

"Raya doesn't want pups, not right away. She wants to travel and teach." My sister interrupts my morbid thoughts; she obviously felt more inclined to share her thoughts with me now.

This will not be happy news for Brandon. His mate wanting to be an Edor is problematic, seeing as only the unmated are allowed such a role.

"Well, maybe she will feel differently now." I try to reassure her until our mother enters Fallon's room, carrying a long dress bag. "I hope that's not for me!" I try to muse, but my mother impatiently tuts before ushering me to do her bidding.

"No, it's not for you, it's for Fallon. I think it'll be perfect for covering your legs for the ceremony. Here, help me hang this." She hands the garment to me, and I hang it onto the front of Fallon's wardrobe and unzip the garment bag.

As the pale purple silk comes into view, my blood runs cold. I know this dress; I've seen it before. From the gasp Fallon makes, I know she recognises it too.

"Th-th-that's Alessia's dress," Fallon stutters out in obvious distress. "I can't wear her dress; she hasn't given her permission."

"You know she wouldn't mind you borrowing it for today," our mother counters, and her direct coldness shocks me. "Why don't you try it on. It'll cover the casts on your legs completely, and you'll still look elegant and respectable."

This is the final straw for my baby sister. Her loud sobs reverberate across the bedroom. "Where is she? Why can't we find her? And how can you be so blasé about it, mother? Your daughter is missing- presumed dead, and you act like nothing's wrong."

"Control yourself, Fallon." Our mother stands tall and continues to remove the dress from the hanger. "Today is not the day to be falling apart and making a spectacle of yourself. You are Fallon Ward, Lady of the Veil and the Alpha's daughter. Act like it."

My sister asks me to leave so she can change into the dress, but I wait outside the door, unable to rest until Brandon returns home.

"Today is a joyous day. My son and heir, the Future Alpha of the Reverent Moon, has found his mate." My father's booming voice travels from the grand hallway, up the staircase and to the landing. "Tonight, we will witness her unveiling and their first mating, and Goddess be good, in a few months' time, our family line will be stronger than ever!"

It's a surprise to hear that Brandon has permitted a witnessed consummation. Deacon never did, and I just assumed Brandon would prefer privacy too. I know

I would. I hope I am not called upon to bear witness. The thought of watching my brother mating is gross. I do not want to be privy to what happens between him and his mate in the privacy of their bedroom.

Fallon's shouting from the bedroom stops my pondering entirely, and I return inside her room to stop her and our mother from tearing each other apart. This is going to be a long day.

~ Brandon ~

Claiming my mate is going to get me into a world of trouble with my Queen, but I'm finding it hard to regret my actions, especially when my excitement grows at her unveiling later this evening. After informing Mrs Burke that we are mates and that I want to unveil Soraya this evening, I watch in awe as the two women set about organising everything.

Mrs Burke sends me to the seamstress to ask for ribbons and clips for Soraya's hair, and being the Future Alpha means my presence does not go unnoticed. By the time the manager's wife has helped me pick out the ribbons for Soraya, half the pack have sent their well wishes and congratulations to me through mindlink.

Of course, I sent word home to my parents, who are now busy making all the arrangements for the ceremony later this evening. Everything is rushed, but I wouldn't have it any other way. Tonight will be the beginning of the rest of our lives. Even waiting another night feels impossible. I need her to be mine. I need her like my life depends on it.

Once Soraya is ready, I help carry her bags up to the Alpha Quarters. I can tell that she is nervous about what is expected of her and sad to be moving away from her family and community, so I try my best to reassure her that we will visit regularly. Her sisters seem quiet and withdrawn. One has a large welt across her cheek that closes her eye. One of the sisters' mates is very talkative and overfamiliar, and I get the feeling that Soraya doesn't much like him. I will ask her about this later, but for now this is about her official unveiling.

I leave Soraya and her family with my mother while I take my place beside my father in the Ceremonial Hall. My brother Deacon stands at the front in his Ceremony regalia. This will be his first unveiling ceremony. My mother wheels Fallon down the aisle and takes her seat on the second row with Euan taking a seat on the front row, as is custom. Fallon doesn't smile when she sees me, and I can tell from the tears in her eyes that she is upset.

Don't ask her; you'll get an earful off her, just like I have. It's the dress, Euan links me, warning me not to engage with Fallon right now. I don't immediately understand, but taking more notice of my sister, I know that the dress she is wearing belonged to Alessia. My bowels turn to ice water, and sweat beads on my brow. My condition must be apparent to all the guests, because Deacon approaches me and attempts to calm me.

"Don't worry, big brother, the next part is most enjoyable. You don't have to worry about the ceremony. Everything is going to be fine. In fact, your mate is ready."

The large wooden doors open to us and standing in the doorway at her mother's side is Soraya, covered head to foot in a white lace veil. Maverick purrs in satisfaction. The doors close behind her, and the music begins as she makes her way to me. I smile back at her, trying to reassure and encourage her. The petals drop off the flowers in her hands as she shakes with nerves. It will be a miracle if there are any petals remaining by the time she reaches me.

Mrs Burke returns my smile, and I take a moment to thank the Goddess for Soraya's mother supporting our union. Her tears cling to her eyelashes, but she whispers happily to her daughter, sharing one last moment before I claim her as my mate.

Everything is completely perfect, a moment of tranquil bliss, as Mrs Burke places Soraya's hands in mine and whispers to me, "Please, take care of my baby."

"I promise, I will," I vow to her. However, before we can continue with our unveiling, the hall doors swing open, clattering against the walls either side of them. The whole congregation turns to the calamity, muttering and murmuring, as Clayton strides in. Trust him to make a scene and steal the limelight.

"You weren't going to unveil her without me, were you? Goddess above, where are your manners, brother?" He saunters up the aisle towards me. "Well, I am here, come on, let's get this done with."

Rage builds within me, and all that keeps me sane is the tiny hand that trembles in mine and the repeated warning of my wolf that it is bad luck to kill someone on such a special day.

~ Soraya ~

When we arrive at the Alpha Quarters, Luna Beverly shows me to what will become my shared rooms with Brandon. "Let the Omegas know if there is anything you need. We will be waiting in the Ceremonial Hall for you in around an hour's time." My mother repeats our thanks and quickly gets to work on making me presentable.

Feeling like a pampered princess, I have a hot shower. My sigh of bliss echoes loudly around the bathroom as the warm water cascades down my back and relaxes my muscles. This is something I am really looking forward to, hot running water! I lather up my body with the fragrant soap, allowing the lavender to soothe me. The apple scented shampoo invigorates me, leaving me feeling energised and hopeful.

"Mother, please have a shower while I dry off. It is divine!" My mother, knowing that this might be her only chance, does not waste time and quickly chases me out of the bathroom once my veil is covering my head once again so she can enjoy the hot water too.

Taking the opportunity to look around without my mother watching me, I glance around at my new home. As well as my dressing room, where I now stand, and the en-suite bathroom, there is an office for Brandon, a large sitting room and a master bedroom. I don't enter the office; it is not my place to pry, and I will have to await Brandon's permission to enter that room. The sitting room is large and comfortable with luxurious couches and solid wood furniture. It will look nice here once I add some personal effects too. The sitting room alone is bigger than my mother's whole hut, and I wonder why anyone would want or need so much space. I walk through the room which leads to the bedroom. At the centre of the room, the focal point is a large four poster bed draped in rich red material. The curtains around the bed are a mix of organza voile and red velvet. My heart begins to pound when I realise that this is the bed I'll share with my mate, with Brandon. Tonight!

"You don't have to be afraid." My mother's voice, so unexpected, causes me to jump. "You do know what is expected of you. Especially as Brandon is our Future Alpha. He'll want a son and heir as soon as possible. He has been kind so far; I can only hope he'll be kind in bed too."

I do know what is expected of me, and that is what I fear. Every other dream and desire now no longer belongs to me. After tonight, I will simply be a brood mare for the Future Alpha, nothing more than a means to an end.

"Will it hurt?" I ask my mother bluntly, not holding back, for I need the truth, even if I do sound pathetic.

My mother slowly nods at me. "Yes, it will hurt, but if you cooperate and don't resist, it'll hurt less, and it doesn't last long. It's over before you know it." She smiles at me, pityingly. "However, eventually, you'll get your reward. You'll deliver your mate his son, but you'll also have a child to love for the rest of your life. There is no greater gift."

Resigned to my fate, I hug my mother and blink away my tears. I cannot change what will come but I can and will learn to embrace what the Moon Goddess has intended for me.

My mother stays in the other room while I use a small hair dryer to style my hair, adding curls and ribbons to the long yellow locks that will finally be unveiled to the pack and, most importantly, to my mate. My nerves simmer and bubble in my tummy, twisting my insides uncomfortably, until finally my mother helps me to attach the white veil to my head.

The white veil is long and intricately designed. I remember watching it in awe when my sisters were unveiled too; however, theirs took place in the courtyard, not in the pack's Ceremonial Hall in front of every high-ranking wolf in the pack and our ally packs too.

"It's time, Soraya. After tonight you'll no longer be a Daughter of the Veil but a mated respectable female of the pack. I am so proud of you and the young woman you have become." She wipes away her tears that spill over before continuing. "May the Goddess bless you and give you everything you need for a long and comfortable life."

Guiding me so I don't misstep and fall, my mother holds onto my arm and guides me out of the Alpha Quarters and over to the Ceremonial Hall. There are crowds outside, already responding to the rumours afoot that their Future Alpha has found his mate and she is about to be unveiled. Despite being covered, my cheeks burn at the thought of everyone looking and seeing me. It's overwhelming. What if Brandon finds me unappealing? What if the pack does? I quake even more, and I want nothing more than to run away and hide behind my veil forever.

We reach the Ceremonial Hall. This is the first time any of my family have been granted access, and my mother reassures me that Sirah and Savana are already sitting inside with their families.

When we arrive outside the grand hall doors, they are opened for us by Omegas, and as I step inside, Pandora howls her appreciation, sensing Brandon close by. *Mine!* She chants in my head. *My Mate!*

The Ceremonial Hall is filled with fresh flowers, and the opulence of the room leaves me in awe, so rich and beautiful. The dozens of guests get to their feet as I walk in. My legs tremble, and I am convinced if my mother lets go of me, I will crumble to the ground.

And then I see him. My mate, my future and the reason I am here in the first place, and the whole room washes away. All that matters is that Brandon and I are unified today, because together we will be strong and able.

I float down the aisle to my fate and barely remember my mother until she hands me over to Brandon. My body reacts on its own as it seeks the completion of being reunited with my other half. The warm tingles of our bond course throughout my body, igniting a desire deep within every nerving ending. Nothing has ever felt as right as being here with Brandon in front of our family and friends. I know in my heart and soul, in this exact moment, that this is my destiny. This is what the Moon Goddess intends for my life. This is one hundred percent right.

Then as soon as the moment started, it disperses with a loud bang. I don't realise what the issue is until I feel Brandon's anger radiating off him. Worried that he is dissatisfied with me, I quickly check his reaction and then search around the hall, where all our guests are chatting amongst themselves, gossiping about the disturbance to my unveiling.

Clayton walks down the aisle towards us, and I now understand Brandon's anger. Clayton has arrived late and is causing a scene during our ceremony. This is a major disrespect to Brandon as the Future Alpha and to our union.

A fire burns in Brandon's eyes. Without even thinking, I reach up and touch him on his cheek, breaking the fierce stare he is giving his insolent brother. He leans into my hand with a small smile. I like his response to my touch, and I watch in fascination as his anger disperses. I am under no illusion that this insult will be addressed later, but for now it is insignificant, and we can return back to our ceremony.

"We are gathered today for the commitment ceremony of our Future Alpha, Brandon Ward, to his fated mate, Daughter of the Veil, Miss Soraya Burke, and to bear witness to her unveiling." My eyes fill with tears as I am overcome with sentiment. I am being unveiled, and my mate is about to make his solemn commitment to me.

"Hey, stay calm, sweetheart. Try to enjoy this moment. I know I will," Brandon whispers through my veil to me. We are so close to each other, and yet, he still doesn't know what I look like. Panic floods my senses, filling my chest to capacity... What if he doesn't like me, what if I displease him?

"Do you, Brandon Ward, pledge your life to your mate? Do you promise to honour and protect her, face happiness and adversity together and live within the teachings of the Moon Goddess?" My panic eases slightly as Brandon gives his solemn promise to me and to the Shaman. I hear both my mother and Luna

Beverly sighing in contentment as Brandon holds my hand and recites the vows back to me.

"And do you, Soraya Burke, pledge your life to your mate? Do you promise to obey his command, to honour and respect him. To support him in his role and endeavour to provide him with an heir as dictated within the teachings of the Moon Goddess?"

"I-I... I..." I stumble when I realise that my vows are different to Brandon's and to the ones my sisters had to pledge to their mates. My mouth is dry but also watering, my sight blurs at the edges and my tongue is too big for my mouth. "Don't worry about the exact words, pledge to be my mate, and I will more than return what you give to me. Can you do that?" Brandon, sensing my panic, whispers to me once more. I nod to him and give my pledge.

"I can now pronounce you blessed in the eyes of the Moon Goddess. It is my great honour to permit you to unveil your mate." Shaman Deacon congratulates his brother, and I begin to kneel in front of Brandon so he may remove my veil.

"No! I'd like you to stand, please. I want you to be level with me when I remove your veil." It is custom for the female to submit to her mate, to stand is highly unusual, but it's what Brandon has requested, so I do as he asks.

Brandon gently lifts my heavy veil, careful to not pull my hair, letting it spill over my shoulders and down my back. When the fresh air hits my face, I look up at him, meeting his brown eyes, finally, without anything in the way.

"Wow!"

Chapter Eight

~ Brandon ~

When my brother finally gives me permission to unveil Soraya, my hands tremble. I have wanted to see her face for what feels like the longest time, and now my moment is here. I lift her heavy veil, careful to not pull on the clips that hold it in place.

Finally, I get the end of the veil over her head, allowing it to slowly flow over her shoulders, revealing honey-blonde hair and the cutest face I have ever seen. Her eyes are a clear, deep blue, full of curiosity and trepidation. My voice catches in my throat as one word escapes my mouth, "Wow!"

My exclamation pleases her; her eyes widen and then she grins back at me. "Hi," she replies simply to me, and as much as I want to pull her into my arms and claim her fully in front of the whole congregation, it would be unseemly. Instead, I thread my fingers through hers, and hold her close to me.

Her scent fills my nose, and the sensations of our bond flow between us. I am in awe of both the magic of the Moon Goddess and my beautiful mate, who shyly looks away, unable to keep my gaze without blushing. Goddess above, how she pleases me. She is nothing like the picture in my mind when I fantasised about this exact moment, for I had imagined the most glorious young woman I could... but Soraya more than exceeds every fantasy I have had. Her hair, so silky and fair in comparison to my own, glints in the light. Her pale skin is creamy and flawless, and all I can think about is how magnificent we will look when we join together, with my dark, hard skin pressing into her delicate, soft fairness. I cannot wait for a moment alone with her.

My mother, however, reminds me that there is a lot of fanfare before either of us will be allowed such graces. "It's time for your reception. You and Soraya will greet your guests who are forming a receiving line."

Holding on tight to my mate's hand, I don't let her out of my sight. Many of the pack offer their congratulations, including my best friend and future Beta, Daniel. "You kept this quiet, Bran. How long have you known?" he asks me curiously.

"About three months, but Soraya only came of age yesterday, and so I had to wait." He slaps me on the shoulder in merriment and offers his congratulations to both me and my mate. I look at Soraya with pride, noticing her button nose and full pink lips. The Moon Goddess has truly blessed me.

Once the line starts to dwindle, I finally notice Soraya's family bringing up the rear. The little girl who seems attached to my mate shouts to us, "Ray-Ray, look, I got flowers!" And her mother scolds her in response. In the distance, I observe the older sister being admonished by her mate. I have no doubt he caused her facial injury; no wonder Soraya dislikes him.

"Anais, don't forget to bow to our Future Alpha, just like I showed you." The little girl bows low to me with the flowers still in her hands, and when I tip my head in recognition, her eyes light up and she gives me a toothy grin. The joy in Soraya's eyes confirms to me that this little girl is a source of love and happiness to my mate. It is my job to enable their relationship to flourish.

"That is such a pretty name, Anais! Will you save me a dance later?" She nods yes, before her mother and father proudly move her along to allow the rest of the line.

After greeting the rest of Soraya's family and accepting their words of congratulations, the line finally comes to an end, and so I take my mate's hand once more to escort her to the reception room. Until my brother swaggers up to the table.

"Congratulations to the happy couple, Brandon. I must confess that I am extremely jealous of your good fortune. An honest and devout, pure and innocent Daughter of the Veil and she is a beauty too." My hackles rise at his insubordination. Maverick hovers on the brink, wanting to shift and remove Clayton's throat once and for all. "I am looking forward to getting to know you better, sister-in-law. I want to know *everything* about you and your family."

I watch in horror as he kisses Soraya's hand, smiling sickly at her. From Soraya's reaction, I know she feels sickened by Clayton's actions; she recoils away from him, and this infuriates me even more. "Is that a threat, *brother*?" I shout at him as I grab him by the front of his shirt, lifting him from his feet in a cold hard reminder that I am his Future Alpha. I am stronger and more powerful than he is, and he will not threaten what is mine. Soraya steps back, her eyes wide in shock but also ablaze with fiery fury.

"No, not a threat, Brandon. A promise. Have a great night. I can't wait to watch your consummation later. This is going to be so much fun." He straightens out his shirt, as he laughs, and then walks off into the reception room.

"A witnessed consummation? You consented to them watching me, us. That!" Soraya's cheeks are now a deep red. She looks at me with a disappointment that tears away at my heart. Honestly, I haven't even given the process any thought. Sure, I couldn't wait to be as one with Soraya, but no one has even mentioned the witnessed consummation to me.

"I didn't. I forgot. It is customary for the Alphas and Future Alphas first mating to be witnessed, but I will tell them no." Her shoulders relax as she exhales. The relief in her confirms that she trusts me and that the private act between us should be kept that way. There are other ways to confirm our mating.

"You would do that for me?" she asks with a squeak. I smile back at her. Soon she will realise that I will do anything for her. Anything within my power at least.

"I will try my best to give you everything you want and need, always. On that you can rely on." I pull her body close to mine. There is only us around now, and I can't resist the chance to really connect with her. My cock reacts instantly, and Soraya's blush returns with a vengeance when she feels the evidence of my attraction to her.

"It won't be your first-time mating, though, will it?" It's my turn to blush; however, no matter how uncomfortable this situation is, I want my relationship with Soraya to only be based on the truth. I will not hide anything from her, and I only hope that my honesty about my indiscretions will show her that I can be trusted.

"No. It won't be my first-time mating. I'm not going to lie to you. It will be my first time with my fated mate, though." She nods at me, before quickly glancing around to see if anyone else can see us. "You may not be my first, sweet Soraya, but you will be my last. About that day, in my bedroom… what you saw—"

Placing one finger on my lips, she shushes me. "I've made my peace with your past, Brandon. Maybe you should too. What matters from now on is the present and future." I kiss her fingertip, and she shivers in response. I want to see her do that again. And again.

I run my fingers through her hair, which resembles spun gold, and finally touch her face with my fingertips. Her skin is so soft. She really is utter perfection. However, before I can kiss her, my father interrupts us.

"Brandon, come on! Alpha Rio of Pyro Moon pack wants to talk to you about the troubles in the east." He doesn't take any notice of my new mate; it's almost like he can't even see her, but to my father, she is just another she-wolf, another pup maker. I will not allow this slight.

"Surely Alpha Rio can wait for today, father. I would like to introduce you to Soraya, my mate." The anger on my father's face appears almost instantaneously.

"Have you lost your mind, boy? Don't be turning into a lovesick werewolf now that you've had a sniff of your mate. There are more important matters at hand." Without barely a backward glance for my mate, my father marches back into the reception room. However, before he completely leaves the hall, I call back out to him.

"I refuse to have our mating witnessed. I will provide other evidence." I keep my voice as hard and firm as I can despite my fear of standing up to my father.

"What does it matter? If you're going to provide other evidence as you say?" His horrified look and questioning tone tests my resolve, but I need to demonstrate to Soraya that I will fight for what she wants and needs. I use logic as my final weapon.

"Exactly, Father, what does it matter? Pretty soon it will be obvious to everyone that we have mated, so what does it matter?" My father, noticing that I have outwitted him, relents.

"I will agree to this on the basis that you provide other evidence. And that you come with me now and speak to the Pyro Moon Alpha about the trouble in the east." Shock mingles with my joy for having secured this for Soraya, and the relief on her face is payment enough.

"Brandon, you go with your father. I would like to catch up with Fallon." I wink at her in thanks for not making this difficult as I know a fair few other mates would. "I'll wait for you." She bows her head to me, and my father looks on admiringly.

"She will make a good mate and also a loyal Luna when the time comes, son. She knows her place." For my father, this is the height of appraisal. A woman who knows her place, but for me, I want Soraya to be free to explore where she wants her place to be. I don't want her to feel bound by our bond. I want it to enhance her life, as she enhances mine. However, I have to take my victories where and when I can.

Ultimately, I need to know my place too.

~ Fallon ~

My heart hurts, probably more than my legs. I am wearing Alessia's dress, and the thought alone repulses me. She should be here, wearing the dress for herself. My family all continue to celebrate and rejoice; meanwhile, Alessia is missing, and her absence festers inside me like a rotting corpse. How can they forget?

The only solace I had was Raya, and now she belongs to Brandon. I am bereft all over again at the loss of my only comfort, my confidant, and filled with fear for her safety too. Clayton will now have ample opportunity to take advantage of her, especially if Bran goes back to the troubles in the east. Raya will be left here, alone, and it scares me now that I know what Clayton is capable of.

My veil, despite being the finest lace, still smothers me. I am choking not only because it is covering my face but at what it represents. I'm ready to rip it completely from my head when Raya walks into the reception hall with Brandon, who kisses her hand before joining our father. Raya seeks me out, and my breath catches in my throat when I see her face again. She's even more beautiful than I remembered.

It's been ten years since I have seen her face, with both of us taking the veil at eight years old, as is compulsory in our pack. I have often wondered about the slight, pale-faced beauty with the flowing yellow hair. Her eyes are a more brilliant blue than I remember. Her hair still shines golden on her head, and her face is even more glorious now.

As she approaches me, I attempt to gain some composure, some decorum, for I am not just a Daughter of the Veil. As the Alpha's youngest daughter, I am a Lady of the Veil too. "Congratulations, Raya. It was a beautiful ceremony and a joyful unveiling."

Raya smiles back at me radiantly. "Thank you, Fallon. I'm relieved it went as well as it did. Although, I can tell Brandon is furious about Clayton being late." Her assessment doesn't surprise me.

The tension between my two older brothers has been building for a while. I had always believed that Bran felt threatened by Clayton because our father seems to confide and favour his second born son more. When Alessia disappeared, the rumours were that Bran made her vanish. Now, I wonder. I wonder about so much that it consumes my sleep as well as my waking hours. Clayton is evil. I now know this to be true. Will Brandon be the same?

"Don't worry about my brothers tonight. This is a celebration of your liberty, enjoy it, Raya. You have a life of duty now as the Future Luna." Her eyes widen as realisation dawns on her. She is the mate of the Future Alpha, which makes her the Future Luna, and while most girls would have been overjoyed at the news, the serious and conscientious person that Raya is prevents her from seeing this as less than a mammoth task.

"I moved my stuff into the house before the ceremony. I'll be able to visit you every day now while you recover." We hold hands as we talk and watch, and an hour must pass by before Brandon comes back to collect his mate.

"Thank you for keeping Soraya company, little sister. I know you'll be happy to have her nearer to you." Keeping my voice steady, I tell him how much of a joy it is.

"Soraya, I'm sorry to interrupt, but my mother is insisting on us having our first dance to start off the festivities."

Raya practically runs to him; her pleasing smile almost tears my stomach apart. I've seen the mate bond before but this time it hurts fiercely.

Tears fill my eyes as I watch them walk away together. She looks so free, so happy and utterly cherished in my brother's arms. It's everything I could and should wish for my best friend. The lump in my throat grows as the tears fall, and yet, no one can see me because of my veil, and so I make no effort to hide my heartache.

I should never have been so careless; it was inevitable that someone would notice my distress.

"You're in love with her, aren't you?" Euan whispers to me. Icy cold dread grips the back of my head and neck, and fear constricts my chest, making it hard to breathe. What he speaks of is an abomination, punishable by death in our pack.

I don't know what you are insinuating, but stop right now, Euan. I use our mindlink to prevent others from overhearing for I would be stripped of every entitlement, every privilege and shunned for being so *unnatural.*

I can see it from your interactions and from how much you are grieving right now. It's okay, little sister. Your secret is safe with me. He pats me on the shoulder and says no more. Is that why I'm so sad? Am I really in love with Raya?

I never knew I was. Euan smiles sadly back at me. *I promise I never knew I did.*

The heart loves who it loves. But she is Brandon's now. She is mated to the Future Alpha, so you have to forget this, put it out of your mind. I nod my agreement to him, fresh tears streaming down my face, as I accept that I wanted something more than just a best friend and that will never happen.

I hear my brother talking, as my wheelchair begins to move. "Mother, I'm taking Fallon back up to her room; she's not feeling well." I accept the help Euan gives me. Tonight, I will grieve, and tomorrow I will be back, ready to fight for the truth and then justice.

The last thing I see of the celebration is of Raya, laughing and dancing with Bran spinning her around while her golden curls fly out around her. Her melodious laugh and her innocent happiness crumbles what remains of my heart and resolve. I cry all the way back to my room until, eventually, I feel nothing. I am empty inside.

~ Euan ~

Fallon falls apart after our little chat, and so I support her in the small way that I can. She really had no idea that she had developed deeper feelings for her friend, and as open-minded as I am, I need to counsel her, because the rest of the pack, our father in particular, will not tolerate it. And another one of my sisters in danger is the last thing I want or need.

I link Brandon on the way out so he knows that Fallon is safe and can at least enjoy his mate this evening without worrying. I have never seen my brother looking at anyone or anything the way he stares at his new mate. Jealousy bubbles up in my chest and relief fills my mind. I have no mate yet, one less person to care about, one less person to protect and one less weapon to be used against me. How can I both envy and pity my brother in equal measure for having found his mate?

When we reach Fallon's bedroom, I push her inside and wait to see if she asks me to stay.

"How could you tell? Do you know others... like me?"

It breaks my heart that she is discovering her true nature this way. Personally, I don't see an issue, but no one has ever asked for my opinion and nor are they likely to either. I don't know why I noticed Fallon's feelings for her friend, I just did. She seemed devastated beyond the worry of her friend potentially being hurt. Perhaps just looking at her more closely this past week made it obvious for me to see.

"Yes. There are others. Not in our pack but definitely in other packs. You know why you have to hide this, Fallon. You know that I love you and will support you no matter what. But you will not get the same support from Father." Her veiled head nods in response.

The Omegas arrive to help Fallon out of her dress and into bed, so I bid her goodnight and take the opportunity to slip away and change too. I will stand sentry outside Fallon's bedroom tonight.

After quickly showering and changing into sweats, I head back to Fallon's room, but I'm distracted by lights and mutterings inside my father's office. Creeping closer, I recognise Clayton's voice straight away.

"Once he goes away to the east again, we can interrogate her about his movements." His laugh causes me to shudder in revulsion. "No, he refused to have it witnessed. He's a pussy. Before long, my father will see it too and will name me Future Alpha instead."

I struggle to contain my wolf, Flynn. His anger at Clayton's betrayal and backstabbing grows by the second. I need to warn Bran, and I need to keep close to Fallon at all times. Who knows what else this mother fucker has planned for us.

"I'll have to wait until she is marked or with pup. I'll have the healers keep a close eye on her and blame it on what happened with Heidi. Then, as soon as we know they are fully bonded, we will be free to use her to weaken him."

Having heard enough, I creep away and return to my sister's room. As luck would have it, Fallon is safely tucked up in bed with a dark night-time veil covering her face. "Goodnight, little sister, I'll be right outside if you need me."

I will have to tell Brandon all I have overheard. It's the only way we can prevent the past from repeating itself.

Having assured Fallon earlier that her friend would be perfectly safe in our home, a wave of anxiety now attacks my peace of mind. No matter what happens, no matter the cost, I must help my brother protect his mate. Soraya is my Future Luna and my sister by law, and it is my solemn duty to ensure her security.

Brandon deserves to have one night of care-free mating. Once I give him my warning, he'll not rest until his mate is out of danger.

In the early hours, I see Brandon and his mate as he takes her into their new bedroom, just down the corridor from Fallon's room. Earlier, I envied my brother, but knowing what I do now, I feel nothing but sore hearted for what he must overcome.

Chapter Nine

~ Brandon ~

The rest of the evening goes by perfectly. Soraya dances with me, with her pretty white dress swinging around as we move and her long yellow hair flowing down her back. My heart feels like it could just burst out of my chest at any moment. Being with her makes me feel content and complete. I can only hope this is how our night will end.

When she stifles a yawn, I take the opportunity to suggest it's time for bed. Her cheeks flame in embarrassment, and the fear is clear to see in her eyes, but so is the desire. Of that I am in no doubt.

Saying our goodbyes will certainly draw attention to us and cause my mate further discomfort, so instead, I decide to allay her fears by making our leaving the party into a little game.

"Shall we sneak away before anyone notices us and makes a big deal about it?" I whisper to her, and butterflies fill my stomach when she smiles radiantly back at me.

"Yes. Please. I've had enough drama and attention for one day." We laugh together as we plan our escape.

"I think we should cut the cake and demand everyone have a taste, then, while everyone is busy, we can sneak off. We might have to leave separately, though."

"I will go to the bathroom, and then, you could come and meet me when you're able?" I kiss her hand once more; I appreciate her cunning and cooperation more than I can explain.

"Yes, my sweet. That sounds like a plan. Follow my lead, okay?" As she nods to me, her eyes twinkle conspiratorially, and my body reacts involuntarily, causing the blood to rush straight to my cock. Who knew I could find her innocence and cooperation so endearing. The pull to be alone with her is fairly overwhelming me now. I've never been so desperate for a moment alone with another person. I still haven't had an opportunity to kiss her, never mind anything else.

Interlocking my fingers through Soraya's, I call out to my mother. "We would like to cut our cake now and share it with our guests please, Mother." My mother, the obliging host, navigates the Omega's so that we are ready to cut the cake within a couple of minutes.

"Now, before Brandon and Soraya cut their cake, they must make a wish. Join me in prayer to the Moon Goddess that their wishes are granted." Forming a circle around us, the pack collectively chant their prayer while Soraya and I close our eyes and stand with our foreheads touching as we make our wish.

I wish for my mate's eternal safety, keep Soraya safe from harm. I repeat my wish over and over until the pack prayer is finished, meeting Soraya's beautiful eyes when I open my own as the pack cheers for us. This day, even with its hiccups, has been almost perfect. I just hope the rest of the night can match up, if not for mine, then definitely for Soraya's sake.

We cut the cake, and I playfully reach out to smear cream on Soraya's nose. She shrieks as she tries to dodge me, and I get to see a cheeky side to her nature when she rubs her nose against my neck, smearing the cream back onto me.

"Hey!" I shout to her through my laughter, and for a single moment, everyone else ceases to exist; it's just me and my mate in a charged, happiness filled moment.

It's over in a matter of seconds, but the desire for another moment like this one, but in private, spurs me on to ensure that we are able to slip away from the party without causing a scene.

Leaning down to Soraya's ear, I whisper, "Are you ready to make a run for it, sweetheart?" It pleases me that it takes her a second longer to gather her wits after our little moment together.

"Yes, I'll see you soon!" she tells me as she makes her way to the bathroom. Without wasting a second, I remind my father he has yet to dance with his Luna. He thanks me for the reminder before taking my mother by the hand and pulling her onto the dance floor.

Seizing the opportunity while I can, I grab a couple of slices of cake and a bottle of champagne before making my way to Soraya.

"Are you leaving, Brandon?" Deacon's voice calls out to me as I leave the hall. He is hiding in a corner, obviously avoiding the crowd.

"Yes, my mate is tired, and we wanted to slip away without a fuss." He nods to me in agreement.

"Very wise, I wish I had thought of that." He visibly blanches at his indiscretion, obviously mortified that he has mentioned his own union. "Heidi probably would have appreciated getting some rest that night, but we stayed at the party until 6am and then slept all the next day." He smiles sadly at the memory. "Cherish these moments, Brandon, for when they are all you have left, you will hate yourself for not realising that happiness is in the little moments we share. It's not a destination."

He stands and walks back into the hall with a promise to hold everyone off for a few minutes. I take the chance and call out to Soraya. She pokes her head out from the ladies' bathroom, smiling at me when she realises we have escaped.

We walk to our new home together, as we embark on our life as a mated pair. I can't resist pulling her close to me to experience the mate-bond tingles I have been hearing about my whole life. I must admit the rumour vastly unrated how amazing it feels to hold hands with your fated mate. Even though most of her flesh is covered, I still get to experience feeling whole with the other half of my soul.

"I hope you like the rooms allocated to us?" I ask her, and she nods back enthusiastically with a blush high on her cheeks. "Good, I'm glad you like them. They are yours to do whatever you please with."

Using the key given to me by my mother, I open the door to my new home and pull my mate in behind me. I bolt the door behind me, placing the champagne and cake on the small table in the lounge area. Soraya stands near the doorway with her arms crossed and wrapped around her.

"Are you cold?" I ask her, and as she shakes her head at me, I notice her hands trembling too. I stride across the room to her, closing the distance between us. "What is wrong, my sweet? You're shaking." Stroking her cheek again as I look into her eyes, I'm alarmed when tears fill those beautiful blue orbs.

"I'm scared. I don't know what to do, and I'm frightened that I'll disappoint you," she tells me honestly, her voice trembling.

Her fearing me is the last thing I want. It's heart-breaking that she thinks this way to begin with. "I'm so proud of you, and that you are my mate. You could never disappoint me, Soraya." After hearing my assurance, she finally makes eye contact again. Goddess above, she is exquisite. "You don't have to fear me or what is to come."

"I know what my duty is, Brandon. I know I have to do my duty but... I'm not completely sure of the... mechanics." With her eyes glistening and her cheeks bright red in embarrassment, she explains to me that she knows what she must do, but I'll need to teach her. "I'm asking for you to be patient, because I do want to please you and make you happy."

"Woah, hold up a minute. Let's back this up and go back to the start. You don't know what to do because you're a virgin, my virgin. You do not apologise for that." I sit down on the sofa and pull her down into my lap, making her yelp in surprise. "I know you want to do your duty. And I do too. But I also want us to do this because it's what we want. I want to be with you. I want to pleasure you and make you mine. I will make it enjoyable for you."

"My mother says it will hurt. And I'm worried about having pups; I'm not ready to be a mother yet." I rub her back, as she pours out all her worries to me.

I really like that she is willing to share her innermost thoughts and feelings with me. "And what if I'm really bad at it, Brandon? I mean, I saw you naked that one time and I just don't know how we are meant to... you know... fit together."

I don't know if she has finished, so I continue to rub circles on the small of her back and smile in satisfaction when I feel her physically relax against me. She might be apprehensive and scared but she trusts me. She wouldn't have told me all that and still be sitting on my lap as she is doing if she didn't trust me.

"All your worries are valid, Soraya. As I told you this morning, there is no rush. There is one thing I want from you tonight, and if you can give me that, or at least try, then I'll be more than happy." She starts to tense in anticipation of my request, of what I will ask of her. "I want to kiss my mate. It's been driving me wild all this time. I am so desperate to kiss you, Soraya. Can we at least try that?"

Taking me completely by surprise, Soraya slides off my lap, into the seat beside me and turns towards me. "I'd really like to kiss you, too," she says plainly, and the very air between us buzzes with anticipation and built up tension. I hold her face in my hands and drag my thumb across her bottom lip.

I have fantasised about this exact moment and now, it is finally here. The hundreds of fantasies I have had fail to live up to the reality of kissing my sweet mate. I know this for sure when my lips finally connect with hers.

Soft, plump, sweet lips against my warm, hard ones. She keeps her mouth firmly shut, which makes me smile. She said I'd have to teach her, and I will relish every tiny moment of it. Placing my thumb on her chin, I apply a small amount of pressure so she follows that I want her to open up her mouth for me. As soon as she yields, I gently probe her mouth using my tongue, and it floors me when I finally realise how amazing she tastes. She gasps against my mouth; however, she quickly catches on to what I want her to do and returns my kiss just as passionately as I anticipated.

We kiss for a few seconds, and when she makes a quiet moaning sound at the back of her throat, I allow my tongue to duel with hers and growl in satisfaction when she timidly copies my motion. This is the hottest moment of my entire life, and all we are doing is kissing.

I pull Soraya back onto my lap and our kiss becomes frenzied. I can't get enough, but I hold back, wanting to respect her boundaries.

"Ahem, it seems the young love birds are starting without us." A deep voice muses, and Soraya rushes away from me, full of embarrassment. I should have realised that our moment of privacy wouldn't last. "We knocked, but when you didn't answer the door, we used the key your father provided us with." When I look up, three elders stand inside our apartment.

"Elder Dorien, Elder Simon, Elder Randall; what do you want? What are you doing here?" I ask distractedly, as I look searchingly for Soraya. I hope she is okay. We weren't doing anything wrong. We are mates and in the privacy of our own home. I already want to get rid of them as soon as possible so I can resume kissing my mate

Instead, my insides twist in horror when Elder Dorien tells me why they are in my room. "We are here to witness your consummation, of course."

Chapter Ten

~ Soraya ~

The whole day is a whirlwind, and the majority of it passes pleasantly. Apprehension builds inside of me when I consider tonight, but for reasons unknown to me, I trust Brandon to guide me. Despite not knowing him very well, I know deep in my bones that he will keep me safe, and that is rare in a pack like ours. Most ladies can only wish for their ordeal to be over quickly and as painlessly as possible. From his conduct and consideration today, I can't envision Brandon ever deliberately hurting me. Quite the opposite in fact.

A part of me cannot believe my luck; maybe Brandon and I can be really happy and make a decent life together. He has shown me nothing but respect since he realised he is my mate. If this continues, I know I have been extremely blessed by the Moon Goddess.

Despite my worries, when Brandon suggests calling it a night, I don't hesitate in agreeing. I crave a moment alone with him, no matter how much being alone with him and what it will lead to scares me. I know it'll be okay, because Brandon will make it so.

I try to be brave, but being alone with Brandon in our new home overwhelms me. My whole-body shakes and trembles, as I stand in the entrance of our sitting room, but the warmth in Brandon's eyes chases away most of my reservations. Before I know what is happening, I am sitting in his lap, telling him my every worry. Even more astonishingly, Brandon is listening to me and soothing me. His hand touches my back, and an instant tranquillity comes over me. Everything in the world is okay, because I have my mate, the other half of me.

Brandon does everything he can to reassure me, and as I look into his eyes, the room around us pales. Nothing else matters, only us. With curiosity piqued, I wonder what mating with him will be like. Will it hurt as much as I fear? Will I be able to please him? And what of pups? That consequence is what stalls me the most. I am not ready for such a task.

"All your worries are valid, Soraya. As I told you this morning, there is no rush. There is one thing I want from you tonight, and if you can give me that, or at least try, then I'll be more than happy." I tense involuntarily as I wait to hear what he expects from me, hoping that whatever it is he wants is something I can do, because I do want to please him. "I want to kiss my mate. It's been driving me wild all this time. I am so desperate to kiss you, Soraya. Can we at least try that?"

My heartbeat escalates rapidly, as he waits for my reply. His frankness emboldens me to be honest. I move to the seat beside him so I can face him. "I would like that too," I admit, and the smile that Brandon gives me in return further encourages me.

I look at his mouth because I don't feel brave enough to make eye contact after my bold statement, but I quickly realise that this is a bad decision. Once I look at his lips, I can't stop thinking about what it will be like to have his lips pressed against mine. Until finally, Brandon takes mercy on me and brushes his lips against mine. The warm sensations flood and overwhelm my senses. I am his and he will forever be mine after tonight. All reservations fade away as I allow Brandon to show me what it is he wants me to do. The kiss initially starts very chaste and innocent, but within seconds my tongue is mating with Brandon's.

He holds my face in his large, calloused hands, and I want nothing more than to be closer to him. The craving and yearning to be with him floors me, so fierce and strong and insistent. I have never known a feeling quite like it.

Then, in a blink of an eye, the whole mirage shatters, and when I look up, the pack Elders are there telling us they are in attendance to witness our consummation.

I run from the room, away from the Elders and their expectations. Away from Brandon and his power to make me forget who and what I am. Horror seeps into my bones, and anxiety and panic war with my body. I want to run and hide. I want to be free from expectation. However, I now want to be free with Brandon.

"I told my Alpha father that I refuse a witnessed consummation. Why are you here?" I stand at the door obscured from their view and listen to what my mate says. Pride bursts from my chest when I hear the way he stands up for us and the sweet words in which he uses in reference to me. Brandon makes me feel brave and worthy.

I re-enter the sitting room with my head held high as I listen to my mate admonishing the Elders for their interruption.

"You had no right to enter my home. What if Soraya had been here alone? I want you to leave right now." Brandon stands tall, towering over each of the Elders. I proudly take his hand and stand beside him, feeling my full strength shining through in my mate's presence.

"Okay, dear boy, I can see you will have no trouble bedding your mate, and so we will leave you to it, no matter how much we were looking forward to doing our duty, too." The older gentlemen chuckle amongst themselves, making my skin crawl. "We will require further evidence, but the fact that you've wooed her already reassures us that there will be no objections to your pairing." Brandon takes the key from them, as they leave, and once they are gone, he bolts the door and also pulls a wooden stand to block anyone else entering unannounced.

He stands in front of me, and I realise there is quite a significant difference in size between us. I am eye-level with his very firm sculpted chest. If we were to stand toe-to-toe, I would have to crane my neck all the way back to look into his eyes.

"I'm sorry about that, sweetheart. Where were we?" he says to me, and my whole body throbs in response once again. However, the moment, our moment and our first kiss, has passed. "Come to me. I'd like to make a toast to us."

I walk back to his side and accept the glass of champagne he pours for me, before pouring his own. "To my beautiful mate, may we have a long, happy and fruitful life together." He holds his glass up to me, and I repeat the motion, having never done this before.

Brandon drinks his champagne, and I tentatively sip at mine, pulling my face at the taste, causing Brandon to laugh in response. "Was that your first time?" I nod my head, believing he is asking if it is my first-time drinking alcohol.

"We would never have anything as extravagant as champagne in the Huts. The men may make moonshine, but the ladies would never take any of that." Brandon smiles at me as he takes my glass away, which is probably a good thing because my face is feeling very hot all of a sudden.

"I wasn't talking about the champagne. I was asking if that was your first kiss." He places down the glasses and takes my hands once again.

"You know it is. My first kiss belongs to my mate. You know the vows the Daughters of the Veil take." If my face weren't red before, it most certainly is now. I look down again, unable to meet his intense stare. "It wasn't your first kiss, though, was it?" I ask back, both desperate for the answer and knowing full well his honest response will shatter me.

"No, it's not. But it was my first time kissing my fated mate. It was the most sensational kiss I have ever experienced." Chancing a look up at his face to see if he's mocking me, I am relieved to see that he seems sincere. "I want more of those kisses, with you and only you."

I don't make a conscious decision to kiss him again, but somehow, that's exactly what I do. Brandon appears to like my forwardness because he picks me up and spins me around as I kiss him, and he kisses me back with passion.

"I will never get enough of you, Soraya. You're so fucking sweet and delicious. And you're all mine!" His words, so unexpected, seem to reach me deep down in the pit of my stomach, flooding me with an unfulfilled desire. "I want to take you to bed, I want to mate. But I will take your lead. What do you want, my Sweet?"

What do I want? I know I want Brandon; I know I'm ready to be his, but a niggling doubt still stops me. "I don't want to be a mother just yet, Brandon. I know you need an heir, but I just need a little time to adjust."

Kissing down to the place where he will eventually mark me, waves of delight warm every nerve in my body when he kisses me there. "That isn't what I asked. I asked you what you want. Putting heirs and duty and customs aside, what does my sweet Soraya want?"

The ache in my stomach travels to the junction between my legs as Brandon continues to pepper my sensitive marking spot with his warm kisses.

"I don't know," I tell him plainly as I shudder, his touch overwhelming my thoughts and senses. "I'm not sure of the words to use."

"Do you want me to do something about the delicious arousal I can smell coming from you?" I gasp and try to move away, but Brandon holds me steady. "That is all mine, Soraya. We don't have to mate, but I would like to make you feel good and do something about your needs because your scent is driving me crazy."

I moan involuntarily when he nips at my marking spot, alternating his gentle little bites with teasing swipes of his tongue. "Do you like that?" he asks me, and his hot breath against my puckered skin is working even Pandora up into a frenzy.

Say yes, tell him we need him. We need more. She tells me insistently, *our mate has the power to make us feel better, say yes.*

Caught up in the mixture of feelings, I simply tell him, "Yes," which raises another grin from him, causing me to blush even deeper than before.

"Yes, what? My Sweet. Do you like that? Do you want me to make you feel good? Can you trust me?" At the end of a rope of my own making, I finally surrender to him.

"Yes. Yes, and yes. But if we don't mate... everyone will know." I don't understand what Brandon's intentions are. All I really know is that my body feels tormented, and he has promised to help relieve that.

"Don't worry about anyone else, just concentrate on you and me. I would like you to remove your dress and lie down on our new bed." He removes his shoes and his tie and unbuttons his collar. "Would you like me to help you undress?"

I nod to him, turning my back to him and showing him where my dress is tied at the back. After untying the ribbons, Brandon loosens all the loops and fastenings before turning me around to face him again.

"Come on, sweetheart. Take off your dress so we can go to bed."

"But, Bran, first about pups... I'm concerned."

"I will not be putting a pup in you tonight, Soraya. Please trust me. We will not mate until I can prevent it from happening, for now."

"But you want me to undress?" He finally smiles as I reach what I am confused about.

"I do want you to undress, but what I want to do tonight will not create a pup. Trust me. Tonight is purely about being with you and bringing you pleasure."

With his reassurance, my worries are temporarily appeased, and so I finally allow my dress to fall from my body and onto the floor.

~ Brandon ~

Soraya's responses are so honest and refreshing to watch, I want to see her every reaction. Her open and innocent remarks consistently remind me of her inexperience, but her big, blue eyes look at me with such trust and curiosity. No one has ever looked at me in this way. People look at me with fear and intrigue. Sometimes they even look at me to see what they can gain from interacting with me or to compare me to my father and now my brothers. The look Soraya gives me is something I have never ever experienced before. She delights me. I don't have to second guess her because I know she'll tell me honestly if there is something she wants or needs to share.

The alluring scent of Soraya's arousal fills the room; it's an involuntary reaction that no one can control. Maverick purrs with superiority that our mate wants us. She doesn't realise it yet, but she does. And all I want to do is ensure that after tonight she will not only know that she desires me, but she will want to do something about it too.

Alessia was the person who informed me that females can receive pleasure in mating. Until that point, I thought it was a means to an end for me and my fulfilment. How she laughed at me when she informed me of the ignorant and selfish lover I was and that I had a lot to learn about the female form and how to worship it. At first I thought she was pulling my tail. Women give pleasure and carry pups. But Alessia insisted it could be both satisfying and euphoric for a woman, if her lover treats her right, of course.

I had never concerned myself with pleasuring a woman before that. Why would I? I would often seek the service of a Scarlet Woman, but it was a mere transaction which was to benefit me. However, once Alessia planted the seed in my head, I had to see for myself if it were true. The next time I sought a Scarlet Woman, I looked for an older lady and asked her directly. Her coy smile confirmed what Alessia had told me, and so for a couple of weeks I returned to the older woman, who showed me everything I needed to know for when the time came to satisfy my mate.

And that time has arrived. I'm worked up in anticipation. Tonight is completely about Soraya. I need to keep myself, and Maverick, under control, but it's a hard task because I can't wait to see her in all her glory.

My anticipation causes butterflies to flap about in my stomach, but I try not to show her my nerves. It's already blatantly obvious that she is nervous enough for the both of us. Regardless of this being my first time lying with my mate, it's her first time ever, and her needs are paramount to mine.

The trust she places in me satisfies me more than any sexual act could. She is mine, and I will look after her. She is my world now. When she turns her back to me to help her with her dress, it takes all my willpower to not bend her over and claim her right here and now. My natural instincts as a werewolf plague me now. *Please let me do this the right way, Maverick. Let me do this my way for my mate.* I reason with my wolf, and after furiously rebuking me, he submits to me but tells me to hurry up and get her claimed, or he will do it for me.

Soraya stands before me, and I reassure her that I will not be planting a pup in her tonight. With this tiny amount of reassurance, she lets her dress float off her tiny frame, exposing her creamy skin to me at long last. She wears simple white underwear as a sign of her purity, and my heart swells with pride. My mate, she is mine.

"You are flawless, Soraya. My perfect mate." My hands span her waist. Her skin is so smooth and soft. We really are like day and night, and it's an incredible mix. I finally kiss her again, and this time she knows I want her to open her mouth. She moans again when I scrape my teeth across her bottom lip. Goddess above, she tastes delicious, so sweet and intoxicating. I clearly cannot get enough.

Sweeping her up in my arms, without breaking our kiss, I carry her to our new bedroom. The spacious room is tastefully decorated in deep reds and gold and is filled with sturdy dark wood furniture.

The four-poster bed must have seemed ominous to her when she first saw it; however, now it will be our sanctuary. She will grow to love our place here. It is adorned with the finest silks, and the Evidential sheet, the one that proves our consummation, is already laid out for us. I rip it from the bed and throw it into the corner, out of both of our sights and, therefore, thoughts.

Placing her down in the centre of the bed and covering her body with my own makes me sigh in delight. The cool silk sheets are not even comparable to how Soraya looks and feels to me. I am amazed that she is so receptive to my touch. She quivers and trembles at the tiniest of movements and yet she accepts it all too.

The sensation of her skin against mine leaves me euphoric, and to my delight, our bond continues to grow and knit closer together. I gently slide my hand down her body, relishing the responses it sends throughout my own body. I could never deny the way she makes me feel. Like a whole person, a proper man. Like a mate.

I graze my hand over her pert breasts, and even over her chemise, I can tell she is in perfect proportion. A growl erupts in the back of my throat in admiration. "So, fucking beautiful. Every inch of you is just perfection." Her eyes are now heavy lidded and full of passion as the yearning takes hold of her. "Look at how amazing we look together, sweetheart. Individually we are so different, but together we are simply magnificent."

She looks down at our bodies but doesn't say anything else. My dark hand splays across her milky abdomen. "I can't wait to see us fully joined together, sweetheart; it will be phenomenal when we finally become one. But that is for another night. For now I want to tend to that arousal of yours. Tell me, my sweet, have you ever touched yourself?"

From the way she frowns, I know she hasn't. My Soraya is as pure as the day she was born. "That's okay. We can discover together what you like. I would like to touch you, right here." I lightly touch her pussy with my fingertips and feel her panties are already damp with arousal for me. The emanating heat reminds me of the burning desire in my own underwear. "But I want to do it under your clothes. Will you permit that?"

"Yes. I give you permission, Brandon. I feel strange inside... I can't describe it." I kiss her again, before she becomes overwhelmed. Her first encounter is bound to be overwhelming, and I don't want it to frighten her. I smile in appreciation as she helps me to remove her undergarments, catching my first glimpse of her fully naked.

"Shhh, my sweet, let me take care of it." Slipping my hand in between her thighs, I gently and tantalisingly stroke up to the junction at the top. She moans against my mouth, gasping for air, as I touch her for the first time. A shiver of delight runs throughout me as I explore her wet folds. "Oh, baby! You feel even better than my wildest fantasies. This is mine now. All of you belongs to me. You are mine."

"I am yours," she reaffirms to me. She's out of breath, panting, as I continue to probe and explore her. Using my fingers, I spread her lips wide and ever so gently rub my fingertip across the little bundle of nerves at the crest of her womanhood.

"Brandon!" She calls out when I do, and I shush her once more, I know the new sensations are taking her by surprise. The power I wield over her body, the ability to give her something so incredible, is fascinating. As I circle her clit, her legs begin to shake. I sense her rapidly beating heart and her irregular breathing when the sensations take her higher and higher to oblivion. I cannot wait for more, so I kiss down to her breasts that are at long last exposed to me, topped with light pink peaks. Her breasts are full, rounded and pert, and just right on her frame.

I continue my assault on her clit. Using my thumb, I finally allow myself to touch her entrance. She's wet but so, so tight. No wonder she worried about the mechanics of us mating. Even one finger inside there is bound to hurt. I continue to lightly probe around the entrance of her glorious hole until she calls to me.

"Bran, something... oh my goodness... Brandon!" Her eyes are now almost completely closed, her lips swollen from my kisses, and the blush on her cheeks is no longer from embarrassment alone. "Brandon, what is happening?" I watch in awe as my mate cums on my hand, all through my doing. Her body shakes and spasms, and she calls out my name as waves of illicit pleasure attack her whole entire body.

"Oh baby, you look incredible when you cum. That is just the start of me worshipping you. Do you like it?" I peek back up at her when I ask; however, she continues to look back at me, dazed, but passion instantly ignites in her beautiful eyes. "I want to try and do it again, but this time, I need to see you."

"You want to look at me... down there?" she asks me in a strangled voice, alarm rising in her.

"Soraya, I'm not going to just look, I'm going to kiss you there, and lick and suck, and you'll like it. I am going to love it!" Her eyes widen at my brazen declaration, but there is no denying the desire and want her body exudes.

"Are you sure this is okay? Is this what mates do?" she asks me even as she allows me to spread her legs apart.

"It's what *we* do. I don't give a fuck about other mates. My sweetheart is going to be worshipped by me, every single millimetre of her." I look up into her eyes as I swipe my tongue up her pink slit, gently poking at her clit once more. Her sweet and tangy taste explodes on my tongue. My cock is now ferociously demanding attention as it stands thick, hard and throbbing in my pants, which seem to have gotten a lot tighter in the past ten minutes.

"Oh, my sweet Moon Goddess!" she cries as her head drops back against the bed, and her body shudders once more. She bunches up the silk covers in her hands as the pleasure rolls across her.

I smile as I explore the very heat of her with my mouth, but not before reminding her, "Not Moon Goddess, Soraya, it's Brandon! Call my name, sweetheart, mine and only mine."

Chapter Eleven

~ Soraya ~

My whole-body floats on another plain. Brandon has been touching me intimately, but has also turned my mind to mush. I do not know what this witchcraft is, and if I am honest, the way I feel right now, I don't care what witchcraft it is. I want to get on my knees and thank all the Goddesses for my blessings. Not only is Brandon kind and considerate, but he is spending time to bring pleasure to me. I expected pain tonight, but this is a long way away from pain. This feels amazing.

Now, he uses his lips and tongue on my most private parts. At first, I thought maybe he had it wrong, surely, he didn't mean to kiss me there, but now, I know, I have never felt anything so right. Brazenly, I hope he'll want to do it again. And again.

Wow. Who knew my mate could make me feel this way? That he would want me to feel this way. Fresh waves of pleasure roll over my body as Brandon continues to kiss me between my legs. There is one ultra-sensitive spot that he concentrates on, and every time he licks, kisses and even bites that spot, my legs shake, and a warm glow seems to emit from inside me until euphoria bathes every millimetre of my body, ebbing and flowing, and elevating me to an ethereal height.

"Brandon!!" I call out as my entire being convulses in pleasure. But even as my body is in raptures, I feel myself tear inside, bringing pain where there was once ecstasy. I flinch away from his hand and his mouth, not wanting the discomfort to continue.

"I'm sorry, sweetheart, I didn't mean to hurt you. You're so innocent and pure. Let me make you feel better again." I shake my head no, but deep down I know Brandon wouldn't hurt me on purpose. "Mating will hurt you a little at first, Sweet, but I'm hoping I can prepare you as much as possible to minimise that hurt. Your maidenhead is still intact. Fully intact in fact!" I lower my head, embarrassed about the topic.

"I'm sorry, Brandon. I do want to make you happy. Is there something I can do to fix it?" He chuckles and raises his eyebrows at me causing my stomach to somersault.

"Just leave it to me. I will take it eventually; I just need to figure out the least painful way to do it." He sits up on our bed, leaving me naked and exposed, and so I try to cover myself with the sheets. "Are you trying to hide from me? Did you forget so quickly where I just had my tongue, Soraya?"

Looking at me with an expectant expression, I moan as my embarrassment hits full force. "Brandon!" But his laugh is infectious, and eventually, I laugh along with him.

"Did you enjoy what we did?" For the first time, he's the one who looks vulnerable, and my instant reaction is to reassure him.

"I think it was pretty obvious I did! I never knew… I didn't know it could be like that." With all my inhibition forgotten, I kneel up, lean over to him and kiss him fully on the lips. "Thank you for worshipping me, and for being mine… I think it's my turn to worship you now."

Clearly, I have no idea what worshipping my mate will entail, but what I do know is that I want to give Brandon what he has given me. I want to make him feel how he made me feel. I want to share everything with him.

"Don't worry about me; I think you've had enough of an education for tonight. I don't want to completely corrupt you just yet!" But I insist. I begin by unbuttoning his shirt, noticing how my hands shake as I do. "You are amazing, Soraya. I will never, ever tire of you."

His encouragement is all I need to continue. His approval makes me brave, and so once I have completely removed his shirt, I gently rub my hands over his firm, toned body. Where I am light, he is dark, and where he is powerful, I am soft. "Where can I touch you to make you feel good, Brandon?"

His reactions fascinate me: the way he shudders as I run my fingertips lightly over his pecs and nipples, his breath catching in his throat. It's powerful knowing I can make him feel like I did before.

"You mean aside from the obvious?" I've lost track of what I asked him, so I nod at him and hope he doesn't notice.

"What you're doing right now is pretty awesome, but I suppose you'd have to touch me in similar places that I have touched you." I chance a glance at his lower region, and the bulge in his pants only seems to have gotten bigger. Imagining what it would be like to hold him and stroke him as intimately as he did me has fresh stirrings of arousal building up inside me again.

"Would you like me to show you?" Nodding to him, as I unbuckle his belt, he gasps again. "Just tell me if you want to stop at any point and we will."

"I will, Bran, I promise." He kisses me hard, and my passion is now reaching a fever pitch. How is it that I want to kiss him so much? I push my hand down from his chest to his abs and lower again, over his pants. He is so hard and masculine. When he gasps again, I worry I've hurt him. "Did I hurt you? Do you want me to stop?" I ask him, slightly panicked.

"No, don't stop, sweetheart. The touch of your fated mate really cannot compare; your touch is spectacular." His praise and obvious enjoyment inspires me to continue. However, I need space; there is not much room to manoeuvre inside his pants.

"Can I undress you please, Brandon?" He doesn't waste time in aiding me, and now, as he lowers his pants, I see his manhood without restriction. It looks bigger than I recall from that time I walked in on him with the Scarlet Woman. A lot bigger! Panic rises in me, starting in my chest that pounds erratically and then spreading to the pit of my stomach and up to the whirling thoughts in my head.

"Hey, please don't panic. It's going to be okay." Brandon encourages me to stand and wraps his thick, muscular arms around my slight frame. His comforting embrace, the tingles that shoot through my body and everything we have already done this evening suddenly hit me; this is a lot for me to take. "Did I scare you?" he asks me softly as he pushes my hair off my face.

I nod to him, and to my internal disgust, tears swim in my eyes, clouding my vision, and I have no other option but to explain myself. "It's a lot to take in. And I'm still worried about how this is going to work physically between us."

He holds me close and rubs my back again like he did earlier, in gentle circular rhythms that my body cannot help but relax against. My body moulds to his, and suddenly, I know it'll be okay; the Moon Goddess fated us and it will be ok.

"If you cannot believe me and what I tell you, do you trust the Moon Goddess? Do you trust that she sent your perfect match as a mate?" I nod to him because I do trust her and her plan for us all. "The Moon Goddess blessed us, and this will work because she has foreseen it and made it so."

"I'm sorry I have so many doubts, Brandon. Truly, I am happy that we are fated, but it looks so big, and I struggle to see how it will fit." His deep chuckle that I am now growing to love warms me.

"Let me tell you, baby, it will fit, and it will work. Just give your body and mind time to adjust, and I promise, we will fit together. It's going to be breath-taking!" I accept his assurances because I honestly cannot process anything more at this moment. "Shall we go to bed now? I don't know about you, but it's been a long couple of days, and I can't wait to get into bed and sleep next to you."

When I turn to get my clothes, Brandon lifts me once more and carries me back to bed. "I'd like for us to sleep naked. Is that okay, my Sweet?"

He's asked so very little from me thus far, and I do trust him, and therefore, as alien as it feels to sleep in my bare skin, I decide to do it to please Brandon. He pulls my body close to his own, and with my head nestled in the crook of his arm and my hand on his chest, I have sincerely never felt safer.

"Sweetheart, tomorrow, outside of our home we have to keep to customs. You must address me as sir and obey my word." I already know this. Although this night has been full of surprises, I never expected it to continue, especially not outside of our cocoon. "However, when we are here, just you and me, I'm your Brandon and this is how I want it to be between us. I want you to be yourself and be happy."

He kisses my head as I fall asleep, holding me and stroking me. "Good night, Brandon. Sweet dreams."

"Good night, my Sweet."

The following morning, I wake up in the exact same position I fell asleep in. Complete with a puddle of drool travelling down my cheek and glistening away on Brandon's chest.

"Morning! We are late for breakfast, but you were sleeping so soundly that I didn't want to wake you."

Self-consciously, I try to flatten my hair. He is staring so attentively in my direction, but if he wasn't, I would have pinched my cheeks to add a bit of colour. I have never been concerned about my appearance before now. However, this is the first time Brandon is seeing me in the morning without my clothes as well as my veil. I want to look appealing to him.

"You're so cute!" He teases me as I hide away from him. "How am I ever going to keep my hands off you for a whole family breakfast?" His comments warm me inside, despite feeling exposed and self-conscious. Brandon still desires me and finds me appealing even with uncombed, messy hair!

Breakfast is a busy and loud affair for the Ward family. There are terrines and platters of food. More food than I have ever seen at one time. As my eyes greedily attempt to see everything at once, Brandon keeps edging me towards my seat next to him at the table. Everything seems to be going well until Clayton enters the room.

"Good morning, love birds. Why don't you show us all your mate marks?" Instantly, all heads in the room look at Brandon and me. As panic rages inside me, Brandon holds tightly to my hand. "Father... she's unmarked! I cannot see her mate's mark." He smiles wickedly at us, and Brandon, having had enough provocation, stands abruptly from his seat, forcing the chair to clatter as it topples over.

"And? We haven't marked each other yet, but we will." Brandon spits out at his brother. I can feel the animosity rolling off him and so, I stand next to him to show my support.

"You brought a whore into my dining hall?" our Alpha roars across the room. From the satisfied smirk on Clayton's face, he wanted this to happen.

"She is no whore; she is the absolute opposite of a whore. She's my mate! MINE!" Brandon roars back at his father, who paces rapidly towards us. Before I can defend myself, the Alpha grabs me by the hair, pulling my head back to expose my neck and, more importantly, my marking spot.

"I don't see a mark, and she's definitely not wearing a veil. Therefore, she is a WHORE!" the Alpha growls back at his son, unhappy with being contradicted. "No evidence. No mark. Are you keeping a whore here?"

I fall sideways as Brandon pounces on his father. "GET YOUR FUCKING HANDS OFF HER NOW!" Brandon yells at his father. "SHE IS MINE! Soraya, go back to our rooms now!"

"Yes, sir." I reply, as I scurry from the room as fast as I can. The shifting sounds and growls that follow me out scare me, but there is no way I'm going to disobey Brandon's order.

Unable to hold back the torment, I cry as soon as I reach our rooms. What is going on? Is my mate going to be okay?

~ Brandon ~

Maverick rages at the insult hurled at our mate. *Kill them now, take their throats.* But I wait until the doors close behind Soraya, ensuring she is safely from this room, before I respond. Euan shifts and stands loyally by my side. Clayton smirks from behind our father's shoulder, and Deacon sits at the table, engrossed in his porridge.

"How dare you touch my mate! How dare you speak of her in such a disgusting manner. I am the Future Alpha, making her our Future Luna, and you will show her the respect she deserves." I begin. I do not look at Clayton but at our father instead. He taught me these rules. He taught me that she-wolves are inferior to us men, but the Luna, or Future Luna in this case, is to be worshipped and adored. As the mate of the Alpha, people need to see why she is worthy of such a position.

"She isn't your mate, *yet!* She does not bear your mark, and therefore, she isn't yours *yet.*" My father shows no weakness; he will not relent on this point. "Why didn't you mark her? You assured me you would provide alternative proof. The Evidential sheet has not been presented. She has no mark. Did you forget?"

I shift uncomfortably, not wanting to betray Soraya's confidence, but I have to defend her and defend us, too. "She is a devout Daughter of the Veil, father. Just as you intend the females of our pack. This is all new to her. I will provide evidence, but I want to be patient with her too. She has done her duty, and she will continue to do her duty; of that, I have no doubt."

"Patience? Are you crazy, boy? Fill her with your child and have done with it, Brandon. You know what is expected of you. Your consummation will be witnessed this evening. This time you will not wriggle out of it." Clayton giggles at my father's speech, riling me up even more.

"What would you have me do? Hold her down and force her?" I ask the man I once idolised more than any other.

"If that's what it takes, then, yes." he replies, sitting down to his bacon and eggs, thinking this discussion is done.

I slam my hands down on the dining table, causing glasses to smash and food to bounce off their current holders. "I will NOT rape her!"

"She's your mate, how can it be rape? Just get it done, Brandon." He looks up at me with cold, evil eyes. "I'll attend myself this evening with the Elders. Do your duty, or tonight, I'll personally ruin her myself and declare her a Scarlet Woman at breakfast tomorrow. Is that what you want?"

He repulses me to the point that I don't recognise this waste of organs. My mother sits with her head bowed. Is that how her fate was sealed? Is this why she is so closed and cold? Her mate is threatening to rape mine, and she sits cowering.

"Fine. I will see you this evening. But make no bones about it *Alpha*. She is mine and no one, not even you, will ever touch her again." My father looks at me admiringly and tips his head in recognition of my defence.

Clayton, however, doesn't read the truce between us and continues to prod and goad me. "Brother, perhaps you don't know where it goes... shall I give you a little lesson on the art of lovemaking?" Before I have a chance to respond, Euan lunges at Clayton, grabbing his throat threateningly. "Get off me! You big mongrel!"

As Clayton wriggles on the floor, I stand over him, exuding my authority. "Euan has vowed to serve me; he is loyal to me. You insult me or my Lady Mate again, I'll allow him to rip that toxic throat clean from you. DO YOU UNDERSTAND?"

"BOYS! Stop fighting and get some breakfast." our father rules, as he cuts into blood sausage and fried tomatoes. The colour of his food forces me to think of what is to come. "Clayton, do not speak such words in front of your sister again." Suddenly, I have no appetite, and my overwhelming drive is to go to Soraya and ensure her safety.

"I've lost my appetite. I'm going home," I tell them as I walk from the room, with Euan at my heels. "Thank you for your loyalty, little brother. I have another task for you. I need you to guard the door for a while. Fallon should be okay with mother today."

Staying in his wolf form, my brother stands sentry outside the door to my rooms. I don't relish the idea of telling Soraya what has been said, but I have to inform her so she can be involved in how we progress. Although I have a couple of ideas of what we could do now, all of them seem drastic.

"BRAN?" Soraya shouts as I open the door. "Oh, my Goddess, are you okay, Brandon? I was so worried!" I'm ecstatic when she practically leaps into my arms.

"I'm okay, sweetheart. I can't apologise enough for what happened at breakfast. My father is furious, and I know that is not a pleasant experience for anyone."

"We forgot about the marking complication. I do understand, now. I should have stayed shielded until we marked each other. We were both so happy and easily allowed ourselves to be swept away with finding each other," she explains in reflection.

"I still do not believe we have done anything wrong. We have just found each other; you shouldn't blame yourself for getting carried away. That is what happens when you find your mate and you are happy," I assure her, because I don't want her to blame herself.

Although she offers me a small smile, I can tell she still blames herself. "What will happen now, Bran?"

I pull her back to the same couch we shared our first kiss on last night. This time she climbs onto my lap, filling me with contentment and arousal. "My father says he's returning with the Elders tonight to witness our consummation. He will declare you a Scarlet Woman if you aren't marked by morning."

Resting her head against my shoulder, she doesn't shake with upset and worry like I anticipated. "Oh! I see," she simply replies.

"We have a couple of options. Euan is standing guard for us right now. We could make a run for it. I know a little place we could go, but... I'm not going to sugar-coat this. This is dangerous, and it won't be an easy life. But we would be free to be mates and do things at our leisure. And we could avoid those old trouts from demanding to witness our special moment."

"Would we be free, though, Brandon? Truly? You're the Future Alpha. They aren't going to just let you run off." As she strokes my neck gently with her fingertips, I am soothed and calmed by her. "Would I still be able to see my family? Will they be safe here once we leave?"

"I don't think they will be, Soraya. I'm sorry. I cannot guarantee that. But what other options do we have?" Everything is falling apart. I'm falling apart because I want to protect her, but I can't. "The other option would be to allow them to witness our consummation. I don't want that, not like that. This shouldn't be about them. This is about you and me."

She holds my head in her tiny hands and looks into my eyes with her beautiful big blues, as she talks to me. "Or there is a third option... and my favoured option," she tells me shyly; her reddened cheeks already inform me that this is a delicate matter. "We mate and mark now, before they arrive this evening. On our terms with no witnesses."

She'll never fail to surprise me; that is for sure. "But I told you we would wait until you were ready. I hate this. I wanted it to be your choice." As I lower my head, she raises it back up. This time she looks confident and sure.

"Brandon. This is something that is going to happen, and given the freedom to choose from the options we have, my choice would be option three." She smiles down at me, my shining ray of light, and I once again thank the Moon Goddess for my good fortune. "Yes, it would have been nice to wait a little longer. But I am yours, Brandon. I'm ready to be yours and for the whole world to know it, too." And with that, she leans forward and kisses me soundly, just like I taught her last night.

~ Fallon ~

Once Brandon and Euan leave the room, everyone starts talking at once. I clear my throat and address my father. I have heard my brothers talking before, but my father has never spoken freely like that in front of me before. I obviously know more than the average Lady of the Veil because of my brothers and their friends frequenting the Alpha Quarters; however, my mother and father don't know how knowledgeable I am. To them I am their little girl, Fallon. So, I am going to take this opportunity to make my father feel uncomfortable.

"Daddy?" I call to him in my sweetest, sickliest voice, causing my mother to snap her head in my direction, warning me with her eyes, like only a mother can. "Daddy? What is rape? Would you allow my mate to rape me if I said no?"

"Fallon. You will not talk about such things. Stop this immediately," my mother admonishes, but I overlook her and continue to press my father, under the guise of curiosity.

"With all due respect, dear mother, I am trying to learn to be a good mate for the future and Lady of the Veil for the present. Please allow father to answer." My father looks between my mother and me.

"You know what your duty is, Fallon, and I know no one will have to force you because you wouldn't dare disgrace me by failing to do what is expected of you. Would you, my dutiful baby girl?"

My skin crawls in revulsion, but I have to maintain my pretence. "Of course not, father. I know what you've destined as my fate."

I need to speak to Raya. There is no way either one of us can stay around while these pathetic excuses of men and leaders administer draconian standards on us. As soon as Brandon leaves on his duties today, I'm going to persuade Raya to run away with me, to a better life. To freedom.

My rebuke in the dining room earns me another sermon from mother and Shaman Deacon, and then I have to do afternoon prayers before my appointment with the healers, jeopardising my opportunities to seek out Raya. My legs tingle and Rogue is itching to run. Perhaps, this time, I won't let her stop.

Chapter Twelve

~ Euan ~

Having shredded my clothes when I shifted in the dining room, I opt to stay in my wolf form outside Brandon's new rooms. I seem to spend most of my life patrolling this corridor now. My heart is still pounding as Alpha adrenaline rushes through my veins. I might be the youngest son, but I am of Alpha blood all the same. I have learnt everything at my oldest brother's heel: to fight, defend and lead. I may not be Alpha one day, but I will live to my potential as the offspring of one.

For a long time, I harboured suspicions about Brandon. I thought him cold and calculated, but when Heidi died, I realised he is reserved and resourceful, because he must be. When the time comes for him to challenge our father, I will stand by him and add weight to his claim. I know that this is the only way to ensure Clayton does not trick our father into naming him the next in line.

The way I see this all panning out in the next five years or so is with their defeat and probable death… or ours. There isn't a way to co-exist. Not like mother or Deacon seem to think.

Deacon's actions, or lack thereof, sicken me. He could and should have stood for Brandon and his mate. He has experienced first-hand what forcing someone does to a bond. To think he shares the same blood with me is mind boggling. Where he once had a voice, he is now silent and weak. I no longer recognise the shadow of man he has become. Maybe I should cut him some slack; he is obviously still grieving. But if I can see history repeating itself, surely, he can too and will do what he can to stop our brother going through the anguish he did. Deacon used to be so strong and opinionated. He refused to have his consummation witnessed. There wasn't as much pressure on him as the third son of the Alpha, but he still stood for his principles. Now, I don't know what he stands for or even who he is.

After sitting for around thirty minutes, Brandon comes to the door and throws some sweats at me. "I need your help again, but I need you to be discreet. Can you do that, Euan?"

I shift and change my clothes, but before I can respond to him, he mindlinks me.

What I tell you must be kept in confidence. I know I can trust you, but I want you to understand the importance of your discretion.

My discretion is yours; you know that to be true, brother!

Brandon smiles back at me. *I do. Soraya would like us to mate and mark now before the cronies arrive. We want to prevent pregnancy for now. I need you to go to the Scarlet Women and get me some sheaths. No one can know, Euan; you know this is forbidden.*

I stare at him as I process what he has just told me. My emotions have just experienced a rollercoaster, but the ending isn't good. It leaves me feeling scared.

"But, Bran–" He shushes me and places a finger on my lips.

Don't embarrass Soraya. She'll be mortified I've involved you. Can you do this for me please, Euan? Can you help me prevent a witnessed consummation for my mate?

I reluctantly agree to help him. *I'll be an hour- tops.* But inside my stomach turns as I remember Heidi. Of her punishment. And her death. I will help Brandon this time, but then I have to tell him what I know, or his mate could face a similar demise.

The Scarlet Women reside in the run-down area of the territory, called the Ruins; so-called because it is the home and workplace of the ruined females of the Reverent Moon pack, who once besmirched, are disowned by their families and left to fend for themselves by doing the only thing they can to earn a coin or two; selling their bodies. There is a wide selection of women in the Ruins, ranging from the old, seasoned and well-oiled grandmothers to the recently disgraced Daughters of the Veil. There is always a clutch of pups, as well as dirty children that roam around aimlessly, looking both bored and undernourished. The whole area stinks of deprivation and desperation. And yet the population continues to grow, year in, year out.

Sure that a woman I have visited on a few occasions can help me get the protective sheaths Brandon is in need of, I go directly to her division in the dilapidated block not far from the deserted pavilion. Esme smiles when she sees me. In another place and time, Esme is a girl I would have been proud to have as my partner. Long red hair, a sprinkle of freckles across her little button nose and green eyes that dance with mischief. She is roughly the same age as me and became a Scarlet Woman after being disgraced when she lay with a man two years ago.

"Euan, come in, it's great to see you again," Esme tells me as she invites me in. I wish I could stay just a little while, just to catch up with her and see how she is, but time is precious right now and I've promised Bran that I will not let him down.

"I can't stop, Esme. As much as I wish I could. I'm actually here to ask for your help." Looking around, she closes the door discretely before directing me into her tiny room.

"What's up? What can I do to help?" Her easy acceptance of my request is just one of the reasons why I find her so attractive. Nothing is ever too much trouble for her. It kills me inside that while I find that endearing, many other men would take advantage of her because of that trait.

"I need to secure a small number of protective sheaths. No questions asked and no one can find out about it." Without hesitation she picks up a basket from the floor with the illicit sheaths packed away in.

"I can probably spare three or four without the general making too much of a fuss, but... you'll have to leave a coin so I can pretend we used them." I place five coins in her hand, and she blushes. "Sorry, I just can't afford for him to beat on me again. I was laid up for three weeks last time."

"Can I come back and spend some time with you soon? I wish I didn't have to leave straight away." Her dazzling smile at my request just melts my heart. She isn't my mate, but this is what I imagine having a mate feels like.

"It's always a pleasure to see you, Euan. Thank you for the coins. And good luck." She points to the four sheaths in my hand, smiling once more.

I race back to the Alpha Quarters, and the whole time I wish I had told Esme that the sheaths aren't for me.

Brandon comes to the door of his bedroom with his shirt off and perspiration on his forehead, and I hand over the sheaths I procured from Esme. *Just in time, Euan. Thank you. I'm bolting the door, but send a warning if anyone approaches.*

Resuming my position, I stand guard outside my brother's door. I hear a tell-tale cry out about an hour later. I can't help but grin for my brother and his success in mating and marking in time to defy our father and the old cronies.

If I am ever fortunate enough to meet my mate, I hope I can defy them too.

~ Brandon ~

As soon as Soraya kisses me, I know protesting out of principle is a lost cause. I want this, she wants this. The only fly in the ointment is my father and the Elders insisting on witnessing the consummation. However, my sweet girl already has a solution to our problem.

"Let's do it now, this afternoon before they come to witness. We can present our Evidential sheet and show our marks too... if that's okay, Brandon?" I growl as I pull her to me, causing her to yelp in the way that I'm growing to love.

"You are mine; I want every person in the world to know that you are mine. I think it's a great idea, but only if you're sure, Sweet." I want to keep reassuring her and providing an opportunity for her to say no if she is so inclined.

"I've never been as sure of anything. I'm still worried about being a mother, but the Moon Goddess blessed me with you, and I must have faith that she knows what she is doing." Her faith and ability to accept her fate humbles me. "I want to do this correctly, Brandon. I am going to take my shower and lay out the bed as required. If you could arrange the candles, I will light them when we are ready."

I pull her back to me. Every word she speaks resonates within me. My soul recognises her. She is mine. I'm overcome with admiration and respect for this beautiful, intelligent and spunky woman I have been blessed with. I am falling deep and hard for her, and even if I could stop it, I wouldn't want to.

"If you get your shower, I'll just make a couple of arrangements to ensure we aren't disturbed, okay, sweetheart?"

With one last attempt to keep my promise to Soraya, I go to Euan to ask for his help. If he can procure the forbidden sheaths from the Scarlet Women, then we can mate without the worry of Soraya getting pregnant yet. I completely understand and accept her reasons for wanting to wait. I have my own reasons for not wanting a family just yet too. The instinct to reproduce has been strong since I found my mate, but I cannot and will not bring pups into this shitstorm of a situation. The pain that my mother feels at the disappearance of her child is a constant reminder of what I stand to lose, and I couldn't bear to bestow that pain on Soraya.

Our pack has a consummation ritual, passed down through the generations. I know the ritual off by heart because it is drummed into us all: the importance of the ritual. But for me personally, it'll be my job as Alpha to uphold these traditions and customs so that they continue to be of importance to the next generation. I always thought it dumb, but hearing Soraya say that she wanted to do this correctly filled me with amorous pride. If my sweetheart wants most things done correctly, then that is what we shall do.

Eagerness and excitement mix with the nervousness building within me about our mating. I want this to be perfect for Soraya and the least I can do is keep my promise to her about preventing a pregnancy. To occupy my mind, I work out, doing weights and press ups to dispel some of my nervous energy before getting my own shower, and after arranging the candles as Soraya requested, I break out into a sweat, trying to think of a reason to hold off mating until Euan returns. I want to kiss him when he arrives at my door with the protection I requested.

Relief floods me and wars with the building desire in my gut, I have the sheaths. I am not breaking my promise to my sweetheart.

"Are you ready, Bran?" Soraya calls out to me.

"I've never been more ready for anything in my life before, my love."

~ Soraya ~

My relief when Brandon returns home safe is overwhelming, and it comes as a shock how much I care about him already. When he tells me his father's ultimatum, I know there is no alternative. If I want to do this on our terms, we must act soon. Brandon appears to be very upset about the situation, and so, as nervous as I am, I attempt to be as calm and as reassuring as possible for his sake. After the way he reassured me last night and this morning too, it's the least I can do.

He seems so shocked at my suggested plan, but if I am honest, I am happy to be doing this. As kind and generous as Bran's offer is to wait, I don't want to risk being labelled a Scarlet Woman. I belong to him now, and he belongs to me in everything but the mate's mark. The time has come to be a woman and take control, and I am glad it's with Brandon. I am so happy he is my mate.

After showering and brushing my hair, I complete the first stage of our pack's consummation ritual by anointing myself with Neroli oil to symbolise my purity to Brandon. I dress in the customary ceremonial gown, which is essentially a white shirt that barely covers my ass. Then I carry my chastity statue of the Moon Goddess, the rest of the Neroli oil and the clean Evidential sheet to our bedroom.

"Are you ready, Brandon?" I call out to him as I enter our bedroom, not feeling half as confident as I did when I initially made my suggestion to my mate. However, when he comes up behind me and wraps his arms around my middle, pulling me close to him, his familiar scent soothes me.

"I've never been more ready for anything in my life, my love. Shall we light the candles?" A shiver runs through me in anticipation. The candles are a symbol of hope, the second step in the ritual. The light is said to guide the new mates on their new journey. There are two candles in a gold holder, and in the middle is a place for me to place my statue of the Moon Goddess. Every Daughter of the veil is bestowed with their own statue to pray to. Mine will now pass to my own daughter unless Brandon becomes Alpha before then, in which case she will be given a precious stone version as a Lady of the Veil, just like Fallon was.

Eagerly, I set my statue in the holder, and then we stand side by side while we each light our candle. Handing me the lit matchstick after he lights his candle, Brandon watches as my shaky hand lights the second candle. Brandon blows out the match when I am finished and kisses me on the cheek before placing his offering before the candles.

"What is it?" I ask him, my voice coming out in a whisper. I stand on my tips toes to try to get a glimpse of the curious green stone.

"It's a ring for you. It's healing Jade, quite rare but powerful and beautiful. Just like you." I blush at his compliment. All nerves about our impending consummation evaporate, and in its place is the all-consuming yearning, similar to how I felt last night, but even stronger and deeper.

"It's beautiful, Brandon. It's so thoughtful and kind of you. I–" His mouth covers mine and devours me, kissing me deeply and passionately. My tongue tangles with his, causing me to whimper with surprise and wanton need. "Bran!" I moan both in chastisement and desire, although what I *need* is still raw and new to me, and relatively unknown. However, my body responds in earnest at Brandon's nearness, our kisses and the building tension between us.

"Come on, Sweet, if I carry on kissing you, we'll never finish this ritual. You make me forget everything, apart from you!" I laugh with him, happy that I affect him as much as he affects me. "Do you have the Neroli oil?"

"Yes, sorry! You make me forget everything too!" I hand him the little vial of oil, and after applying a small amount to a cotton wool ball, Brandon also anoints me, declaring me pure and untainted.

"I accept you, Soraya Burke, as my fate. My blessing, sent from the Moon Goddess." He stops to look intensely at me, and every single word seems to be more than mere letters and sounds; I can feel it in my gut that he means every single word. "I promise, as a lasting tribute to our mating and marking, that I will love no other, I will remain faithful to our bond, and I will treat our union with the love, loyalty and respect it deserves."

"I accept your promises, Brandon Ward. I freely give my body and loyalty to you." With our pacts complete, we continue with the ritual. I spread the Evidential sheet on top of the bed, and Brandon brings the flower heads; white roses, also a symbol of my purity, which we both pull apart and scatter on the bed.

"Are you absolutely certain, sweetheart?" he asks one final time, as he picks up his blade. I nod quickly before I change my mind. "Then, it is time."

Taking my cue, I remove my ceremonial dress by lifting it up and over my head. Brandon's sharp intake of breath catches my immediate attention. "How is it that you are even more beautiful than last night, Sweet?" His eyes are filled with desire, and his body is already responding to mine.

Holding out my hand, palm up, I wait for him to draw my blood with his blade. However, he amazes me by cutting his own palm first. "Oh, hell! Now I know why I was supposed to cut you first. I don't want to hurt you like that." I take his blade from him and quickly cut my own palm. In my haste, I probably cut a bit too deep, but I will heal quickly enough. I place the blade next to our candles, and without hearing him move, I am quickly in Brandon's arms. Our fingers thread through each other's, and our bond amplifies, strengthens and solidifies as our blood mingles while we kiss.

Last night when we kissed, it was sweet and at times hot, but now our kisses reach fever pitch, and our bodies both seek completion, which can only be achieved through mating and marking with the one person fated to you. "You are so fucking sweet, Soraya. I'm like a bee, greedy for your nectar. I want you so badly."

Despite all my reservations, trepidations and anxiety, I can't wait either. "I want you too, Brandon." Growling at me, he picks me up, my fair naked body splayed across his strong, hard, dark one. "Take me to bed, Bran." I encourage him before kissing him once more. Passion and want ignite deep inside me, and Pandora frantically paces in my mind, wanting fulfilment and wanting her mark too.

I wrap my legs around his waist as he carries me to bed, his body following mine onto the Evidential sheet. "Sweet, let me make you feel good first; it'll help make it less painful for you." My body trembles in anticipation, and desire roars inside me.

"Yes, Brandon. Make me feel good again," I tell him, to his chagrin.

He delights me by kissing down my neck to my clavicle. "That's my good girl. I'm so proud of you for being brave and strong. This is your reward." He kisses down to my nipples that stand and point to attention, craving his touch. "So fucking perfect for me. My sweet, sweet girl."

My body arches against his, wanting more of his touch, wanting more of his words. My breathing hitches, and the ache in my tummy becomes uncomfortable. I need him to touch me, like he did last night. I need him to make me feel good again. "Yes, Soraya, follow your body, follow your instincts, tell me what you need."

"I need you to touch me, again. Just like last night." His hand edges lower, and my heart races. My breath catches in my throat until he finally reaches the heat of me. "Yes, Brandon, there." His fingers skilfully find the pleasure spot that craves his touch. Enjoyment flows throughout my body, but the ache is still there, plaguing me, demanding more.

"You're so wet. You like this as much as me, don't you, Sweet?" I nod to him, not risking him taking away the delight he is giving to me. My body moves involuntarily against his hand, and although I wince when he presses a finger inside me, it's nowhere near as painful as it was last night. It actually feels... wonderful, like he is able to massage that ache right out of me. After a little while, he stretches me further by placing another finger inside me. "Does that still feel okay?" His movements slow slightly, and my hips buck against him.

"It feels better than okay. Don't stop, Brandon." He continues to pump two fingers deep inside me, while using his thumb to apply pressure to that wonderful little spot, and my body vibrates as I reach new heights. "Brandon!" I call out, as fear begins to creep in. How is it possible to feel this deeply about someone?

The bed moves with Brandon's weight as he removes his trousers. He shows me a small package. "It's a sheath to stop us making a pup. No one can ever know, Soraya. Do you agree?" I nod, not trusting my voice. I'm scared, grateful, eager, and unsure. I watch as he rolls the clear covering that resembles a sock onto his manhood. "Lie back, Sweet, and place your feet on the bed with your knees bent."

Following his instructions, I try to get a grip of my fear. It's just mating. It's just mating with Brandon. Feeling his body press next to mine, the panic continues to build. "Soraya? Talk to me. What's wrong?" My silent tears roll down my face. I am such a coward!

"I'm scared." He kisses me soft and sweetly, without any judgement or pressure. His kisses soothe me until I move restlessly against him once more.

"I'm scared, too. I want this to be perfect for you, but what if I fail? I can't wait to bear your mark, to proudly show you as mine and to be in a position to protect you properly, too. But I worry about falling short and letting you down too, Soraya."

"But you're doing so great," I tell him, eager to reassure him, but also finding solace in the confession he gives because it shows me clearly, like nothing else could, that we are in this together. We will be in this together, forever, me and him. I have nothing left to fear. "It's going to be okay, Brandon. You are doing such a great job. I'm ready now." I look into his dark brown eyes as I give my clear instructions.

His hardness presses against my most private parts, and we look into each other's eyes until he finally pushes into me, hitting a barrier.

I don't mean to shout out. It's only when my ears stopped ringing that I realise the noise came from me. "Baby, are you okay? Soraya, did I hurt you?" He tries to move away, but I trap him with my legs so it doesn't hurt again.

"Don't you dare move!" I tell him fiercely through my shock and tears. My insides feel like they've been shredded apart. My core pulses and burns where my body merges with Brandon's.

"It's sort of a requirement, Raya. You have to move to mate," he concurs with me in a strained voice, and I can't help but giggle at his reasoning. "What are you laughing at? Your pussy clenched my cock when you laughed; it felt so good!"

Well, this makes me laugh even more, which makes Brandon laugh too. He looks gorgeous and carefree and younger! The throbbing starts to ease slightly, and the yearning returns with a vengeance. "Okay, you can move now."

He looks relieved when I permit his movement. "Thank the Goddess for that!" he says as he withdraws from me and then sinks back into me. It's still sore, but not painful, and now the waves of fulfilment roll throughout me, pleasure mingling with the discomfort. "Oh, my sweet Moon Goddess, you feel fucking amazing! It's never felt like this, never this good!"

I brazenly look into my mate's eyes and repeat back to him the instructions he gave me last night. "No, Brandon. Not Moon Goddess! My name is Soraya. Shout my name!"

Chapter Thirteen

~ Brandon ~

Being with Soraya, becoming one with Soraya, mating, loving and cherishing her like this is like nothing I have ever experienced before. This perfect, beautiful and beguiling woman is all mine. As I plunge my sheathed cock into her, I know from her tightness and gasp that it hurts her; however, when I try to withdraw and make it better, she forbids my movement.

"It's kind of a requirement, Raya. You must move to mate," I tell her gently, feeling my resolve to hold back, to worship her and be gentle, starting to wane. It's only amplified when she clenches the half of my cock that is inside her. As pleasure courses through me, I tell her what it feels like, which makes her laugh again. It feels so good that I worry my poor cock is going to go off before I have brought my mate to climax, which is when I intend on marking her.

I found out through another pack I often visit for my Alpha training that they mark during climax because it lessens the pain and strengthens the mate bond. I want Soraya to be coming before I mark her. I want our bond to be unbreakable, and I want her to be at the height of pleasure so my bite doesn't hurt her as much.

I'm still not even fully inside her, but it's enough. It's enough for now. We are mating, and that is what matters right now. It will be another amazing experience when I can bottom out inside her too.

"Sweet Moon Goddess, you feel fucking amazing! It's never felt like this, never this good!" I confess to her because it's the truth. It never has, and now, this is what forever will feel like. All others pale in comparison. Soraya is the Goddess, and how I will worship her!

Just when I think she can't surprise me anymore, Soraya looks right into my eyes, laughter and enjoyment dancing in hers. "No, Brandan. Not Moon Goddess! My name is Soraya, shout my name!"

"Oh, I will shout your name, baby, but first, I want to make you come and mark you. Wrap your legs around me." She follows my instructions and places her hands on my shoulders, my body shuddering from the added delight her touch brings. "Baby, you feel so good. Does it feel good for you too?"

She nods to me; her face is flushed from the exertion. "It doesn't hurt anymore. Should I be doing something more, Brandon?" Her body instinctively moves in rhythm with mine, and her hips rise to give me better access.

"You are perfect, darling. You are doing amazing." We kiss as we mate, and once or twice, I almost lose myself completely, so engrossing and all-encompassing the whole act has become. I slide my hand down between our bodies and find her clit once more. "Brandon!" she calls out to me, and I can tell from the way her body trembles that her orgasm is imminent. I keep my movements measured but quicken my pace and continue to rub her sensitive spot.

She cries out my name again, and when her body surrenders, pulsing and squeezing me, I lick her sweet spot before plunging my elongated canines in, marking her as mine. As she continues to ride her orgasm, I have no option but to surrender to my own. Soraya's name echoes around our new bedroom as I completely empty myself inside her. As my own waves of enjoyment drench me, I feel her little tongue caress my own marking spot and hiss as she marks me too. Both of us continue to move and pant, and once Soraya has licked my mark to help it heal, I kiss her again. This time even my lips tingle with our strengthened bond.

I look down upon my mate, as we both bathe in the glow of our post-coital bliss. "That was amazing... you are... you are everything to me, sweetheart." To my utter dismay, she bursts into tears, big, heavy, hot, tears that fall like rivers down her face. "Oh no, what's wrong? Are you okay? Did I hurt you... Soraya, please, talk to me." She cries some more but she seems more in control than she was before.

Reluctantly, I pull out from her, not wanting this moment to end but also wanting to ensure she is okay, and she winces as I do, confirming it had hurt her. I bring her body closer to mine and hold her safe in my arms. "I'm just overwhelmed. Everything happened so quickly; three days ago I turned eighteen years old and now I am an unveiled, mated woman. It's just a lot to take in." I murmur words of encouragement to her and allow her to cry in my arms until she is spent. I need to discard this sheath, no evidence of what we've done to prevent a pregnancy can be discovered.

"Are you hurting, sweet? Is the pain bad?" I ask her. I don't want her to be in discomfort. I just need to know how to make it better. She nods to me and buries her head into my chest. "Tell me how I can help."

"I'm just dreading looking at our Evidential sheet. I'm not looking forward to everyone else getting a glance at it too. It's so embarrassing." I understand her embarrassment, but I'm also confused as to why she is dreading to look for herself. The Evidential sheet is our proof of her purity and our consummation. I want to hang it from the wall with pride.

There is only one thing for it. "Come on then, Sweet, let's check it out for ourselves. Let's get it over with and then you can stop worrying about it." She agrees with ease, and I smile, as I kiss her head, pride filling me when I think of my brave beauty. All my pride vanishes when I see our Evidential sheet. I do not want to hang this from the wall. I want to burn this sheet and forget it ever existed. It was meant to be proof of Soraya's purity, but all I can see is the proof of my brutality. Crimson covers it. We are told to expect blood and pain when deflowering our mates, but this is simply barbaric. "I'm so sorry," I whisper pathetically to her. I fall down to my knees and beg for her forgiveness, for I never ever want to hurt her. I just didn't realise how fragile a virgin would be.

To my alarm she kneels next to me. "What are you apologising for, Bran? I don't understand. We have our clear evidence; no one can dispute a thing now, can they?"

As shame plagues me, I explain how I feel. "I've hurt you and made you bleed; for Goddess' sake, I made you cry! I'm not proud of that, Soraya. I only want to worship you." She looks back at me strangely.

"Brandon. It was amazing! Yes, it hurt, and yes, I've bled enough to warrant some concern, but I cried because I was overwhelmed with how strongly I feel… about you, for us and most importantly about our consummation." Her honesty and humility stun me. How am I blessed with this incredible creature as my mate? "We need to do something about… that!"

Following her gaze and pointed finger, I realise she is talking about my still sheathed cock. Pulling the sheath off gently, careful to not spill my seed until I reach the Evidential sheet, I allow just a couple of droplets to mingle with Soraya's blood. I flush away the rest of the fluid and then throw the sheath into our open fire watching until it burns away completely.

"You need to put your dress back on. They'll be coming soon to 'catch us'." Her eyes widen, because I haven't told her that part of my plan yet. "I had to do something to help Euan gain favour with my father and Clayton again. Plus, I don't want there to be any comebacks. They have to catch us in the act."

It is evident from the fierce stare Soraya is giving me that she is not happy in the least with me about this. She walks away from me, limping slightly as she does and slips her ceremony dress back on. "You could have told me beforehand, Brandon. But, we will discuss this later."

Goddess above, she pleases me; she is fiery and passionate. She will keep a man like me honest and in line. I climb up on the bed between her knees "I'm sorry, we will talk about it later. But, they are almost here." She places her hands around my neck again and pulls me down to her, kissing me passionately. My wayward cock instantly swells and lengthens, ready for round two, but the poor thing hasn't figured out that this is an act. "Yes, baby, open your legs more for me," I shout as I hear the front door opening.

"Brandon, ouch, be careful, please!" I growl at her and that twinkle in her eye as she giggles internally.

"What is the meaning of this? Your consummation was to be witnessed in four hours' time. Explain yourself." My father is the first person in the room. I quickly jump from the bed and face him.

"I didn't want to wait any longer. I did what I am supposed to, remember?" My father nods back to me. "Besides. We have now consummated; you can have our Evidential sheet and then you can leave us be to make the pup you desire. There is no longer any need for a witnessed consummation. You have all gotten more than an eyeful, and if one of you even attempts to look at my mate, I will rip your fucking throats out."

Standing naked in front of my father and Elders, with my cock still rock hard, standing proud and glistening with bodily fluid, there can be no denying what Soraya and I were doing. "Soraya, pass me the sheet." She keeps her head lowered as she scoots off the sheet and passes it to me.

Handing the blood stained sheet to my father, he cringes ever so slightly, standing aside for the Elders to receive it instead. "Good boy! This is an excellent sheet, and your lady mate must have been a model Daughter of the Veil. Look how much her flower has bloomed for you. Excellent work, Future Alpha. We will leave you to it, blessings on your attempts to make a pup."

"Father, how did you know? This just happened naturally, or we would have waited for you to witness. I couldn't miss the chance, you know that." My father looks back into the room as I escort them out. Soraya sits on the bed with the sheets pulled up to her chin, only the top of her golden head is fully visible to us.

"Euan told us he heard your mate crying out your name. Great work, son. Now, get in there and make a son." He claps me on the back as he leaves. I bolt the door, this time blocking it completely. It's now time to look after my sweet, to ensure her every need is catered for, and I will permit no one else in here until I am done.

She shocks me when I find she is no longer in our bed, but standing, with her hands on her hips and fire burning in her eyes. "Don't ever do anything like that again without telling me first, Brandon!" I hold my hands up in surrender. I don't want to fight with her, and she has every right to be mad at me.

"Sweet, I promise. I'm sorry, I should have been more considerate." She nods her head, satisfied with my contrition. "Now, come back to bed. I want to kiss you better!" Her face flames in that utterly irresistible way, and I can't wait until she falls to pieces in my hands again

~ Fallon ~

No matter how hard I try, I cannot shake my mother off after breakfast. She stays glued to me as though she already knows I'm going to try and do something forbidden. No matter what excuses I provide, my mother remains at my side.

At my mother's insistence, we join my father and his upper team as he makes the announcements about Brandon having a mate. He leaves out that they haven't mated or marked yet, as he arrogantly believes he has everything under his controlling grasp. How I want to wipe that disgusting smirk off his face!

The pack's Beta, Gamma and Delta teams congratulate my parents and begin to make arrangements for Soraya to be guarded. "Why does Soraya need so much protection?" I ask without thinking. This might make our escape a bit more complicated than I initially thought.

"She isn't just Brandon's mate; she is the pack's Future Luna. She is now Brandon's weak spot. To make Brandon the strongest and most invincible Alpha, we must ensure no harm can ever come to his Luna," my mother's Gamma explains to me. "She will be shielded from the rest of the pack as much as possible. She won't leave the Alpha Quarters without good reason, and Brandon will always escort her personally, with a full guard."

Tears well up in my eyes. It's too late. I left it too long to get myself and Soraya out of here. "What? But she's just Raya, my friend. You can't do that to her. It will feel like a prison to her." Grateful for my veil, I continue to hide my distress.

"You are a woman, Fallon. You have no business getting involved in pack safety and security. I mean, look at you! You can't even look after yourself." Clayton's chastisement causes Rogue to rise within me, especially when he smirks at the others in the room. "You just concentrate on finding your mate so you can be of some use and further the line."

Before I can respond, Euan bursts into the room. "Father, come quickly; I think Brandon is doing his consummation without you and the Elders."

My father and the Elders rise to leave. Clayton begins to stand too, but my father pushes him down by the shoulder. "Stay. This doesn't concern you." Which does make me smirk in response. "Euan, tell me, what makes you think Brandon has started his consummation without us?" I hear my father asking Euan.

"I heard the girl cry out in pain and lots of movements and groaning." My father grins in response, but in that tiny moment, I realise Euan fooled me. I can't trust him either. He's a snake for ratting out Brandon and Soraya like this. He is just as bad as the others. However, I secretly hope that he is wrong and that Soraya remains pure and unmarked so we can escape together.

The alternative doesn't seem appealing. It's becoming abundantly clear that I really am all on my own, especially if Euan is correct and Raya has mated and accepted Brandon's mark. There will be no escape for her now.

With my heart unable to take any more disappointment, I feign illness. I just need time and space on my own. "Mother, I feel unwell. I want to go back to my room, please." My mother nods at me absentmindedly, but my stomach twists uncomfortably when I hear my father give instructions in her stead.

"Clayton, escort Fallon back to her room please. She isn't feeling well." I look through my veil pleadingly at my mother, but she lowers her head, offering me nothing. Where is her spine? Did they remove it when my father marked her? Is this what happens when you are 'blessed with your mate'? The Moon Goddess can shove that notion up her backside. I want out of here, away from this life, away from this damned family.

"Come on, little sister. I'll see you back to your room!" My blood runs cold, not from what he says, but how he says it. Just as I consider mindlinking Euan to help me, I remember he's a dirty snake too.

I am completely alone.

~ Euan ~

Brandon's mindlink took me by surprise. He didn't mention anything about informing our father before he went to mate and mark. Maybe the thought has only just occurred to him? I don't know, I simply do his bidding as instructed. Fallon's eyes burn into me, and even from behind her veil, I can feel her hatred for me. I might have fooled father and Clayton that they can somewhat rely on me, but I lost Fallon's trust in the process. If only she would trust Brandon. Maybe with Soraya on board, Fallon will drop her guard. However, for now, I feel lower than a snake's belly for deceiving her this way.

Taking my position back outside Brandon's door, I can hear most of the shouting from inside. The Elders leave first, carrying a heavily bloodied Evidential sheet. Then a fully naked Brandon shows out our father, winking at me before closing the door.

Job well done, Euan. You can go and rest now. I have everything under control here. He informs me through our mindlink.

Congratulations, brother. We may have a problem with Fallon, but it can wait until morning.

I wait for his reply, but I know I've lost him. *I'll speak to her tomorrow. I'll see you all tomorrow.*

Knowing that I will not sway Fallon this evening, my thoughts quickly return to Esme. Maybe all is not lost this evening. Perhaps I can salvage something nice for myself.

Before I know what is happening, I am running for the Ruins. For tonight I can forget my responsibilities and the past. I don't have to worry about the future. I can live in the moment with a lovely woman who makes me feel happy. One night is never enough, but right now it's all I have.

~ Fallon ~

My heart is pounding in my chest and in my ears when I arrive back at my bedroom. Clayton has pushed me in my chair back to my rooms and whistled cheerfully all the way. The noise is ominous and creepy and fuels the fear inside me until it is almost completely out of control.

Once I'm back inside my sanctuary, I hope with all my might that Clayton will go and leave me to it; however, to my further dismay, I hear him bolting the door closed behind him.

"What are you doing? You can leave now; I'll summon the Omegas to help me." I try to keep my voice level, but fail miserably. I know that Clayton is aware that I'm scared from the way his lips curl in a menacing grin.

Without even speaking to me, he strides right back across the room to me and rips my veil from my head. "I think it's time for us to have another chat. You don't seem to understand that I could ruin you, just like that!" He finishes by snapping his fingers. I lower my head and refuse to acknowledge him. This is now the second time he has seen me without my veil. He knows as well as I do that this is strictly forbidden. I worry for my safety, for my reputation. Nothing prepares me for the terror that now courses throughout my body as Clayton lifts me by the throat, out of my wheelchair and high above his head.

Squealing like a pig, I plead with him. "Please let me go." But this only fuels his desire to crush me. He laughs at me as he toys with me and my emotions.

"Do you want to know what happened to Alessia? She was a whore, the local bike that every wolf had ridden... even me! You see, sister, I have no doubt you're still innocent, but it would give me the greatest pleasure to destroy that and have you buried just like Alessia was." He laughs as he casually confesses his crimes to me. "Alessia had to be taught a lesson; I had a duty to uphold our family name and values. I will simply tell father you did the same as Alessia, and he will turn a blind eye to anything I do to you."

Full of hatred, I spit in his face. The second I do it, I know this will only make things worse, but how dare he speak so cavalierly about our sister and about annihilating me in a similar way? I will never bend to him and his vile conduct. "Go fuck yourself, Clayton. If you lay another finger on me, I will rip your fucking arm off. You don't scare me. I'm of Alpha blood, too. You think because you have a cock and balls that you are superior to me? That's your first mistake. Get the hell out of my room and don't come near me again."

Scrambling away from him, I scream in horror as I feel his hand roughly groping my bare flesh under my dress. "I will punish you, Fallon. Then, I will publicly ruin you so father will want you to vanish, just like Alessia. Want to see our sister again? I wonder if they let whores into the Promised Lands?"

Using all my strength, I push him away, and when he raises his hand to slap me, I bite his hand. I clamp down as hard as I can on his filthy, abusing hand and refuse to let go. It gives me great satisfaction to hear him scream in pain. With my mouth otherwise occupied, I have no option but to mindlink him.

I hate you. Did you kill her? Did you kill Alessia? Through his haze of pain, he laughs at me as he refuses to answer. *You traitorous coward, I'll fucking kill you for hurting her!*

I didn't kill her. Father didn't give me the honours. Stunned by his admission, I relax my jaw, and Clayton seizes his opportunity to slip out of my grasp. He grabs me by my jaw and throws me down on the floor, knocking the wind right out of me.

"I didn't kill her, little sister. But Future Alpha Brandon did… I just hope the honours for disposing of you will fall to me this time. Don't ever disobey me again, sister. Remember: you belong to me, you fucking little whore. You are mine to destroy."

As I weep for my sister and for the murdering bastards I am related to, Clayton violates my body with his hands to remind me that I am beneath him, here only to be used and abused because I am female. As he roughly pinches my breasts, I offer no resistance; I am numb to the pain and humiliation.

"Our mother is outside. You breathe a word of this to anyone and I will punish your friend, too. Got it, whore?" I nod hopelessly to him. "You agree with everything I say, and you play along. I'll be back tonight to take what is mine."

He lifts my broken body and plonks me on the bed, throwing my veil over me, which I clip into place before he unbolts the door.

"Why was this door bolted?" our mother demands to know. Clayton shrugs at our mother, which causes her to blush. He doesn't answer because, to him, she is below his station despite being his mother and the pack Luna.

"Fallon is upset about Alessia again. I didn't want the Omegas to disturb her grief, so I bolted the door to give her privacy." My mother rushes to my side to comfort me, but no matter what she does, it is not enough. Clayton has broken my heart and soul, and nothing will ever be right in the world now.

My plan to get out of here is even more vital now. My thoughts automatically swim to Raya. I need to get her away from Brandon before he marks her, thus claiming her as his forever. I have to protect her from the evils that lurk in plain view in the guise of my family.

The remnants of my heart are shattered when my mother confirms my worst fears. "Brandon and Soraya mated and marked each other this afternoon; we should be celebrating our family's joyous news. Something tells me we will be hearing the pitter-patter of many little paws soon."

I'm too late. She's now fully mated to a monster.

Chapter Fourteen

~ Soraya ~

In the weeks that follow my mating and marking, my life changes dramatically. I can no longer go to school with Fallon like I have always done, only veiled females are allowed to learn. Mated females learn to look after their mates, breed pups and keep a nice home. Although I had always felt stifled by my life as a Daughter of the Veil, I begin to crave the freedom I once had. The irony isn't lost on me.

After a week of living as a mated couple, my moon blood arrives, signalling that we have been successful in avoiding pregnancy. Though this should fill me with relief, disappointment at not carrying Brandon's pup attacks my peace of mind. Do I now want a pup? Or is this just my natural instincts as a wolf interfering with my emotions?

Regardless, Brandon detects my discontent; although he is way wide of the mark when it comes to understanding why. "Hey, Sweet, don't worry. We can mate again in a day or two when your cramping stops." Smiling at him as I kiss him, he looks questioning at me. "What? What's so funny, sweet Soraya?"

Giggling, I explain, "You just assume I will miss mating with you!" He feigns a shocked expression as he teases me some more. His next form of attack is much more successful in raising a confession from me. He roughly and possessively grabs my chin and crashes his mouth over mine. Stars explode behind my eyelids and desire despite my unclean state begins to stir deep inside me.

He pulls away from me abruptly, his eyes flash black, showing me he senses my arousal, and he reciprocates it. "Are you saying you won't?" he demands to know. I bite my lip, unable and unwilling to lie to him.

"You know I will, but that wasn't the reason I felt sad. I'm not ready to be a mother but I was unhappy to not be carrying your pup too." Although confusion flares in his eyes, he tries to understand.

"Even if we hadn't been as careful as we have been, you know it probably wouldn't have happened in such a short space of time, don't you, Sweet?" I nod to him; I cannot explain why my feelings have changed so much in such a short time. "If you want a pup, I will give you a pup. I would give you the world, Soraya."

The impulsive, irrational part of me wants to say 'yes! Let's have a baby!', but Bran's own doubts about having a child also ring out in my mind.

"You said danger was coming and that it wouldn't be safe. I know the right thing to do is wait. I think my hormones have just got the better of me." He holds me tight in his arms, and it only further confirms that when the time is right, I will be overjoyed and blessed to carry his pup.

A few days later, my moon blood has stopped, but I wake up feeling wretched. There is an uncomfortable pain all throughout my body, and I am not sure why. When I go to the bathroom, I look at my reflection in the mirror and see that my pupils have dilated, making my eyes look almost black. My cheeks are flushed, and my skin is hypersensitive. When I wash my hands, it feels like little needles are stabbing me everywhere the water touches.

The pain in my tummy brings me to my knees, and I involuntarily cry out. Bran calls out my name, responding to my cry and the distress he can sense through our bond. No matter how hard I try, I cannot answer his call. I lie down on the ceramic tiles in our bathroom as tendrils of pain plough through my body.

"Soraya, can I come in? What is wrong?" he shouts through the locked door, and through our mate bond, I can feel his panic and alarm, and my overriding desire is now to comfort him.

"Brandon," I call out. My voice is weak, but it's enough he hears me and breaks down the door and rushes to my side when he realises I am on the floor.

"Sweetheart, are you sick? What happened? Are you okay?" I can't answer him because another wave of cramping starts causing me to cry out again.

Bran checks my pulse and places his hand to my brow, looking into my eyes as he does. When he lifts me from the floor and wraps his arms around me, I realise his nearness helps. I begin to feel better, much better, and the pain begins to subside. Bran nuzzles me and inhales my scent deeply, smelling me, and almost instantly, his worry is replaced with a massive grin.

"I can fix this, baby; don't worry, I have got you; I will make you feel better". His words reassure me, but I am still confused as to what is happening to me.

"What is going on, Bran? I feel awful," I explain to him, wanting him to help me understand.

"Sweetheart, you've just come into your first heat," he tells me with authority. How does he know, and yet I do not? "The cure is remarkably simple: you need me. And I am all yours."

I try to recall my sisters having their heat, but all I can remember is howling and banging. I blush as I realise what it must have all meant; I had been too young to understand before now. It had completely slipped my mind that this may happen soon. The Edors told us very little about mating and the reproduction process, only that we were to do as our mates instructed. It's only now I realise their ignorance.

Brandon places me on our bed before he undresses me. The discomfort, fever and chills return with a vengeance when he isn't as close to me, but Brandon's touch against my skin chases it all away again.

"Soraya, the next few days are going to be rough for you, but I will cater to your every whim and demand. I want your promise right now that whatever your body asks for, you tell me straight away so I can give it to you. Promise?" He smiles at me, giving me the reassurance I need. I know everything is going to be okay. Because Brandon said so. I have no doubts when I place all my trust in him, once again.

"I promise, Bran. It felt a bit better when you were holding me," I tell him honestly; I am completely naked now and Bran just has his underwear on. The cramps start again, and I whimper and hold myself, but Brandon closes the space between us and lets his instincts take over.

"I don't want you to just feel a bit better, I am going to make you feel amazing," he says to me as he fondles my breasts and kisses me. "This is your most fertile time; we have to be extra careful, but I can't make any guarantees, okay?" he tells me solemnly. I tell him I understand and that I am willing to take the risk. "I am too. Who knows? The Moon Goddess may know better than us what we need right now."

It is amazing to share this time with him. The excitement and anticipation builds up between us as he pulls my legs apart, growling of satisfaction before he plunges his gifted tongue into the heart of my femininity. My body instantly reacts, shivering and tingling in sheer pleasure and eliciting a moan of delight from me. He licks me with his rough tongue, using long strokes and little flourishes, all the way up my delicate folds until he reaches my sensitive bud.

"Yes, Bran, there!" Oh, dear sweet Moon Goddess, how does he do it? He drives me insane with his nipping and sucking directly on my most responsive point. I no longer feel sick, I feel alive. He pushes two fingers inside me, and it's almost too much. The vibrations of my release already begin, while Brandon continues to lap away at my folds and thrust his fingers inside me.

The warm pleasure courses throughout me, filling me with sunlight and glory. But I am far from satisfied; my body demands more, I need more. Brandon strips out of his underwear and kneels between my open legs. Lifting my hips to meet with his, he slides almost his full length into me, filling me to capacity with his manhood. I hear him groan as he moves on top of me, and the feel of his skin and weight soothes the beast of lust inside me.

Now, I am feeling sated with my man on top of me, completely penetrating me, touching me, teasing me. I love it. Brandon warned me that the next few days are going to be hard, but this feels amazing to me. As he ups his pace, he pulls my hands to my private parts.

"Touch yourself, sweetheart. I want to watch you while you do." I do as he asks, timidly at first. He bites his lip and groans when he sees me getting pleasure from my little circular motions on my sensitive spot, and I like that I have this effect on him. It makes me braver and more confident. I close my eyes as my body floats to a higher plain of indulgence, and I move my fingertips faster over my wetness, making me moan loudly; Brandon thrusts deep and hard inside of me, and I continue to rub and touch myself. It's the most exquisite experience of my life.

"Are you close, baby? Or do you need my help?" I am so close, so close to fulfilment once again. I am not sure what to say or do, I just need to carry on.

"Don't stop, please don't stop, Bran. Don't Stop! I am coming. I'm coming!" I shout the last part, and my shouts mingle with his grunts of completion as ripples of delight fill me.

I trap him with my legs. He is mine, and I am keeping him close by to fulfil my needs. Eventually, we untangle and Brandon stands to get us drinks.

As soon as he moves away from me, the cramps start again, and I cry out, "No, you can't go, it hurts."

He scoops me up and places me in his lap. "I am right here, baby. I will never leave. I will give you anything you want or need, I promise."

He is so eager to not only please me but to keep me from the discomfort. Bran is attentive, dutiful, and enduring. As a Future Alpha, his athleticism is rivalled by none, and at times like this, I guess I could praise the Moon Goddess even more for that blessing.

For the next few days, I am an unquenchable beast, demanding and taking everything my accommodating mate has to offer.

In moments of quiet, when Bran has managed to sate my wolf for a short while, I hear Brandon sending the guards to the grocers and kitchens to pick up supplies for us. I am not even a tiny bit mortified when I hear him tell them I have my first heat and to reschedule all his plans for the time being because he is needed. They bring food, juice, and ice as well as bath salts and massage oil.

I have never known a need like this; it is another level of arousal and lustiness. Bran tells me it's because it's my first heat; apparently, the first one is the hardest one.

We no longer finish a marathon session when the gnawing starts in my stomach again and the fevers and chills come within minutes. The aching in my chest, like my heart is trying to strangle itself, and the shooting pains throughout my body start next, and the only thing that will soothe it is Brandon's touch and nearness. I cannot think about anything else, only him, us, and mating.

Bran holds me close and kisses me to take away the badness. He fills hot water bottles, and then he fills pillowcases with ice and uses each one to chase away the flushes and chills. He showers me with love and affection, bathes my wanting body and massages all the bad away; however, the only thing that works fully is mating. Pandora, my wolf, has completely taken over. She is lapping up all this love and affection; she is rolling around in delight, chirruping and basking in her wanton glory. She is brazenly demanding positions, oral, deeper penetration and harder, more ferocious lovemaking. And my body is just her vessel to get that.

Bran is in his element, and I could never doubt his loyalty to me. I am grateful that his desire for me is also insurmountable. He laughs heartily when I channel Pandora's cravings and never ever lets me down; he rises to the challenge each and every time and never seems to tire of my wanting.

Until now, I never really understood the purpose of heats for a she-wolf. However, after three straight days of insatiable mating, I fully understand now that it is mother nature's way of ensuring the werewolf race never dies out. Once you go into heat, there is nothing else that matters, only mating; and mating usually leads to pups.

After four days, normality finally resumes, and Bran laughs at me when I become shy in front of him after the way I have been acting. "Don't laugh, Bran; it's embarrassing!"

"Why are you embarrassed? It's only natural, Sweet. It's not like you had much choice, is there? I have loved the past few days; I loved sharing your first heat with you." I smile back at him in mutual feeling because, although I thought our bond was tight before, we are on a whole new level of together; we are one now.

Once Brandon leaves for training, I sit and contemplate our time together. My feelings for him are already growing deeper than I ever thought possible. He says he has loved sharing this time with me, but he's never said how that translates to how he feels about me. As I fall for him, I hope he's feeling the same. I'm going to have one mighty crash to earth if not.

~ Brandon ~

The demands on my time are coming from all directions. Diplomatic missions, training, the Hidden Queen, my family, and although she doesn't demand my time, the moments I am able to steal with my sweet Soraya never last long enough. I recall her heat that finished around two weeks ago. That will always be one of my favourite memories of our time as a new couple. Since those few days, when we were both consumed by the heady haze of arousal and satisfaction, the strength of our bond is now superior to anything else I have ever felt. She is everything and more to me. Her heat allowed her to become more liberated around me, and her wolf's demands now allow her to express her own, knowing I will do anything to bring her comfort, fulfilment and joy. I cannot wait for her next heat.

"Brandon! Are you paying attention? I swear to the Goddess, since you found your mate, your head is in the clouds." My father slams his hands down against the conference room table. Everyone jumps with a start, and then all but one stare at me. "You must go today. Now in fact. This cannot be delayed any further. How long do you need to assemble your team?"

"There is no need to be so hasty, Alpha. Perhaps the east will quieten down soon!" one of the Elders advises, but my father is insistent.

"You will leave today. Assemble your team. No more excuses, Brandon. You are first and foremost my heir and the Future Alpha of the Reverent Moon Pack. Start acting like it."

Deflecting diplomatic missions from my father isn't the worst of my transgressions since I claimed Soraya. My Queen has obviously heard that I have claimed my mate despite her warning and instructions and has summoned me twice in two days. I have to go and explain myself, and take further instructions on how to proceed, but I can't bring myself to leave Soraya. Partly because I can't get enough of her, but mostly because I'm terrified of something happening to her.

It is clear to see that her life here with me is not everything every young woman would want in life. She's isolated away from everyone, including her own mother and sisters, and me leaving too would make her feel absolutely cut off. Therefore, I have been holding off on leaving for as long as possible. But I can't hold it off much longer.

Although Soraya tries to hide it, I know she is hurt by Fallon's disinterest. My sister puzzles me, and I don't know what to do with her anymore. One day I couldn't keep her home so she would be safe, the next she will not leave her bed. I know Alessia's disappearance weighs heavily on her, but even with taking that into consideration, Fallon's change in behaviour is disturbing.

The mission I abandoned to claim Soraya has hit a critical point. If I don't return to the negotiations, it could result in a full-scale civil war. The Queen has expressly told me that this cannot happen. If the war in the west starts, then her rise to power here will be stalled. Since I already defied her by claiming Soraya, I need to prove my loyalty once again both to her and her cause. I also do not believe my mate will be safe until the Queen takes her rightful place. Soraya and any pups that will come along before long at the rate we are going at.

Leaving is the last thing I want to do right now. I am falling hard for my mate; she never ceases to please and surprise me. I no longer remember my life before her. I never want a life without her in it, but to keep her safe in the future, I need to make this journey now.

"I will have my team assembled in a couple of hours. I think I should take my mate; it could be part of her Luna training, and I don't want to miss an opportunity to further our line." My father smirks at my request. I hope he will allow this one indulgence.

"The girl is a distraction to you, Brandon. Far too much of a distraction. She stays here, like every Future Luna has done. Send a messenger when you have news, son." And with that he dismisses me.

Leaving the room, I mindlinking my team, instructing them to be ready to leave in two hours' time. The only person who doesn't respond is Euan. I need him to keep a watch over both Fallon and Soraya while I'm away.

After failing to find him, I have no option but to entrust Soraya into the care of Josh, who is the head of her Gamma guard. Frustrated, I leave a note for Euan, before heading home to tell Soraya, wishing I had more time to enjoy her before leaving.

Chapter Fifteen

~ Euan ~

I have returned several times to the Ruins. I think I'm in love with Esme; I know that every moment we spend together is never enough. Her profession has me turning with jealousy, but she isn't mine to lay claim to, and her position here in the Ruins is secured only by her trade, and as we aren't fated and she's unmarked, I have no right to feel the way I do.

As the son of an Alpha, I have no right falling in love with a Scarlet Woman, but it snuck up on me, taking me by surprise. She is incredible, pretty, strong, and fierce, but this latest development leaves me reeling. Looking at the small, plastic cassette she places in my hands, I'm so shook that I cannot speak for a full minute.

Esme cries with her head in her hands as I stand staring at her with my mouth hanging open. "You're pregnant? Is it mine?" I want to kick myself as soon as I say it. It doesn't matter to me if it's mine or not. It's Esme's baby, and if she permits me to be involved, I will do it regardless of whether the child is biologically mine or not.

"I don't know, Euan. I want to think so. But I can't tell you that for definite," she tells me honestly, and for that, I love her all the more. She has always been completely open and honest with me; I can never deny that. I know what the hazards of her profession are, and I love her anyway.

"We'll mate and mark tonight," I declare, but she cries even more as she shakes her head at me. "What? Why? Why are you saying no?"

"You know, as well as I do, Euan. This will never be allowed. You're the Alpha's son, and I'm a whore. This child may not be yours." I try to protest, but she raises her voice, preventing me from making further interruptions. "This is an abomination; you know the Bastion and the Elders will declare it so. Your father would have my baby ripped from me and my throat taken before he would allow a son of his to be mated to me."

"Fuck my father. I'm my own man. We could be a family. We'll move somewhere else, away from the Reverent Moon." She holds my head in her hands, her eyes wide with love and longing. "I could take care of you and junior. I love you, Esme."

She looks back at me startled, before wiping away the fresh tears before they fall. "I love you too, Euan. I never thought it was possible to feel the way I do about you." I brace myself as I wait for the inevitable. "But it doesn't matter how we feel, we cannot be together. I will not have your blood on my hands."

As Esme pulls away from me, a tightness settles in my chest. I cannot let go, not now, not ever. "If I can get us out of here, find us another pack or a safe place to be together, will you be mine?"

"Don't, Euan, you're making this harder than it needs to be. Just walk away." She pushes my shoulders back, but there is very little force behind it.

"I love you. If you don't love me, I will walk away and wish you well. But I know you feel the same way, baby. I know you want this as much as I do." She is overcome with emotion, and I catch her before she falls to her knees. "I want to be with you. Please, let me love you. Let me figure out a way to make this work."

She rests her head against my shoulder and finally addresses her main concern. "But what if the baby isn't yours, Euan. Will you still want me then?"

"I don't give a shit if he's not biologically mine. I claim him as mine. I claim you as mine!" Despite her delicate condition, I'm far from gentle when I claim her mouth to reiterate how I feel about her. As my mouth slants over hers, and my tongue rubs against hers, I know I've won her over when she melts in my arms and returns my fevered kiss. "Be mine, Esme. You're all I'll ever want in life."

"My heart is already yours. If you can find a way, then the answer is yes, I'll be yours, Euan."

~ Soraya ~

Brandon and I have been mated for around five weeks, and in this time, I have seen my mother twice. After spending every day with her until this point, I ache with longing for the closeness we once had. I miss her and my sisters. The simplicity of life at the Huts, something I had once found mundane, now haunts me. How I wish to live that life now. However, I would never give up Brandon in exchange.

Fallon has become distant towards me. I thought us being sisters by law would have made our friendship bond tighter, but she is short tempered and uninterested in me now, and it hurts that this woman was once my closest friend. Although her legs are fully healed, Fallon spends copious amounts of time in bed, not washing or changing her clothes. I know her mother, Luna Beverly, is deeply concerned about her.

My new home is beginning to feel more like my own now that I have added some personal effects. At times it feels more like a prison than the sanctuary that Brandon promised me, but I know he makes my life as easy and as comfortable as he possibly can.

Brandon is a revelation. Not only is he kind and considerate towards me, but he is also fun and generous. Spending night after night wrapped up in his arms is the only thing that keeps me sane right now. My mate has done everything he can to make my transition from Omega's daughter to Future Luna as smooth as possible. My Luna training keeps me busy through the day and at night I lie with Brandon, just talking, planning, kissing and occasionally mating.

Leaving our room is only permitted with either Brandon or with a full Gamma Guard, which was assembled the day after Brandon and I mated and marked each other. My every move is watched. After almost four weeks of living in the Alpha Quarters, an Omega began coming into my home every morning to make my bed and do my laundry. Having done these tasks by myself since I moved here, I am perplexed at the sudden assistance.

After a few days of her attending to me, I pluck up the courage to approach the Omega, who I know by sight from the Huts. Her name is Sally, and she is a middle-aged, mated female. "I can do this myself; I know how. Who asked you to do this?"

Sally's face flames in embarrassment. I wonder perhaps if she has been told to not talk to me or tell me why I need an Omega all of a sudden. "The Alpha ordered it to check for your moon blood. He hopes to be the first to congratulate you and Future Alpha Brandon on your new pup." My insides freeze in horror, the audacity of that man! Out of anger I almost kick her out of my room, but I know that Sally is acting on orders that she cannot refuse.

"Thank you, Sally. I can let you know if my moon blood arrives." But Sally shakes her head at me, I can see the pleading in her eyes, she is afraid.

"I'm sorry. The Alpha wants me to bring evidence. I must check. Please don't tell him that I told you." I nod my agreement and leave her to do her duties, but inside I am both scared and angry. Pushing it to the back of my mind for the time being, I will discuss it with Brandon later and ask him the reason why.

Later this evening, he arrives home with the head of my Gamma Guard. "Soraya, I have to go away for a few days. Please do not leave the Alpha Quarters while I'm away. Josh will be here to protect you, and I will return as soon as I can."

Josh, the Gamma wolf, looks stoically ahead, showing no surprise at this announcement and making me believe I am the last to know about this trip. Josh is okay, and like most other males in our pack, he will protect me, but he will not talk to me or interact with me in any way.

Wishing we were alone so I could speak to Brandon freely, I use the etiquette expected of me because I am the Future Alpha's mate. "When must you leave, sir?"

"I have to go right away. I have an important errand I must run for my father." His words are short and cold, so unlike the way he whispers to me when we are alone.

I'll be back as soon as I can, Sweet. Stay safe and don't miss me too much. The tightness in my chest eases at his mindlinked words, and I give my promise to him and tease him that he'll miss me more.

"Have a safe and speedy journey, sir. I look forward to your return home." Brandon's eyes flash black, just like they do when I know he wants to mate.

"Josh, wait outside. I'll be leaving in a moment." Josh leaves without hesitation, and when the door clicks behind him, Brandon sweeps me up in his arms. "You're too irresistible. I wish I could take you with me, Sweet," he tells me, as he peppers me with featherlight kisses that tickle and make me giggle.

"When will you return, Bran?" I want to tell him about his father checking for my moon blood, but when his brow creases, I can see genuine worry and concern in his expression. I swallow down my own troubles not wanting to add further burden to my mate's load.

"It's a full day's travel there and another back. I hope to be no longer than a week. Stay home as much as possible; I need to know you're safe." I nod my agreement to him and try my best to hold back my tears as he leaves.

Being in our rooms without Brandon serves only to amplify my loneliness. Luna Beverly visits me every day to give me my lessons on being a Luna, but under the watchful glare of the Gamma Guard, we are both careful and cautious in our interactions.

On the fourth day of Brandon's absence, Luna Beverly tells me that Fallon has taken to her bed again and would appreciate a visit from a friend. I inform Josh that I want to visit the Alpha's daughter, and after doing a security check, he escorts me to Fallon's room, waiting outside of Fallon's bedroom for me.

"Hey, stranger, how are you? Your mother says you're feeling ill?" I keep my voice light and bright, but Fallon keeps her back to me. "Please talk to me, Fallon. I miss you. Our friendship means the world to me, and I don't want to lose that." She moves around in her bed, and my hopes begin to raise, maybe today she will talk to me again.

"I'm not wearing my veil, close your eyes." I do as she instructs and wait for the rustling to finish. "Okay, you can open your eyes again now. What's up?"

Her abruptness shocks me. Fallon has always been sweet and warm with me, but I don't recognise this person. "How are you feeling? How is school?"

"I feel like shit and school is shit too. You should go back to your rooms, Raya. Come back and see me when Bran gets home. Until then, you should stay in your rooms and lock your door." My mind races as I wonder why Fallon is pushing me away. At first, I thought she may find it weird that I am now mated to Brandon, but this feels deeper than that. I almost feel like she hates me.

I find it hard to keep the hurt out of my voice. "If that's what you want. I'll leave the books and chocolates on your drawers. You can always link me if you want to talk, Fallon." I stand up, and as I do, Fallon sits forward, as though she is going to do or say something; however, my hopes are crushed when she tells me to shut the door tight on my way out.

"I'd like to return to my rooms please, Josh, and I would appreciate it if someone could go to the grocers for me. I need some essentials." Josh gives a curt nod before escorting me down the corridor to my room. No one speaks, and the silence is deafening me. I've never felt so alone. I can't even visit my family and can only hope they are able to get time off work to come and see me instead.

Josh takes my shopping list and waits at the door until I lock it behind me. He doesn't tell me if he will go to the grocers himself or if he'll delegate the task to another, and once I close the door behind me, I don't give it another thought. I'm back in my sanctuary.

Josh returns with my groceries, knocking lightly on the door when he does. I thank him as I take the paper bag from him. "Will you be requiring any further assistance this evening?" he asks me, still as formal as ever.

"No. Goodnight, Josh and thank you once again." I close the door to his back and take my groceries into the lounge. Bubble bath, toothpaste, bananas, and sanitary pads as my moon blood cramps started this morning.

As I sink into the bathtub with my orange blossom bubbles, I sigh in relief as my muscles relax. I think of Brandon and wish for his return, and as my whole-body surrenders to the bliss of the hot fragrant water, I begin to doze off.

I am woken by a loud bang in my home. The door to the bathroom, where I am, is hit with a great force and swings open. I attempt to shield my nakedness with the bubbles. "Leave at once or I will inform Future Alpha Brandon that you imposed here."

A sickening laugh stops me in my rant. I open my eyes and, to my great dismay, find Clayton Ward standing over me, staring at me. "You've been summoned by the current Alpha. Are you ready to answer for your crimes?"

He catches me off guard, what crimes? "I don't know what you mean. Please come back when Brandon returns. JOSH!" I summon my guard, but this makes Clayton laugh even more.

"Your guard was very brave, but he should know better than to stand in my way. He'll wake again in about eight hours. Last chance, get out of that bath or I'll drag you out." Although I am scared, my anger takes paramount. How dare he come into my rooms and violate me in this way.

"GET OUT OF THIS BATHROOM NOW. I AM BRANDON'S MATE AND YOU WILL RESPECT THAT." He steps away from me, as though the mention of Brandon reminded him of who I am. "Tell your father I will join him shortly. Now leave."

To my utter astonishment, Clayton does as I say, and once I am sure the apartment is clear of them all, I quickly get out of the bath and dry myself before redressing. I slip the jade ring that Brandon gave me back onto my finger and hold the cold stone against my lips for good luck.

My hands shake as I open the door, and I cry out in distress when I find Josh sprawled out on the floor with a large bump on his head. No one else has come to his aid, and I don't know where the rest of the Gamma guard are.

With no one else to summon, I give in to the inevitable and make my way to the Alpha's office. My wolf warns me of impending danger, but the Alpha has summoned me, and I cannot deny a request from him.

I take a deep breath before knocking on his door. Shivers of dread run through my body when I am given admittance and see a room full of importance.

Whatever I have done wrong must be severe and that means the punishment will be too. I have no alternative than to face this alone.

~ Brandon ~

Leaving the territory has never bothered me in the slightest before. Going on diplomatic missions and taking secret excursions to get instructions from my Queen has always been a task I revelled in. Until now. Now, the pain of being away from Soraya tears me up inside. I am absent minded, sloppy, and grumpy without her here. My father called her a distraction. Well, I call his bluff. I am distracted without her. My physical body is right here trying to negotiate, while my mind and heart stayed with Soraya. Being without her is a far bigger distraction.

The wolves of the west have never taken the Reverent Moon wolves seriously. They laugh at our customs and think we are unintelligent. They poke fun at our worship and belief of the Moon Goddess and think we are an anomaly among werewolves. At first it bothered me to be thought of as less than them based on the way I have been raised and my belief system. Do they sincerely believe they are superior to me? First and foremost, I am an Alpha wolf, a trained and competent warrior. Then over time, I began to use their own ignorance to my advantage.

The first time I came here to negotiate with them, I brought Clayton. This happened before I became aware of his sadistic and double-crossing ways. They liked Clayton; he was realistic to them because he basically renounced every pack custom and belief we grew up living by. The change in him was so spectacular that it took me completely by surprise. As he spoke to them on their level, jealousy rose within me. Why was it so easy for him to get them onside? Why did they listen to him but refused to acknowledge me?

The next time, I brought Deacon with me instead, but they hated Deacon more than they did me. Stuffy and private, they couldn't relate to him either. I needed someone relatable, but more intelligent than Clayton, who thought his tentative power was more than enough to gain the western wolves loyalty.

So, after much deliberation, I brought Euan. Of all my siblings, Euan is the most intelligent. He is emphatic and relates to people, and he can adjust his own persona to make others feel more comfortable. If I could choose my Second-In-Command, I would choose him, but tradition dictates that Clayton, as my father's second son, is my Second-In-Command until my own son from Soraya comes of age. Euan also has the unique ability to read people; if Euan says someone is sad or angry, I believe him like he is a tried and tested emotion reading machine. He is almost never wrong.

Trying my best to converse with them on their level doesn't come easy, but the thought of returning home keeps me working hard, and after three days, they seem to relax enough to talk about the feud they have with the wolves from The Edge.

The mountains that can be seen from here are in an area called The Edge. We are told this is because it is the edge of the world. I believe it's because the Edge wolves have an edge over us. Being high up, they can see for thousands of miles. They also have the advantage if anyone does attack them as they firstly know the lands much better than we ever will, and secondly raining down an attack is easier than trying to execute an attack from below.

The Edge is dangerous and traitorous, but you wouldn't believe it when you look out at the idyllic setting of snow-capped mountains of the perils that lurk there. My strict guidance is to not anger the monster; the wolves of the Edge are ferocious and relentless. Any slight against them is repaid threefold. A war with them is the last thing we need to be involved in right now.

After three days of deliberations, we get to the root of the problem. "We need to know if you will come to our aid if they attack us." I contemplate their request before I agree.

"If the attack is initiated by them, as our allies we will always come to your aid. However, if you attack them at The Edge, we will not interfere." The Alpha and his team whisper amongst themselves. I help myself to the water on the table, while I await their answer. I am working on my father's express wishes and my Queen's direct orders; I cannot bend any more than I have done. No matter the outcome, this is the end of our negotiations.

"What if they say it is a counterattack, a retaliation for us attacking them first?" the Elder asks. Although I am distracted, I remain aware of what they are suggesting. I see no harm in confirming our loyalty if the fighting takes place here and not at The Edge, we have a duty to protect our allies.

"If the counterattack happens here, we will still respond. We will not declare war on The Edge. It's a suicide mission; their land is capable of wiping us all out. But we will defend our allies." They seem pleased with my response. "Thank you for receiving me. I will be leaving your territory this evening to personally deliver my findings to my Alpha father."

Having given my reassurance that we will remain allies, they physically relax in my presence. "I almost forgot to congratulate you on finding your mate. May the Moon Goddess bless you with a son very soon. I suppose that is why you are eager to leave?"

I could deny it, but what good would that do? "Yes, I believe she will have her heat again soon so I–"

"No need to explain any further; a she-wolf's heat is a glorious time, especially when it is your fated mate. Go home, my friend, and thank you for your continued loyalty."

Not needing to be asked twice, I give my team instructions to follow me later this evening, and an hour later set off in wolf form to secretly see The Queen before returning home.

It takes me four hours of running with very little rest breaks before I see the crypts again. Its redevelopment is astounding to see. I have been away roughly five weeks and already the place is unrecognisable. The buildings are mostly restored now, and roads and protective trenches are all in place. To the right I can see crops growing and additional building work.

As soon as I enter the territory, I can feel my Queen's power. In the short space of time since I last seen her, her power has grown exponentially. The cobbled stairwell to the Queen's chambers is steep and dark, and I no sooner enter when her voice carries to me.

"Go home, NOW. You need to get them out. Never defy my orders ever again, Lieutenant, but I need you to go now, before they harm her even more." I cannot see her yet, but she can sense me no matter where she is. My trepidation at facing my queen is quickly replaced by an overwhelming sense of dread.

"Who? Who is being harmed? And where do I take them?" I ask as I try to leave. My thoughts go to Soraya, my sweet mate, but the thought of her being harmed brings me to my knees.

"They have Soraya, but Fallon is in serious danger, too. We need to move them both now. You'll have to bring them here. We aren't ready yet, but them being here in discomfort is better than staying there while they are tortured." I agree quickly with her, before turning on my heel to race out of the crypts and start my full day's journey back home to the Reverent Moon. I only hope I am not too late.

I pray to the Moon Goddess, Diana. Please don't let them torture my sweet Soraya. Don't let me be too late. Visions of Heidi when she died and of Deacon's howls and screeches of pain haunt my every thought. Is this why she died? Did they torture her too? Most importantly: Why? Why would they harm our mates in such a sadistic and brutal way?

None of it makes sense, but no matter how much I torment myself with all my theories and reasoning, I know I cannot change the past. The present and future is what I need to focus on.

I've been away, trying to stop a war in the west, a place I do not care one iota for, when I am ready to burn my own pack to the ground if anything happens to my love.

Chapter Sixteen

~ Fallon ~

Sending Raya away almost kills me. I love her, and of course I want to be a part of her life, but getting close to me will bring her into the firing line with Clayton. So if hurting her feelings prevents him hurting her physically, mentally, emotionally and sexually, then that is what I will do.

After the way Clayton has violated and abused me, I no longer feel like a Lady of the Veil. My own brother is a monster, who takes the greatest pleasure in hurting me. My defiance, or rather my refusal to bend to his will, is likely to cost me my virginity. That was his threat last night. Of course, no one knows about it, not my mother or father. Only the despicable, evil, loathsome excuse of a man who parades as my brother.

For the last few days, he has come to my room and repeatedly abused me. My beautiful dark skin is now covered in bite marks, bruises, and scratches. However, this is nothing in comparison to the irreparable damage endured by my heart and soul. He has broken me in so many ways, but he will never take my spirit, and whether it is today or in a million years, he will pay for everything he has done.

He knows that I will do anything to keep Raya safe, so he uses this to taunt me. Now that Brandon is away from the territory, I know it is only a matter of time before he moves on to hurting Raya. I cannot and will not allow that to happen.

As soon as Brandon is back, I'm going to reveal what Clayton has done and entrust him with keeping Raya safe, because I won't be here to do so. Leaving this Goddess forsaken pack is the only option left for me now. A life as a rogue, as unappealing as it had always seemed, is now the only spot on the horizon that keeps me going. Who knows? Maybe I'll find my mate on my travels.

My bedroom is both my prison and my torture chamber now. Any pleasant memories I had have morphed into the pain riddled nightmares where Alessia's own abuse merges with my own.

How didn't I know that she was suffering? Why didn't I see it? I knew she wasn't living as a Lady of the Veil. She had secret boyfriends and lovers, and I was always covering for her when mother would look for her or ask her where she had been. On a superficial level, I envied her for knowing what she wanted and taking it unapologetically. I admired her boldness and her indifference to what people thought of her.

Consumed with my own envy, I didn't see what was right in front of me. Alessia suffered too. Clayton told me she did it to protect me, like I'm trying to protect Raya now. He abused her, and it is all my fault. And now she's dead.

Clayton confirmed that Alessia is dead and by Brandon's hand, which leaves me in quandary. Will Raya be safe if I leave her here with Brandon? He seems to treat her well, but my misconception about Alessia now makes me question if all is as it seems. If I question Raya about it, will she be honest and tell me if Brandon was mistreating her? Maybe I could still get her to leave with me if Bran wasn't treating her right.

You know that is wishful thinking. Stop it! Rogue warns me, my inner conscience not allowing me one last daydream. *Raya is happy and content with her mate. You have no right to interfere there. Concentrate on our fight against Clayton.*

Of course, I know she is right, and despite the crushing blow of leaving Raya behind, I am also happy that she is well cared for and maybe even loved. But what do I do about telling her that Brandon killed Alessia? This is something I do feel she should know. It's something I need to confront Brandon about too.

The mindlinked call for help takes me by surprise. The scream that accompanies it sends chills down my spine. *Fallon, please help me, call for Brandon. Your father and the Elders have found me guilty of preventing an Alpha pregnancy. Get Brandon.*

Where are you? I ask her as I tear out of my bed, wasting valuable time to put on my shoes in case we need to run and pausing to pick up the fire poker from the hearth. In the absence of anything else, it will have to do as my weapon.

Tell Bran to hurry. I'm in your father's office, but they are taking me down to the dungeons. I'm scared. Raya is pinning all her hopes on my brother, when she needs to learn she is in charge of her own destiny.

Just like I am.

As an Alpha offspring, I can communicate with my siblings even from a distance; Raya knows this from when my brothers have sent messages to me. Using all my strength, I send out a warning to Deacon, Euan and Brandon and hope that Clayton is unable to intercept it.

Clayton.

Is Clayton there? I ask as I run out of my room. My heart pounds from the exertion and fear. If Clayton is there, this is bad. As I reach the door to my father's office, Raya's blood curdling scream rings out. I boot the door open and storm inside.

"GET THE FUCK OFF HER, YOU TWISTED BASTARD!" I yell at Clayton, who holds Raya up by her hair. She's no longer screaming, and I don't know if she's unconscious or dead. Her petite body dangles limply from Clayton's outstretched arms.

"Fallon? Explain yourself. Why are you here, shouting and cat calling your brother. WITH NO VEIL ON!" I turn to my father, who looks at me for the first time in over ten years. "I won't repeat myself, Fallon. If you want to join the girl in her punishment, that can be arranged."

"I'm no longer a Lady of the Veil. Clayton has been forcing himself on me and physically punishing me when I resist. He wants to do the same to Raya. Why are you hurting her?" My father's complexion changes comically from a sickened green to a puce anger.

Turning to Clayton, he no longer shouts, but his hushed tones are even more intimidating than his shouts. "You touched your sister? You touched my little girl?" Clayton lets go of Raya. Her battered body smashes against the floor, and I yelp when she doesn't move or make a noise.

"She's lying, father. I did no such thing." Screaming with all my might, I run at Clayton, clutching the poker firmly in my hand. For every time he touched me, for all the taunts and threats, I use every ounce of the badness he poured into my life and wield it against him. I raise the hand holding the poker, and without remorse or care, I jab that fucker right through the eye with it.

The room blacks out around me with Bran and Euan's voices echoing through a distant mindlink.

~ Soraya ~

Lowering my head in respect to my Alpha and Elders, I wait for permission to speak. This is my first time in the Alpha's office. One day this will be Brandon's, but as his mate, I won't spend much time here; the office is for pack and business matters, and the female is only needed in here to bring sustenance.

The smell of polished wood washes over me in waves. All the walls are cladded in rich mahogany. The furniture matches. There is a thick, luxurious, red carpet on the floor, and the seats are covered in oxblood leather. There are jade emblems and decorations throughout. No expense has been spared here.

However, for all that magnificence, the room remains cold and uninviting. Shifting uncomfortably in front of the imposing men, I try to calm my nerves.

"Soraya, mate of Future Alpha Brandon Ward, we bring you here tonight to answer allegations made against you. Namely that you have attempted to prevent a pregnancy by your mate and have taken measures to end any accidental conception. How do you plead?"

Looking up at the old men, who stare at me with a mixture of intrigue and disgust, I am tongue tied. "I don't understand. You know Brandon and I have mated; you saw our proof. Carrying my mate's pup would be an honour and privilege." Clayton laughs and sneers at my comment, but quickly shuts up when I glare at him. He's a bully, nothing more or less, and he doesn't frighten me. "I would never do anything to endanger my child, but it's too soon to know yet, my heat was only two weeks ago."

The Elders whisper amongst themselves, before continuing. "We have a statement that details you having procured sheaths, and a witness reported your guard purchasing raspberry leaf tea and sanitary pads for you. Do you deny it?"

Having never procured a sheath, I can say what I'm about to and not be lying. "I have never procured a sheath. I'm not even sure what one is. Yes, I did send my guard for pads, but that's because I started cramping earlier today, and I thought it was—"

"What about the tea? Taking that tea in early pregnancy causes miscarriage. Are you trying to abort your baby." Clayton interrupts me. He scrunches his face up as he addresses me, spitting out his words with venom and animosity.

My hands automatically go to my stomach, my flat stomach. "I've just told you; it's too early to tell if I am carrying yet, but any child of mine and Brandon's will be loved and welcomed."

Clayton dismisses me and addresses his father once again. "She's lying. The girl said the sheaths were for Brandon because his mate doesn't want pups."

After a moment of silence, the Alpha smacks his hand down on the table. "Bring the girl in then. I want to hear her statement for myself." Clayton strides to another door in the Alpha's office, and I hear him talking in a muffled voice. He holds the door wide, and a red-haired woman I have never seen walks into the office.

"Introduce yourself to the Alpha and the Elders please." The redhead looks at Clayton, and when he nods, she steps further towards me.

"My name is Esme, a Scarlet Woman of the Ruins, former Reverent Moon pack member and former Daughter of the Veil." The woman sounds cold and bored.

"How do you know this woman?" the Alpha asks her as he points at me.

"She is the Future Alpha's mate, the one who asked for the sheaths," she answers, as she looks down at her nails. Indignant at her lies, anger bursts from my stomach and into my chest.

"LIAR!" I shout at her. "I've never met this woman in my life. I have never asked anyone for sheaths."

"How many sheaths did you give her, Esme?" Clayton continues, brushing over my denial and allowing the Alpha and the Elders to believe I am guilty.

"A whole box full. Forty-eight in a pack. She gave me money and told me she would need more soon. Brandon has a ferocious appetite," she says with a suggestive smile and a small giggle.

"You admit to lying with the Future Alpha?" one of the Elders asks He seems more turned on than off, though, eyeing the young woman greedily.

"Oh, yes. I have fucked Brandon and Euan and..." She glances up at Clayton, and he smiles at her, encouraging her. "And Clayton too."

"Alpha this is an outrage. Scarlet Women in the Alpha Quarters, your sons fornicating with them. Your daughter has already been banished for her indiscretions, and now this. Your daughter by law is breaking our most sacred laws by preventing an Alpha pregnancy. You must make an example here. Your children are running amok, and you need to bring them back under your control.

"LEAVE. NOW." The Alpha shouts at the Scarlet Woman. "You too, Elder Dorien. I will remind you once that I am Alpha here; you are an advisor and nothing more. If you ever chastise me in front of an audience again, I will banish you. Now go. Elder Randell will take your leading position for the rest of this evening"

The older man leaves with no further words exchanged. As proud as a peacock, Elder Randell steps forward, puffing out his chest.

"Mate of Brandon, what is your defence?" Overwhelming panic races through my veins; they still don't believe me.

"I think you should question me again once my mate returns; he will not be happy that you have brought me here without his escort or consent."

"You are here to answer for your crimes. Brandon isn't here, and we want to address this now. How do you plead?" Tears burn my eyes, but I refuse to show any weakness.

"I didn't do anything. I'm not guilty." Clayton smiles at my answer, and the wicked glint in his eyes makes the tiny downy hair on the back of my neck stand on end.

"In the absence of remorse and truth, we have no option but to find you guilty of Preventing an Alpha pregnancy," Elder Randel tells me flatly, without any emotion. "You will be held in the dungeon until your mate returns before we hand out your punishment. The Moon Goddess is just, but you are an abomination of her ancient teachings and will face the highest penalty for your crimes."

"No, I didn't do it. Please don't do this. I might be carrying Brandon's pup; I don't know; it's too early. Please, have mercy," I plead with tears springing from my eyes. I know people who are sent to the dungeons don't usually come back alive. Seeing my pleading is futile. I reach out to the last person who can help me. Until now she would have always been the first person, but now I'm not so sure. All I know right now is that I have to fight and find a way to stay out of that dungeon.

Fallon, please send help. As soon as my eyes glaze over, Clayton realises I am mindlinking and punches me square in the face, breaking my nose.

"Who are you linking, you little bitch? You think Brandon can hear you from here?" He yanks me up by my hair until my feet dangle off the ground. "Brandon thought he was so high and mighty getting a beautiful innocent mate, all pure and clean for him. Well, you'll be filled with pups when he returns, but the Goddess only knows if they'll be his, mine, the dungeon masters or maybe even fathers."

Clayton lays into me, hitting and slapping me, and as blood pours down my cheek, I know my eyebrow has split. I try to fight. I manage to kick him in the stomach and balls a couple of times, but as he rains heavy blows onto my head, I begin to lose consciousness.

Images of my time with my loved ones run through my head: my papa swinging me about in the meadow as we picked wildflowers for mother, my niece Anais when she was born, spending time with Fallon. My mate flashes before my eyes: the day he unveiled me, our private moments in our rooms, mating. I must fight.

Through my haze, Fallon's voice travels through, and then my body smashes to the floor. A scream unlike anything I have ever heard before echoes out throughout the office, reverberating off the wooden cladding.

Opening my eyes, chaos has erupted around me. There is blood spattered everywhere. Fallon slumps to the floor but looks unhurt. She grips a poker in her hands as though her life depends on it. Assessing the rest of the room, the Alpha is shouting, and one Elder hurls into a wastepaper basket, while the other leans over Clayton's fallen form.

I scoot closer to Fallon. Although her eyes are shut, she cries soundlessly. Silent, pain filled tears roll down her cheeks. I look back and see the source of her distress. Clayton is missing an eye. And Fallon's poker is covered in blood.

Knowing she can face death for harming her brother, I help her stand and move quickly to the door. "Fallon, please help me, we need to get out of here now."

Fallon wraps an arm around my shoulder, and I support her weight as much as I can. Using the Omegas' staircase, we run as fast as our broken bodies will allow us. But just as we leave the Alpha Quarters, a dark figure emerges.

"Fallon? Is that you?" The disguised voice says; however, once the moonlight hits our faces, he knows exactly who we are.

"Come with me now, both of you. You cannot be seen." I try to object as he lifts Fallon up, over his shoulder. "You've gotten heavy since the last time I did this, kid!"

I get the shock of my life when he faces me, the night sky illuminating him enough to allow me to identify him.

"Deacon?"

"Shush. Yes, it's me. Throw on that Shaman regalia in case anyone recognises you. Brandon is on his way home now."

Pulling on his black smock and covering my head with the large hood, I follow Deacon and Soraya into a stone-built hut frequented by the Shaman. This is their refuge, a place they use for contemplation and prayer.

"Soraya, I need you both to lie low and be quiet. My father is calling for me, so I must respond to keep my cover. I'll be right back."

Chapter Seventeen

~ Brandon ~

Tearing through the land, I plead for speed, extra strength, and the will to get home before they hurt my precious mate. How fucking dare they touch her. She is mine! Under my protection. In my heart. The love of my life. I will have their throats for this.

As the sun sets, I continue to run, stopping only momentarily to drink from a stream or to gather my thoughts and bearings. My communication with my brothers and sister is still not being received. The mindlink won't work from this distance; I need to be closer to our land so I can send the warnings and rally some support. As I travel closer to our land, Fallon's mindlink is the first one I receive. *Brandon, if you hold any affection for your mate, get home now. She has been accused of preventing an Alpha pregnancy, and father and Clayton have her.*

If I hold any affection for her? Is Fallon kidding me? Soraya is my whole world now. It is abundantly clear to everyone else. I don't understand her reticence to accept that my mate means everything to me. My outrage quickly disperses when

I hear Soraya's frantic mindlinks too. Surely the whole pack can hear them, why doesn't anyone intervene?

The next person to answer my call is Euan. I'm perplexed when he gives his location as the ass end of The Ruins. It will add an additional couple of minutes to my journey, but I need him and his support. As much as I want to fly in there and demand Soraya back under my care, they have the numbers to easily overpower me and lock me up. Then my girl will really be in trouble. I contemplate contacting my best friend, Daniel, who is supposed to be my future Beta, but his father's loyalty to my own has prevented me from involving him.

Running directly to Euan, who is battered, bruised and tied up with silver chains, my confusion builds even more. My youngest brother looks as though he has been through hell and back. The haunted look in his eyes sends chills of foreboding through me.

Shifting into human form so I can help him get out of the chains, I look around for one of our well-placed chests that contain clothes, weapons and long-life food for the pack and pick up an axe and strike the silver. The loops around his wrists are wound tight, and from his injuries, I can see he must have been chained up for a couple of days at least. Silver prevents him from healing himself as it is so toxic to us as werewolves.

Retrieving some snippers from the chest, I drop to my knees to finally free him, but his voice, so filled with desperation, distracts me.

"This is all my fault, Bran. If anything happens, I am so sorry," he cries, as he holds his head in his hands.

Wanting to understand, I snip the final link keeping him contained before pulling him to his feet. "What's all your fault, Euan? Who did this?"

He groans again; despite me having removed the silver chains binding him, the long-term effects of the silver oxide still cause him weakness and pain. Although, I do believe his pain to be more of the heart than physical.

"She tricked me. Esme. The one I got the sheaths from. She... She..." He stops as he roars in pain. "I thought we were in love. She was having a baby, and I said

I would take it on as my own, that I would mark her as mine. I didn't realise she was using me for information on you and your mate."

Still confused about who Esme is and where Euan and Soraya fit into this mess, although I dont have time to waste, I need to understand what has been happening. Is this why they have Soraya? Or is this something completely different?

"She's in with Clayton. She fucked me, injected me with something and then invited Clayton in, who rewarded her for her conniving by fucking her in front of me."

So many emotions race through me. Sorrow for Euan, who looks emotionally ravaged and genuinely devastated. He has given his heart to a liar and a fraud. Hatred, pure all-consuming loathing and disgust for Clayton, which is so great that I worry it'll permanently change me. I will kill him today if he lays a finger on my mate; I will torture that twisted monster until he begs for mercy.

"We don't have time for this now, Euan. We will get our revenge. I promise you this, brother, but he has Soraya."

A searing pain, one I have only felt once before, forces both Euan and I to our knees. The echoey, high-pitched scream bounces off the inside of my skull, and then the voice of our sister filters through.

I'm no longer a Daughter of the Veil. Clayton has been forcing himself on me and physically punishing me when I resist. He wants to do the same to Raya. Why are you hurting her? This transmission isn't the same as a mindlink. There is interference and static, like a bad radio signal. I can feel Fallon's presence in the Alpha's Quarters, but it seems like the message is coming from far away.

The primal Alpha roar reverberates from my chest. They have my mate, and he's been abusing my sister! I will kill him; I will destroy him.

However, when we get to the front steps of the Alpha Quarters, Fallon's battle cry blasts us both off our feet. Having been in battle, I have heard a few of these anguish-filled fight to death calls, but none have ever affected me like this. No one has ever shown me this level of power before.

I'm on the back steps. I think Fallon and your mate are coming towards me. I will take them. Then I'll answer father's call. Go to the office and get that bastard,

Deacon mindlinks us, appearing to be the first to recover. I've never been so grateful to have him back on our side. Both Euan and I race up the staircase and along the landing to our father's office. The door remains open, but the tiny blood splatters on the hallway carpet let me know that someone, hopefully Soraya and Fallon, has made an escape.

Looking into the office, I get the biggest shock of my life. Clayton lies practically lifeless on the floor. With Elder Randell summoning the Healers, my father rants at Clayton, kneeling in front of him, demanding answers as he shakes him.

Euan shouts out to our father, and as he turns, I see for the first time the reason Clayton is incapacitated. Where there was once an eye is now an ugly, bleeding, gaping hole. As blood streams down his face, he opens and closes his month soundlessly, reminding me of a goldfish.

"It's a good job you're down now, brother. I promise you, once you are back on your feet, I will make you pay. For what you did to Alessia and Fallon, but mostly, for daring to even look in my mate's direction." Even though I have vowed to myself to come back for Clayton when he is fully able for an even fight, the urge to kick him overwhelms me. My first kick connects with his stomach, but the second one doesn't land as Euan drags me from the room.

However, before I leave, I want my father to know what my intentions are. "It's time for a change, father. I'll be back to take my place as Alpha. You are no Alpha. You are fuck all to me. The moment you allowed harm to come to my mate was the day you lost." My father turns to look pleadingly at me. "Step down, or I'll be back to challenge you. Move away and take that scummy piece of shit with you, or I'll kill the both of you."

"Brandon, wait please. I thought she'd tried to abort your child; Clayton told me." I pick my father up by the throat with one hand, his face turning a deep red as I do.

"I don't give a shit what he told you. You should have waited for me. Tell me… is this what happened to Heidi? Did you fucking torture Heidi?"

"YES!" he screams though he can hardly breathe. "She was punished for not conceiving, but she was weak." I throw him down to the floor in disgust.

"You sick bastard. You hurt her for not getting pregnant? You haven't even given me and Soraya a chance yet. I will make you pay for what you've done." I boot my father, as Euan finally drags me from the room.

"I want him too, but remember what is important. Your girl is hurt and is going to need you now more than ever," Euan reminds me, and I'm glad to see some of the hurt has receded from his gaze and a pinch of fire has returned, burning brighter than ever.

Euan's stark reminder refocuses me. I must get to Soraya; she needs to be okay. I'll never forgive myself for leaving her here in the first place, and if I can't forgive myself for it, why should she?

~ Euan ~

Brandon is a big fella, and dragging him away from our father and Clayton takes everything I have. With the silver still dulling my senses and weakening me, this isn't easy, especially when I know the beast inside Brandon, his wolf Maverick, is ready to emerge and cause carnage.

With my brother riled and my strength deserting me, I have no option but to remind him of his mate. One mention of her and Brandon's eye refocus. Everything else fades away; all that matters is his Soraya.

It's in this moment that I realise that, although I thought I loved Esme, no other mate will ever mean as much to me as my fated one will. I'm hurting now, but it was all based on lies, and eventually, none of it will matter when I finally find my true mate. Until then, I must learn to patiently wait for my destiny to unfold.

Thinking of Esme leaves a bitter taste in my mouth. It is unbelievable to me that the same sweet, caring and kind young woman used me. After injecting me with wolfsbane, persons unknown chained me in silver, subduing my wolf and strength, slowly and agonisingly killing me. They waited for me to rouse, to watch their little floor show. She maintained eye contact with me while she rode my brother, right up to his climax. At first, I thought my heart break was going to suffocate me, but as I watched her, I knew this had been a lucky escape for me. I ensured my eyes burned with the absolute hatred I felt for her for doing what she did. Once or twice, she had to look away, but Clayton would roughly grab her by the chin and tell her to not stop looking.

She means nothing to me, but if that child is mine, I want it back. Bastard or not, if proved to be mine, my child belongs with me, and I will raise him. I will not allow anything but that.

We pass Deacon on the stairs and maintain a distance; Deacon asks us why father has summoned us, and we shrug and tell him he best go and see for himself, but we both know that Deacon is maintaining his front and we cannot compromise him. As we walk away, he links their hiding place to us.

We also have to dissect what our father just admitted to regarding Heidi and her death and find a decent way to share it with Deacon. The death of his mate nearly killed him too. It's only the thirst for the truth that keeps him going, and I worry about what will be left of my brother once we give him that.

As we approach the girls hiding place, we watch the area around it, carefully ensuring we aren't being watched and compromising them. We both stare at each other when we hear the gentle footfall approaching us.

"Brandon? Euan? Is that you?" a familiar voice whispers gently.

"Mother? But... what are you doing here?" I ask her. She looks like a broken woman, aged and fragile, as though the troubles of our home life have added twenty years on to her.

"I heard Fallon's call. Please take me to her; she needs me. Please, boys, I only want to help my baby." The tears spring to her eyes. I have never seen my mother cry before.

"Shush, mother. You are going to get us caught!" Brandon spits out. His exasperation at our mother seems a little overdone for me.

"Bran, calm down," I warn under my breath. "She's worried about us."

"She should have worried when that bastard was fucking us all up in the head. Did you know about Heidi?" Instead of defending herself, our mother weeps even harder.

"Of course, I knew. I know first-hand because it happened to me too. It is what every mated female who contributes to the line faces." We both stand back in horror at the woman who bore and raised us. Never again will I think of her as weak.

"He beat you?" Brandon's strained voice makes me believe that he is as shocked and saddened as I am.

"Yes. Please, take me to Fallon, and I will tell you everything you want to know." Brandon nods stiffly. We sweep the area one last time, and once we are sure we aren't being watched, we move to Deacon's refuge.

Careful to not make a noise to draw attention but also not wanting to scare the girls, we unlock the door and move the lock to the inside.

Brandon's mate comes towards the arch that separates us, and although I can see her hands trembling, she shouts out, "Who is there? I am armed and I will hurt you if you come any closer."

"Soraya," Brandon calls her name, the relief and anguish both mingling in his voice, but his mate takes a step back from him. "Sweetheart, it's me. I came back as soon as I could."

"Who is with you, sir?" Soraya asks him very formally, and I almost feel my brother's heart break when she doesn't immediately respond to his call. We both thought she would be relieved to see him.

"My mother and Euan. Soraya, are you hurt? Can we come in?" She moves further away from him, and panic fills Brandon, rolling off him in desperate waves. "Sweet, where is Fallon?"

"Fallon, do you want to see them?" Even with my werewolf hearing, I cannot make out what Fallon is saying. "She says yes, but do not come too close. She's having a hard time keeping Rogue under control right now."

"Fallon, it's me. Oh, my baby, I didn't know he was hurting you, I'm so sorry." As our mother sobs through her apology, I get my first proper glimpse of my baby sister. It's true that she has abandoned her veil. The war inside her is evident as her eyes rapidly change from her own to her wolfs.

"Did you know he was hurting Alessia, too? Did you know what a twisted beast you have bred?" As our mother shakes her head, I try to move closer to Fallon. "Back off, Euan; I saw you running to Clayton and Father to tell them that Bran and Raya were mating without witnesses. I know you're in cahoots with them."

"No, Fallon. Bran told him to do that. He was trying to help Euan gain favour back after the fallout over breakfast." Soraya's defence of both me and Bran fills me with hope that not all is lost. Her protectiveness of Fallon is both heart-warming and awe-inspiring. Having grown up with several brothers, I never had a need for a best friend. I didn't know this type of bond could exist outside of your blood family.

"Why did father torture or rather allow Clayton to torture Raya, mother?" Fallon sits up from her position on the floor and looks our mother in the eye. Mother quickly looks down at the floor, but I manage to see the shame and guilt in her face before she does.

We all wait with bated breath for the person who can give us the answers, the one who holds the truth we need to move forward. "You act like I have any say in what is going on around here. Soraya was hurt because they believe they have evidence that she isn't doing her duty. Heidi was fatally hurt because they believed she was failing to do her duty."

"So, they are tortured until they provide a child?" Brandon asks with disgust dripping off his every word. He takes a protective step towards his mate, but she steps back from him. "Soraya, I won't let anyone else hurt you. I promise. Come to me."

"No, Brandon. I need some answers first. Just stay where you are so we can see you." United with her best friend, Soraya stands tall and strong as she holds Fallon's hand. The residue of her mistreatment can be seen with the dried blood and torn clothing, but she looks resilient, fierce.

Just like a Luna.

"Mother, were you tortured?" Fallon asks in a very matter of a fact fashion. I look over at our mother to see her response, and recoil in horror when she nods her head to confirm her ill-treatment at the hands of our father. "When? How long did this go on for."

"I was punished for almost a year until I conceived Alessia. I was battered and tortured for producing a daughter and not a true heir: a son." Having heard enough, I go and comfort my bereft mother. Her slight, frail frame shakes as I wrap an arm around her.

"I'm very sorry for what you have endured, Luna Beverly. I needed to know what my future holds as Brandon's mate. I also need to know what sort of man he is and what sort of Alpha he intends to be." Brandon and Soraya look at each other, and the distance between them is more than physical; something has changed. "Fallon has told me something, and I cannot continue as your mate until I know the truth. Until we both know the truth."

Brandon looks between his mate and our sister, and sweat beads on his brow. Only he knows the answers the girls want. It's what Fallon has always wanted. Even I don't know the full truth, but I trust Brandon. I trust that he is honest, and I know he won't guide me wrong.

If only Fallon and his mate could trust him too.

"We want to know the truth. Did you kill Alessia? Clayton told me you killed her. I need to know, Brandon." Fallon doesn't shout, but she may as well have. Brandon flinches away from her words; he can no longer make eye contact. I try to intervene, but my mother pulls me back. She wants the truth too.

"It's not as simple as you think, Fallon. It's not as clear cut as all that," Brandon answers, and as he does, Fallon retaliates. She lunges at him, and Brandon is saved only by Soraya holding Fallon back.

"Did you fucking kill her? Answer the fucking question, Brandon. Answer me!" she screeches at him. Her eyes are wide and crazed, and spit flies from her mouth. If Soraya wasn't holding her back, I think she would have choked Brandon by now. "Did you kill my sister?" she screams at him again.

Brandon falls to his knees with tears falling freely down his face. "Yes! I killed her. It was me. I did it." My ears ring, and my mother cries out loud in distress at the news. Brandon stands and looks at us all. "I killed Alessia."

Chapter Eighteen

~ Fallon ~

As soon as I scream and push that poker into Clayton's eye, an otherworldly power floods my body. Blasted backwards, I am unable to finish the job that I set out to do; I wanted to wipe out Clayton. I wanted to brutally and unapologetically destroy him so he could never hurt anyone else ever again. The hate I feel for him fuels and drives my sinister thoughts, but I believe everything I feel is a product of his actions and is, therefore, justified. I know I at least managed to seriously maim him. Now, his dark, disgusting soul will be ever present on his face.

Only vaguely can I recall how we moved from my father's office to Deacon's sanctuary. All I do know is that Soraya came through for me. Despite her own injuries, she dragged my sorry ass to a relative place of safety.

"Fallon, did you call for Brandon like I asked?" she huffs out, as she checks my body for wounds. She is yet to understand that my hurt is inside, in my heart and soul, and it cannot be fixed. "Fallon, answer me please! Is help coming?"

After coughing and clearing my throat, I answer her with a still croaky voice. "I called. But, Raya, before anyone gets her, I need to tell you what I know. You can't trust Brandon."

She looks at me with her wonderful, brilliant blue eyes. How I dreamed of seeing those eyes again, but instead of the alarm and sadness I see now, I wanted to see joy and excitement. "Brandon is my mate; I trust him with my life, Fallon. He's your brother. Why do you hate him so?"

"I'm trying to protect you! Don't you see?" I shout back at her. "All I've ever wanted is to keep you safe. You will not be safe with him."

"I've never felt safer than when I'm with him, Fallon. He makes me feel safe and protected." Raya looks down at her feet before adding. "He makes me feel... loved. Adored. Like I matter."

With this new information, I question her further. "You love him?" She looks me in the eye and nods her answer. I can't believe she loves him. He's a monster! "Does he love you?"

For the first time, doubt clouds her expression. "I don't know. I think he might. He makes me feel like he does."

"He's never told you, though?" I ask, forcing the matter on its head. "Has he ever given you those words so that you know for sure?" When she shakes her head no, I have a moment of remorse for hurting her, but I need her to open her eyes. Brandon isn't who she thinks he is.

"He hasn't said the words, but love isn't just about words, Fallon. He shows me in everything he does that I am important to him, that I matter." The pleading looking in her expression almost breaks my resolve. "Just like I've never told you how much I love you, you are my best friend and I love you. I hope the way I act tells you that."

There is no arguing with her logic because I know it to be true, for I love her too, and yet I have never said those words to her.

"He's dangerous, Raya. Very, very dangerous. I don't want him to hurt you!" She snorts at this and shakes her head at me as though I've missed the point.

"Of course, he's dangerous; he's an Alpha werewolf! The strongest member of our pack, and I include your father in that assessment too. I know who he is, Fallon, and what he is capable of, but Bran is different with me. He's kind and gentle."

She won't accept what I am saying, and if she doesn't accept it, she's going to come to harm. "He may seem like that now, but he'll hurt you, Fallon."

"What? Like Clayton and your father just did?" She shakes her head at me, and I have to admit her fierce defence of her mate is impressive; if it wasn't so misjudged, I would have faltered by now.

"Clayton says Brandon killed Alessia," I tell her bluntly, for now we have passed the stage of niceties, I need her to know the facts; she will not be swayed by empty accusations. I must give her the information so she can make up her own mind.

My revelation about Alessia stops her in her tracks. "Alessia is dead?" she asks with a strained voice. With tear filled eyes, I nod back to her.

"Clayton told me that Brandon killed Alessia and if I told anyone what he was doing to me, I would be next. He had no reason to lie about it, Raya. There is no trace of Alessia, and Brandon did leave the territory that day. It all fits into place."

"No!" she says with determination. "I know Brandon. I know he wouldn't do it! I've seen the heart of the man; he can't have done it."

Sensing my brothers close by, I put a suggestion to Raya. "He's on his way; he'll be here at any moment. How about we stick together and ask him, right here, right now. If I'm wrong, I'll admit I'm wrong. But I need to know."

"I will stay by your side until you get your answers, I promise!" She holds out her hand for me to shake, and for her loyalty to both me and her mate, I wish for the first time to be wrong. For Raya's sake, I want to be wrong about Brandon.

The first shock I get is that my mother is with Brandon and Euan. Unsure if we can trust her, I mindlink Raya and tell her that Rogue is out of control with anger and to keep them all at a distance.

Raya stands firm and refuses to let anyone approach us. *Thank you for being the best friend any girl could wish for.*

"We want to know the truth. Did you kill Alessia? Clayton told me you killed her. I need to know, Brandon," I ask, keeping my question as direct as possible and my voice as neutral as I can bear to gain his cooperation, but Brandon flinches away from my words, unable to look at either me or Soraya.

"It's not as simple as you think, Fallon. It's not as clear cut as all that," he answers back to me, riling Rogue, who is waiting just under the surface to pounce. Before I can stop her, Rogue attempts to lunge at Brandon, but luckily Soraya holds me back.

"Did you fucking kill her? Answer the fucking question, Brandon. Answer me!" I shout at him, trying to exude some authority before screaming one last time. "Did you kill my sister?"

Brandon falls to his knees in front of me as he finally makes his confession. "Yes! I killed her. It was me. I did it! I killed Alessia."

Soraya lets go of my shoulder, and my body free falls to the ground once more. My sweet sister is dead, and the monster standing in front of me is responsible for it.

"It can't be true. Brandon? Tell me this isn't true." From her desperate plea, I can tell how much this hurts Raya, but now she knows the truth; we all do.

"Sweet, I'm so sorry. I never meant for you to be dragged into any of this mess." Brandon crawls on his knees towards Raya, but she backs up until her back is pressed against the wall.

"Stay away from me! I trusted you. Why? Why did you do it, Brandon?" He shakes his head at her, tears and snot flying at Raya, but she doesn't lose her composure.

"I was commanded by my Alpha. It was the only way–" Brandon starts to explain, but Raya will not allow him to continue.

"You aren't the person I thought you were. I cannot spend eternity with someone who would murder their own kin in cold blood." Soraya runs her hand over her face and takes a deep breath before looking straight at Brandon with a pained expression. "I, Soraya Burke, reject you, Brandon Ward, as my mate."

~ Brandon ~

As Soraya steps away from me, my heart burns, and a tearing sensation starts at my navel and travels up to my throat. I'm so close to losing her and I can't. My life is nothing without her now. "Please, Soraya. It wasn't like that. It's not what you all think. It never has been. I need you to trust me on this."

"Why should I trust you? You don't trust me. If you did, you would have told me what the hell is going on so I could protect myself better." My little mate sounds hurt and angry. "I've just been tortured, Brandon. Tortured by your father and brother. Your mother has just admitted that she was tortured until she produced you. I'm scared, and you're keeping stuff from me."

"I'm trying to protect you!" I shout back at her. I'm so desperate to keep her from harm. Why can't she see that? I'm shocked when she begins to laugh.

"Protect me?! How is that working out for you? Because I don't feel protected." As the tears fill her eyes, I think I am beginning to understand. The truth will be hard to take, but we cannot build our future on a foundation of quicksand. We are a partnership, and for Soraya to truly accept me and the life set out for me, she needs to know the truth. "We are either all in, one hundred percent open and honest with each other, or we reject each other now."

"I don't want to lose you. I will be as honest as I can and tell you whatever you want to make this right." My heart pounds against my ribcage, but no matter how much I betray my Queen, I will fight tooth and nail to keep Soraya. She is all I have left to live for.

"I don't want to lose you either, Brandon. I love you; I'm in love with you. Tonight was terrifying, and life will continue to be terrifying if you keep me in the dark about what is going on. Why did you kill Alessia?" Maverick is still howling in my head at her admission that she loves me, causing her questions about Alessia to throw me.

"I have to start way back at the beginning so you'll all understand. I'm tired of lying and holding this all in. She was my sister too." Despite my reservations about sharing, the prospect of unloading this burden, of the truth finally being out in the open amongst the people who matter most to me, is a welcomed thought. "Alessia was different from all of us. She got her wolf when she was fourteen years old, and at the age of sixteen, she had her first heat."

"She had a heat without a mate?" my mother asks in a high-pitched voice. Heat generally only starts once a she-wolf is mated. "Why didn't she tell us?"

"Diana told her she had to keep it all a secret and that once people found out who she was and what she would be capable of, she would be in grave danger."

"Who is Diana? What has she got to do with this?" Fallon interrupts me this time. She frowns at me in confusion, looking so much like Alessia when she does.

"Diana is the Goddess of the Moon, our idol and highest deity. She has never spoken to a werewolf directly before. Brandon, where are you going with this?" My mother answers Fallon before I can, and from the tone of her voice, she doesn't believe me.

"I'm trying to explain this in chronological order so you understand. Sia was different, Mother. She was special. Her heats eventually became too much, and she had to mate, or it was going to kill her. And after that initial first-time mating when she was nineteen, Regina would not let up. She would push and push and push until the only reprieve Alessia would get would be when she found someone to mate with." I pause, knowing this will be upsetting for my mother to hear. "However, this sort of behaviour never goes unnoticed when you are a Lady of the Veil. You all heard the rumours about her. She wasn't acting out; she was following her natural instincts as a werewolf."

"I get that, Brandon, but isn't that sort of... desire reserved for our fated mate?" Fallon asks. She is the one I need to explain to the most. She is the one who has relentlessly searched for our sister, trying to find the truth, while I have had the information she needed all this time, but have been sworn to say nothing until it becomes perilous not to.

"Yes, usually it is. But as I said, Sia was special. She had been blessed with something no other ever has. You know the legend of the Moon Goddesses?" She nods to me slowly. "It's all true. Diana sent a Queen to remind us of the sanctity of the mate bond. She sent her to our pack because of the way we have evolved to take power from females and rule them, instead of with them. A Queen was sent to return our lands to an even equilibrium. A Queen of Alphas."

The moment of truth is here. My mouth is dry and wet at the same time, and my stomach turns itself into knots as I look at the faces of almost everyone I love and care about.

"Have you ever spoken to Diana?" my mother asks. The doubt is evident on her face, and her eyes are clouded with misgivings. Of course, when I first heard this tale, I didn't believe it either.

"I have never spoken directly to Diana, but she has sent messages, and she informed the Queen when I found Soraya, when I had told no one. Even Soraya didn't know because she was too young." Looking at my mate now, I need her to understand. "She forbade me from claiming you. She said it would put you in the same danger that Heidi had been in. That is the reason I went away. But I couldn't stay away. You see, I love you, too; I think I always have."

"Bran…" Her voice is whisper soft, and yet it caresses me in a way like nothing else ever could. "I'm trying to understand; truly, I am. What happened to Alessia?"

Smiling back at her, I try to continue my explanation, and with Soraya's support and encouragement, it does seem easier. "When Father heard that Alessia had been fornicating again with several pack members, he ordered me to kill her. I tried to get her out of here and meant to fake her death. Unfortunately, Regina, her wolf, would not let Alessia leave. She wanted a pup, and she wanted it as soon as possible. She would send Alessia into dramatic heats that lasted weeks, and no matter how much Alessia pleaded, Regina would not let up."

"So, her wolf wanted a pup, but wouldn't wait for her mate? It doesn't make sense, Brandon. What was the rush?" My mother looks at me, unbelieving, and I begin to panic. I know this is hard to believe, but I am trying to be truthful.

"Alessia didn't have a fated mate, and Regina knew when the time came for her to take the position she was destined for that it wouldn't be as a werewolf. Regina wanted to leave a legacy so she could be born again." Fallon's face drops when realisation finally hits her.

"So, what you're saying is... that Alessia- she was the Queen?" Fallon stutters out at me, her eyes becoming wider with every word.

"No, what I am saying is Alessia was the Queen that was promised. I had to kill her so she could be reborn as the Queen of Alphas."

Chapter Nineteen

~ Soraya ~

My entire body hurts, and that is nothing in comparison to my heart. Of course, I love Brandon, and I never want to be without him. But how can I pledge my life to someone who commands me to trust him but doesn't trust me enough to share massive life altering information. I refuse to live like that. I want us to be equal, and he said he wanted that too. He doesn't get to hide behind 'I didn't tell you to keep you safe', and I am not hiding behind the façade of being a poor defenceless woman.

As I say my rejection, Pandora howls deep inside me. *Noooo! You can't. You're carrying his pup, our pup. I forbid you from rejecting him.* And with that tiny amount of information, I feel stronger, for I am stronger than I ever knew I was. I might be mated to an Alpha wolf, but my body has created and now carries an Alpha too. For my child's safety, I must pursue this, or Brandon will continue to keep me in the dark, and that is no longer acceptable to me.

So, I stand my ground, and surely enough, Brandon tells me and everyone else everything he's been holding in. Watching him from the short distance between us leaves me aching inside. How I wish I could go to him and allow him to take away all the badness. It would be all so easy to do, and yet that is not what is destined for me. I am not Brandon's pet. I am his mate and partner, and it is high time both of us acted like it.

From what I observe, I know Brandon is feeling relieved to share his burden. The tension in his broad shoulders eases and the worry on his face lessens. My mate looks strong and yet, he also looks younger.

"No, what I am saying is Alessia was the Queen that was promised. I had to kill her so she could be reborn as the Queen of Alphas." My mouth drops open. All this time, he has held this inside.

"So where is she now?" Fallon asks impatiently, as she rises to her feet. "I want to see her so I can verify your story."

"You will all see her very soon. Our Queen has been resurrecting an ancient kingdom that had been long forgotten. When she was first reborn, she assumed Alessia's body and form, but she was incredibly weak. She has been biding her time, getting stronger, building up an army and rebuilding her kingdom. She isn't quite ready to take on the Alphas of Veridonia just yet, but everyday she is closer to that goal."

"So, she looks like Alessia? Is she still Alessia? How did you kill her? How did you know if you killed her, that she would be reborn?" Fallon has a million and one questions, and I can't say that I blame her, but my protective instinct is to shield Bran.

"She still has all Alessia's memories and characteristics, but she will never live as Alessia Ward again. She is no longer a werewolf; she is a Queen. Our Queen sent from the Moon Goddess herself." Brandon pauses as he thinks about the next question. "I knew she would be reborn because Diana told Alessia so. I killed her with a silver dagger, as instructed; Alessia was deeply attached to her wolf, Regina, and the only way to let her be reborn as the Queen was to kill the wolf."

Stumbling ever so slightly, my head still pounds from my earlier beating off Clayton. Bran is right at my side but hesitates to touch me. "Can I help you?" he asks softly. His vulnerability is heartbreakingly clear to see. I nod to him.

"I'm sorry, Brandon. I was scared and hurt. And angry. I don't want to reject you. I do love you." Without any further delay, he picks me up bridal style and carries me over to a pew before sitting down with me on his lap.

"I'm sorry too. I should have trusted you, and then maybe you wouldn't have been harmed. How is your head?" With concern lining his face, he traces his finger over my face. The tiny tingles ease my pain, and my whole body feels rejuvenated from our mate bond. "I'm going to kill them both for harming mine!"

Feeling his anger escalating on my behalf, I gently press my hand against his cheek and smile when my big gruff Alpha werewolf leans into my palm, looking for more of my touch. *I have something to tell you,* I tell him through mindlink, wanting desperately for this to be our moment. *Pandora just told me... I'm having a baby. Our baby.*

Initially, he looks at me with an open mouth. I worry I might have broken him, but as tears of joy fill his eyes, and a massive grin spreads across his handsome face, I know he is happy. *I'm going to be a father? We're going to be a family.* I nod to him, emotion filling me as the realisation finally sinks in.

I'm going to be a mother, and despite all my previous worries, I couldn't be happier. The icing on the cake is that Brandon is delighted too. "I love you so much, Sweet. You are the best thing that ever happened to me." Hearing his declaration once again pushes me over the edge; I almost turned him away out of fear. As tears of happiness and worry run down my face, Brandon smiles as he wipes them away. *Hormones already?* he jokes, and I cannot help but laugh.

Can we keep it between us for now. It is still very early on. Noticing the disappointment that flares in his eyes, it surprises me when he acquiesces and agrees to keep it quiet for now.

Okay, we'll keep it our secret for now. Come on. I have to tell everyone what our plan is. He helps me to my feet when it occurs to me to ask him what our plan is. *I have no idea, Sweet. But I'm the Alpha and it's my job to figure out the plan.*

Taking his hand, we walk towards the others. "No, Brandon. We're a team; it's our job now, remember?"

"Yes, Sweet. I remember," he says with a tiny smile. *We ought to move to the crypts. It's not going to be easy, sweetheart, but we will make it as safe as possible. Are you sure you want to do this?*

My family flash through my mind: my mother, sisters, nieces, and nephews. Will they be safe here until I can come back and get them? My hands instructively go to my stomach that cradles the tiny little speck that will become our child. I cannot raise our child here in this pack. Something must change.

Yes, I am sure. Let's do this.

However, before we can speak, there is a knock at our locked door. Deacon, using a prearranged secret knock, waits to be let in.

"We don't have long, and we need to move the girls as soon as possible. They are charging Fallon with attempted murder, and Soraya of preventing an Alpha pregnancy." Deacon rushes around the room, opening small cupboards that look innocuously like walls and seats. He takes out bags and supplies. "Clayton will survive, but he's lost the sight in his eye. He will want revenge; we need to get Fallon away from him right now. He will not harm another woman I love." His voice breaks, and Fallon and Luna Beverly go to comfort him.

"Then it's time for us to join our Queen. I warn you all that this journey will not be easy. but at the end of it, we will at least be safe," Brandon declares, as it's now our only option. The three brothers nod to each other; a silent vow to protect each other and anyone else who needs it.

~ Flashback ~

The moans of pleasure echoed in the cold hall, much to the discomfort of the young werewolf, who sat on a wooden stool. It had been hours of relentless moaning, squeaking, banging, growling, and groaning. However, the Queen had one of her mammoth heats, and despite having no mate, her carnal needs must be met. It would be inhumane to leave her suffering. She is the Queen that had been promised, for Goddess' sake!

After locating a few willing and loyal wolves up to the task, they all, including the young werewolf, made an oath to protect their Queen's reputation. They would do all they could to serve her, even laying down their own lives. The Future Alpha, the Queen's brother, brought her here, away from the main pack, to try and be discreet; however, he could not stay to protect her, despite how much he wanted to. It would draw attention if the two of them were gone for long periods of time. The Future Alpha probably also didn't want to hear his sister in distress or being railed by some of his most loyal men. However, usually he would frequently return, bringing much needed resources, as often as he could. The young wolf began to worry that something had happened because this time, his Future Alpha had not returned for two whole days and nights.

As soon as one man finished pleasuring her, the Queen's pain and discomfort would build up again. The Queen's haunting screams of agony were only sated by mating and sexual fulfilment. Seven werewolves took turns to bring her Highness to ecstasy, but they would no sooner finish, either through exhaustion or depletion, when her need would rise once more. As she moved deeper into her Haze, she became more commanding.

"Don't stop, I need you, now," she cried out, the distress evident in her voice. "I want two of you, at the same time. Please serve your Queen." Her screeches of euphoria, accompanied by the masculine, primal grunts, mingling with the slapping of skin against skin, served to confirm that two men had stepped up to the mark and given our Queen what her body craved.

At first, hearing his Queen being pleasured and knowing what was happening in that closed room made the young werewolf feel ill. The ancient scriptures warn against mating with anyone other than your fated mate. He was uncomfortable with tarnishing her Highnesses morality; however, as the night changed into day, he welcomed the sounds of willing participants. The sound of her distress was simply too much to take.

Being the Queen would come with its perks, but the magnitude of her heat was surely a downfall. Her royal blooded wolf wanted an heir and was doing everything in her power to secure one. It didn't matter who they mated with, as long as it resulted in a healthy pup or two.

The only way to curb the frenzied Haze created by her wolf would be impregnation, and it was the solemn duty of the werewolves present to allay their Queen's discomfort without giving her wolf what she was desperate for.

The young wolf could hear his Queen pleading with her wolf. "Regina, stop, please! I will not give in. I cannot have a pup yet. Pups are sure evidence of my indiscretion, and I would be banished from the pack. We need to stay safe until the time is right. Please stop!"

Evidently, Regina didn't see it that way and so, the Queen's heat raged on for three more nights, with still no visit from her brother. Despite his exhaustion, the young werewolf never left his position until two of the volunteers came to him with a problem.

"There is no let-up; she is still demanding more. This is her worst heat yet; the wolf is going to kill her if she continues. You need to get more protective sheaths; if her wolf commands us to mate without one when we run out, we will be left with no option. Bran should have returned by now; we have to assume something has happened to him."

Without pausing, the young wolf ran to the ruins, a built-up area in the small territory, so called because it is the home and workplace of the Scarlet Women or the ruined females of the Reverent Moon pack. The young wolf looked around for his sister, sure that she would get him the protective sheaths he was in need of.

"Nancy? I need your help, please; it's urgent." He opened the door but quickly closed it again. He didn't want to see his sister's body being used by the fat General. There was a distinct difference in the sounds coming from his sister's room when he compared them to the ones emanating from the Queen's rooms. His sister's false wails and the General's forceful grunts and thumps were not tender or mutually pleasurable. This was an act and a means to an end. Within a couple of minutes, the portly and ruddy General marched past, and the urge to stab him in the eye for being a two-faced condescending prick almost overwhelmed the young boy, but he swore to serve his Queen, and so he quickly returned to his sister to procure the sheaths.

"Who are they for, Nathan? Who needs this many sheaths outside of the Ruins?" He refused to answer her, and hastily left after snatching the sheaths and dropping two coins on the countertop. Running as far as the front door when a familiar figure stopped him. The blood left his face, and the sheaths dropped to the ground.

"You may have refused to answer your sister. But you will not deny me. Show me where you are going." One of the people he had been warned to avoid stood before him, tall, dark and menacing. He may not be the Alpha, or the Future Alpha for that matter, but he was still of Alpha lineage, and still a figure of authority that the young wolf could not deny. Left with no alternative, the young wolf took out his own dagger that had been coated thinly with slither of silver and raised it to his own neck. Slicing into the delicate flesh on his throat, the young wolf sacrificed himself for the greater good.

As the light left Nathan's eyes, the Queen's other brother loomed over him enraged. "Tell me where she is? Where is that whore and who is protecting her?" The young wolf smiled as his soul drifted to the Promised Land, welcomed with open arms by his idol, Diana, the Goddess of the Moon.

They both looked down upon the scene as the enraged brother pulverised what was left of the young wolf with his fists. "The time has come, my dear boy. He knows who the Queen is destined to be and what she will be capable of doing once she claims her position. We have to hide her to protect her, until the time is right to bring balance to this land."

"I am at your service. Tell me what I need to do."

"You will be my envoy to the Queen's protectors. It is time to resurrect my birthplace. Our Promised Queen will be safe there." Taking out an ancient scroll, she pointed out a location to the young wolf, who looked curiously at the aged parchment. "Here, you will find the Crypts of Utopia. It is now your solemn duty to rebuild the Empire."

~ Soraya ~

The imminent future is not going to be easy; I know and accept that for certain. My worries now centre around the family I will leave behind and their safety, and my own little one that is beginning to grow inside me. Brandon assures me we will be safe once we join the Queen; however, where that may be is still a mystery to me and Fallon too, it seems.

"Why didn't Alessia let me know she was safe? Why hasn't she been seen or visited me?" she asks, confusion oozing in her every word. "Doesn't she realise how much I've worried about her? And searched for her?" She looks at Brandon with such resentment that I step between them and attempt to calm Fallon myself.

"I think what Brandon is saying is that Alessia is no longer just Alessia, your sister, anymore. She has returned as the Queen of Alphas. He said they had to hide her to keep her safe and that she was weak at first." Fallon looks at both Brandon and me, and the scepticism in her eyes is clear to see.

"Take me to her. I won't believe it until I see her. I've got my eye on you, Brandon." Fallon doesn't back down from her brother; her strength seems to emanate from every pore. She is a fierce warrior and wants vengeance for her pain and suffering. "I swear to the Goddess I'll rip your throat out if any of this is lies."

Brandon raises his hands to his sister in an act of surrender. "I have been looking after our sister since I was thirteen years old, Fallon. She was my best friend. I have done things I am not proud of." Through our bond I can feel Brandon's distress, and the overwhelming need to comfort him is stopped only by Fallon's increasingly defensive stance. "But this isn't one of them. Our Queen is safe for now, and I am partly responsible for that."

Fallon looks at him doubtfully, still not fully believing his version of events. "What do you mean, partly?" I look at Brandon myself, not seeing this minor detail before, but he smiles back at me when he sees my enquiry too.

"What? You didn't just think this was me all alone, did you? This has been years and years in the making. Our people have been waiting and searching for the Queen that was promised." This I do know to be true. Down in the Huts, when I was growing up, people would often talk about the Promised Queen coming and bringing us back to glory as equal members of the pack. They talked of no longer being ignored or going hungry. I always thought it was fairy tales because I couldn't envision a future like that; all I had ever known was hardship. Then I met Brandon, and I know now that life doesn't have to be unnecessarily hard. It was only living the better life he generously gave me that I now realise this should be something everyone can depend on. "Our Queen has loyal followers, and more join her cause by the day. She is gaining the strength she needs to make a difference here. We just need to join her, and we can all be a part of that. Are you coming?" He asks both of us and I take his hand and nod.

"If you're going, I'm going, Bran." He kisses my hand in a silent thanks and faces his baby sister. Fallon frowns and bites her lip as she mulls over his proposition.

"If Raya is going, I'm going too. You best not be lying, Bran. Now, how the hell are we going to get out of here?" We look around at our band of six, and it is Deacon that steps forward with a plan.

"I think the girls should dress as Shaman and come with me; I can get them off the Territory on a religious mission to the Bastion." Brandon nods to his brother in thanks, knowing that Deacon understands that it won't just be his regalia he loses if he is caught.

"I think we should split them. They are going to be looking for Soraya and Fallon. If Fallon goes with Deacon, Mother can go with Euan and Soraya with me. We all take different routes and meet at the Crypts in a days' time." They all consider my mate's counter proposal and eventually agree there is no other way that can ensure all our safety. This will likely increase our chances of success.

"Mother, I think we will be better off shifting and doing the journey in wolf form. Not many people have seen your wolf recently, and it will be quicker for us." Luna Beverly nods and agrees with Euan, and then he turns to Brandon and asks him what his plan is.

"Soraya has been feeling weak and sore since she was attacked. I'll be in wolf form, and I'm going to insist that she rides on my back." He smiles at me, and a rush of affection for him fills me up with warmth and hope. He covered for me. Now that I am expecting, I won't be able to shift; the transformation alone could jeopardise my pregnancy. Brandon making an excuse for me saves all the awkward questions and guesses. We can still keep our news private for now.

"To test the boundary security, we should send Euan and mother out first. If they are stopped, we know we need to find another way." Bran nods to Deacon to agree with his plan but waits for Euan to make his assessment too. "You'll have to think of a story as to why you are leaving... maybe you're helping our stricken mother, who is looking for Fallon?"

Euan quickly agrees too, although he looks at Deacon with concern. "Yes, that'll work. Are you sure you wouldn't prefer to go with Mother, Deacon. If they catch you with Fallon–"

"I'm well aware of the consequences, Euan. Come on, we can split the resources we have and make a move." Deacon doesn't allow Euan to finish, interrupting him with his stark warning.

We all stand around a rectangle table where Deacon has arranged three black, cloth backpacks. "Each bag has an emergency first aid kit, a light, matches, and food. There are maps and snacks in the front pouch. There are emergency rations inside. They are nothing fancy or special, but they will keep a rumbling tummy at bay for a short while. And we each get a skin for water. Fill it up at every stream you can, and keep hydrated. A thirsty wolf is an irrational wolf, remember that."

I pick up a pack for me and Brandon and secure it to my back using the straps on the arm loops. "What else do you have down here, Deacon?" I hear Fallon asking her brother in awe. And when Deacon turns to answer her, I can really see the resemblance between him and my mate. There is a mischievous glint in his eye, one that often shows up when I'm spending time with Bran. The times I have seen Deacon around the Alpha Quarters he had looked like the light had gone from his eyes. I'm intrigued to know what has fired him up.

"Weapons, Fallon. I have weapons!" Deacon opens up one last cupboard, and it bulges with a massive cache of wears that have one single purpose... to protect us. I hold back and wait for permission to look for myself; however, I watch in awe as Fallon not only takes a few pieces out for herself but deftly handles a variety of intimidating instruments.

Bran watches me intently as I watch his sister. "Have you ever handled a weapon before, Sweet?" he murmurs to me. Shaking my head in reply, I see no point in falsifying my inexperience. Brandon needs to know that I have never even held a weapon before. "Don't worry, I'll show you some basics once we are safely away from here. Once we join the Queen, I will ensure you know how to protect yourself and our pup."

Bran picks out a couple of small hunting knives. "None of these will be any good to me in wolf form. But it'll help us when we go hunting." He adds a bow, a quiver of arrows and a ball of string. "Okay, Euan, are you ready? Mother?"

They both shift into wolf form and Deacon attaches their backpack to the larger wolf's back. "Goddess speed!" I whisper to them as they set off, hoping with all my might that they get through without any issues.

As the four of us remain behind, we wait for the mindlink from Euan to confirm their capture or safe passage so we can then plan our next steps.

Chapter Twenty

~ Euan ~

Through the grass, over the bridge, down the side of the forest. Keeping off the beaten track is my aim. After all, we are less likely to be found if we do. My mother trembles and weeps increasingly the closer to the border we get, until she abruptly stops. *What is wrong?* I ask her through mindlink. *Why are you stopping?* Her wolf, a reddish-brown ageing wolf, looks back at me sadly. And I already know what she is going to say.

I can't leave, Euan. If I leave, your father will reject me and the rejection will kill me. Shaking my head at her in denial, despite knowing this to be true. If she stays she will be punished and tortured. If she leaves, it will most probably kill her. *I have to go back and answer his call. I will try to distract him so you lot can get out. I'm so sorry, Euan.*

Standing in shock as my mothers wolf retreats, I inform the rest of the group before I leave. *Mother has gone back to Father. She said she wouldn't survive the rejection. She is going to hold off Father as long as she can.* I wait for a reply.

Get out of here now, Euan. We are all leaving now. Come on. Not wasting another second, I bound on my way out of the territory, following Brandon's direct instructions. For the very first time in my life, something happens as I leave. The bonds to the pack and my father break, and a heaviness leaves me. Wonder mingles with euphoria. Although I suppose I should be more cautious and contained. This indicates that I am a rogue now and no longer beholden to the loyalty I must show my now *former* Alpha. It will be my honour to declare my loyalty to my new Alpha; however, my first priority is getting away from here as quickly as possible so I am still alive to declare for my new Alpha.

Within a few minutes, a loud siren sounds, indicating an attack on the pack or danger. The borders will be closed down rapidly now that the siren has rang. I just hope the others have had enough time to leave. The only thing I can do is obey my brother's command to get out of here. Since we are now Rogues, we can no longer mindlink to communicate. I have no idea if they made it out or not.

For over four hours, I sprint as fast as I can. When I see a crystal-clear lake, I stop once I have done peripheral checks to ensure I haven't been followed. Not only do I need to rehydrate, but I think I have a thorn or glass stuck in my paw. I shift back into my human form, and immediately pain radiates from my foot, where I can clearly see blood. As a werewolf, I have extremely fast healing powers but only once the wound is clear and allowed to heal. Taking out the basic first aid kit that Deacon had the foresight to distribute, I locate the tweezers and iodine and dig into the open wound in my foot to extract the source of my discomfort. After a couple of minutes, and a fair few expletives, I pull a small twig from my foot. The arch in my foot throbs in protest at the earlier assault. I concentrate on getting my fill of water and resting my foot in the cool lake.

The food reserves, which are kept safe in a fully sealed plastic container, consist of a pouch of porridge oats with instructions to make oatcakes. Although it sounds about as inviting as eating cardboard, my hunger and need for sustenance will not allow me to refuse my meagre rations. Following the instructions, I build a small fire, and using the plastic container, I add a small amount of water to my oats, stirring it into a thick mixture. I add a flat stone to the small fire and drop the mixture to form four circular oatcakes. I use the lid from my plastic container to flip the round discs that actually don't look too bad now.

My stomach growls at the smell of food, but I am worried about attracting unwanted attention. I pack up my oatcakes, refill my water bottle, strap my backpack onto me and shift into wolf form. Already, my paw feels mostly healed. But the hunger continues to plague me.

Running for another hour, still not encountering another person, I find a cave that I decide to make camp in for the night. Shifting back into human form, I do the menial task that will hopefully help me stay alive. I place my belongings inside the cave and then spend time disguising the entrance to it, covering it with leaves, moss and mud. Once I have done this, I set up a few twitch traps. At best I can hope that I might catch a rabbit or two. Worst case scenario is it will give me a few seconds notice if someone gets too close to my resting spot.

The cave is dark and cold, but at least it offers some cover. I drink deeply from my water bottle and eat my miserable supper of oat cakes, which taste like saw dust that someone spat on. They are dry and unsatisfying, and despite eating half of them, my stomach continues to rumble and growl. Opting to sleep in wolf form just in case I must make a quick escape, I strap the backpack to me before shifting again.

Sleep eludes me for the longest time. Lots of questions swirl around in my mind. Is my mother alive, did my siblings make it out of the territory and where are they now? Mostly, the thoughts of Esme, her betrayal and double crossing me with Clayton. That burning look in her eyes while she screwed my brother in front of me. The atrocity of my potential child growing inside her right now. Clayton touching my little sister and torturing Brandon's mate... and most shockingly, finally having my father admit that he killed Heidi.

Despite my troubled mind, sleep eventually finds me. The twitch traps give me a warning that someone is near, and even in my sleep-filled state, I am up and ready to run or defend, depending on who the threat is. When a screech echoes out into the night sky, I don't have to wait any longer. Caught up in my trap is none other than my little sister, Fallon, who shouts at Deacon to free her.

Shifting back to human state so I can help them, I pull on shorts from my bag. "Do you mind keeping it down?" I whisper to them both when I am close enough for them to hear me but not see me. "I am so glad to see you guys are okay. You've bloody ruined my trap though, Fallon."

Upon hearing my voice, Deacon runs at me. "Euan, you're safe. Thank the Goddess you are safe. Have you seen Brandon and his mate yet?" Shaking my head, I swallow down my fear and disappointment. I was about to ask them the same question.

We cut down Fallon, who curses me and my traps before hugging me. "I'm sorry for not trusting you, Euan. It's been hard to know who is faithful and who isn't. I was wrong. I know I'm wrong. And I am so sorry for doubting you."

Hugging my precious sister to me, I know it has taken a lot for her to admit this truth to me. In the light of everything that has happened, gratitude that I am fighting for a better cause is more than I can wish for.

~ Brandon ~

There isn't time to revel in the fact that my love forgives me or that I am going to be a father. I have one aim and that is to get Soraya to safety. No matter what it takes, I must ensure that Soraya and my unborn child make it to the crypts. Having allies helps my mission. *Your father knows Euan has broken his pledge and bond to him and the pack. He's looking for you. He knows you are leaving the territory.* The mindlink of one of my trusted friends does not surprise me. Although this does make things trickier. Without our bond to the pack, my siblings and I can no longer communicate with each other.

It disappoints me that my mother could not find the strength to leave my father and the pack, but I do understand. I wouldn't have the strength to leave Soraya, and they've been together as a mated pair for over twenty years. I do worry about her safety, but I don't have the ability to protect her from her own mate bond.

I shift into Maverick and shake out my shaggy, black fur. Being an Alpha wolf will benefit us greatly right now. Soraya is still feeling weak from being attacked, and we cannot risk her shifting with her now carrying our pup. With the pack from Deacon strapped to her back, Soraya climbs onto my back, causing Maverick to chirrup possessively. *Mine, all mine. Filled with our pup. Mine*! he repeats incessantly.

Ours. Ours. I repeat back to him, laying my claim firmly too. Soraya wraps her arms around Mavericks neck and rubs her face into his fur.

"Okay, you guys, I am yours and yours. And so is Pandora. We are having a little pup, but we must work together to get to safety. Agreed?" Both sides of us unite and eagerly agree with our mate. We would do anything to please her, and that feeling grows deeper and deeper, especially today. To know the woman I love is carrying my child elevates her to a god-like status in my opinion. The strength of my son, who grows in her tummy, flows through her veins now, and I can detect the power she now wields. Running as fast as wolfishly possible, heading for the unbeaten track out of the territory, we don't encounter any issue until we watch from a distance as a small pack chases after Deacon and Fallon until finally, I observe through Maverick's eyes, the golden threads of bonds break in front of me. "Brandon we need to find another way, they know the others have taken that route."

Brandon, your father fell to his knees when the bond with Deacon and Fallon broke. He is searching for your mother. Get off the territory now before it is too late. When this mindlink comes through, I have to accept that Soraya is correct; we do need to take a different approach.

Spinning around, I head to the other side of the territory. This will take us around six hours out of our way, but it's six hours well spent. As the boundary comes into view, I ask one last time, *Are you all sure you definitely want to leave?*

"We have no choice, Bran. Get out now," Soraya spits out, but her overwhelming sorrow fills my own chest through our bond. "Promise we'll come back and save my family as soon as we can." Both Maverick and I make the solemn oath to our mate, her comfort taking paramount as it always should. "Then cross over the boundary and let's get the hell out of here," she adds.

As I cross the boundary, Maverick yelps in pain. *He is renouncing us as Alpha heir. He is taking away our birth right.* As much as it burns and hurts as my soul is shattered as I sever ties to my parents and my pack, I don't stop. I keep running while my mate clings to my back so that we have a chance at happiness, and so our child, no matter its gender, can grow in peace. *We're being followed, we need to hide to keep her safe.* Before I can absorb this information, an arrow slices through the air, heading for us.

"Bran, RUN!" Soraya screams at me, smelling the wolfsbane lacing the arrows at the same time that I do. These hunters aren't looking to stop us and take us back. They've been instructed to aim to kill. Fury fuels me, a hot burning anger like I've never known. It's one thing to punish Soraya for what they perceive as a failure of duty... but to order all our deaths! I can't even comprehend it.

Hold tight, Soraya. As tight as you can. Don't let go. This is going to get rough, but we'll find you a place to hide. I'll keep you safe. Don't let go. I'm winded as something pierces me from the side, and a burning sensation, an uncomfortable, intolerable stinging, starts to radiate from my ribcage outward to every nerve in my body.

"BRANDON!" I hear my love scream as my wolfish body pounds to the floor. Foam pours from my mouth as my body convulses. The world around me begins to swirl and fade. Painfully, my body shifts involuntarily back into human form, and in the process, I begin to hallucinate, because my tiny mate cuts down two tracker wolves before throwing a dagger between the eyes of a third assailant. "Bran. Don't you dare let go. Do you hear me? I'll keep you safe. I'll look after you, but don't you dare leave me."

Raising my hand to her tummy, I stretch my fingers wide to fully encompass the bump that isn't even there yet. "I'll never, ever let go. Do you hear me? No matter what it takes, I will never ever leave you."

Mercifully, our allies arrive, and with the aid of a couple of horses and a guard of six, we are ushered back to our journey to the crypts. After an hour's hard ride, we arrive at a lake and Soraya insists on stopping to stretch her legs; however, I know that she wants to check on my wound and clean it out again. Luckily, the arrowheads weren't silver, but the wolfsbane has done what they intended. Maverick has been silent since I was hit, and I don't know if he is ever going to come back to me. I can't feel him anymore, and I cannot shift. And although the mindlink broke with the others when we left the pack, it didn't break my link with Soraya thanks to our mate bond. But since I was hit and infected with wolfsbane, Maverick has gone, and I can no longer link my mate or feel our bond like I used to.

My father went to the effort of discrediting my Alpha claim, but he probably didn't need to. For what is an Alpha with no wolf?

~ Soraya ~

Brandon seems to drop like a dead weight, with me still riding on his back, and with very little combat training, the only thing that keeps me going is the desire to get us all to safety. My attempts to mindlink Brandon go unanswered, and I don't know if it's because we are now packless or because of his injury, but whatever it is, I don't like it and I feel alone without his comforting voice in my head.

Our Allies coming to our aid save us, because for all my strength and determination, I am no match for the warriors in our former pack.

Within the first aid pack are basics to treat Brandon's wounds, but if I am right, he has been infected with wolfsbane. I know there are some herbal cures used only at the Huts due to our lack of access to professional healers. The flower heads are a light pink, while the black reeds are long and spikey. They are both found near the water's edge. Therefore, when a lake comes into view, I insist that we rest for a little while.

Leaving Brandon propped up against a tree, I tell him to drink from the water bottle and I will refill it once I have refilled my own. Armed with my first aid kit, I get to work finding the cure for my love's ailment. My heart leaps for joy when I spot the herbs I need. Now I just need a way to extract what I need so I can crush it to make a salve. The small scissors are perfect for cutting as much of the long black spikes that I may need. They will also be useful later when I finely chop the reeds in small pieces, before grinding them down.

The little pink flower heads are trickery, like feathers. As soon as I touch them, they fly away in the wind. In the end, I empty the first aid kit into the backpack and use the small pouch to grab the petals before they float away. Satisfied that I have enough to make a few portions of the remedy, I fill up my water bottle and then return to Brandon to get his too.

"Were you trying to make it snow?" he asks me as I walk closer to him. The pale pink petals, almost like cherry blossoms, swirl around us, giving me away. Maybe in another time and another place this would be considered a romantic interlude, but with my mate injured and us on the run from our pack, the mood just isn't right. "I drank all the water like you asked."

"Bran? Do you completely trust the people that have come to your aid?" He regards me before he answers and then gives a solemn but firm nod. "Good. I have a herbal remedy for the wolfsbane; it is an old recipe used by us from the Huts because we don't have money for healers." He raises his eyebrows as I talk, and a warmth returns to his eyes.

"Is that what you were doing with the petals?" he asks knowingly, and I nod to him, feeling shy and self-conscious. "I am your patient, what do you need? The team will be happy to help you."

"A bowl or some sort of dish and a stone I can use to crush and grind the herbs." Brandon quickly summons one of the warriors, Jude, who goes to look for something appropriate. "Brandon, I need to know how severe your injury is. You haven't returned my mindlink since it happened."

A flash of pain crosses his face, and he grimaces. He leans down towards me and whispers in my ear, "I can't feel Maverick. I don't know if he's still a part of me." It's as I suspected, but the grief that plagues my mate fairly overwhelms me too. "Do you think your potion can help?" I nod to him, because I have seen this medicine work wonders and I need to show Brandon the positivity inside me so he believes it too.

"He's just silenced right now. He's still there, and once I make this salve, he should come back to you."

Jude returns with an assortment of rocks and stones, but nothing seems to fit the bill of a makeshift pestle and mortar. One stone looks adequate to place the herbs upon while I crush them, but I have nothing suitable to grind them with, plus a basin to collect and mix with water to make the paste.

"Sweet, what about your ring?" He holds onto my hand, his thick, rough fingers trailing over my slim ones, grazing over the large jade stone he gave me when we mated. "It's rounded and looks just right for what you need." Possessively, and maybe selfishly, I protectively cover my ring with my other hand, bringing it to my chest. My last remnant of home. My only possession I was able to flee with. My Moon Goddess statue, our photographs, and, most importantly, my family have all been left behind. My ring and my gold necklace are all I have left. "It won't break; it's strong. That Jade is one of the strongest gemstones. It's strong and resilient. Just like you, Soraya."

"It won't break?" I ask him as I remove my ring, and he shakes his head back in reply. "But if it does, we will work together to fix it, won't we, Bran?"

"Always," he replies simply, and that is more than I need to confirm that it is just a ring, no more, no less. A ring can never replace my family or the memory of mating with Brandon. No material thing will ever be more important than healing my other half.

"Sorry, I was being silly." Brandon tugs my hand, drawing me closer to him, wincing from his injury that doesn't close because of the offending wolfsbane that lingers inside. Thankful for his support and resilience, I kiss him quickly on his forehead, wishing we had time to embrace and enjoy the pretty view. However, I need to make this salve and treat Brandon quickly. "Can I check your wound before I get started, please."

Tugging up his top to reveal the wound on his ribcage, I want to weep when I see it. It looks a lot worse than it did. I don't have much time. Finding a large flat surface is never an easy task out in the wild. I settle on a large boulder not far from where Brandon rests against the tree. His pallor and complexion look sicklier by the second. On the boulder, I set up my workshop: my scissors, my herbs, the rock to place the herbs upon while I grind them up with my ring. Jude steps forward with the food rations tub from my backpack, a perfect container for mixing the medicine. The men watch in fascination; however, they haven't finished helping yet.

"What are your names, please?" I ask them all. Jude introduces himself again, then points everyone out and names them. Liam, Gerrard, Tony, Alastair and Mikah are our other saviours. "I would like one of you to source some large leaves, big enough to hold my salve in place against Brandon's ribs. Someone else, use up the rations and make us all a snack. Another to go hunting; see if there is anything edible out there. The rest I would like you to man the perimeter and ensure we are not being watched or followed."

"Yes, ma'am. We'll get to it right away." I thank each one of them individually, trying my best to keep their names in order in my mind. When I look back to my mate, his eyes burn with passion and pride.

"You're going to make a perfect Luna, my Sweet. And an even better mother." His praise, always freely given and yet heartfelt and genuine, warms me up from the inside. My own confidence in my ability grows as his belief in me grows. We are an ideal mix because we flatter each other.

Despite my makeshift equipment, I am able to mix a small batch of salve within a few minutes. As I apply it to Brandon's ribs, he jolts in pain and then sighs in relief as the poison begins to ooze from his body. Using the string I procured from Deacon and the large leaves that Tony brings me, I manage to make a crude dressing to hold the salve together.

I am just finishing up my second batch when Liam returns to us. "Brandon, there are people approaching. Probably about twenty minutes away and they don't smell familiar." Brandon quickly arranges for us to move on. Even if they are strangers, they are still a danger to us; we are now rogues, probably wanted for our crimes.

Jude and Gerrard, who turn out to be brothers, help Brandon onto a horse. "Are you able to shift, ma'am?" Mikah asks me. Brandon catches my eye, and in that one look, I know we have to tell the men that have saved us and continue to look out for us, so I bow to Brandon, giving my consent to tell.

"Soraya is expecting. It's still very, very early on, so she didn't want to tell anyone yet, but she cannot shift." Instead of being put out by the news, the men all rally around me, congratulating both Brandon and I on our exciting news.

"A blessing from the Moon Goddess." "The future of our pack." Are just a couple of the phrases I hear, and before I can object, I am lifted gently and placed on the back of a second horse. "Don't worry, ma'am. We are here to look after you, our Alpha, and our Future Alpha."

As good as their word, our loyal men guide us to the Crypts of Utopia, stopping when either Brandon or I need to rest. They try their best to cater for our every whim. When I insist we stop to sleep, they sit sentry around us, keeping us safe, resting only two at a time. They prove their loyalty and devotion a million times over.

When we arrive at the outskirts of the Crypts, I am taken aback at how rough and unappealing the whole area looks. Utopia to me suggests paradise or heaven or even wonderland. This is worse than The Ruins. Brandon smiles at me. The bags under his eyes and fever that is beginning to burn in them worry me. "Don't worry, Soraya. The only way to keep this area safe was to make it look like there is nothing here."

I don't understand what he is saying until we get closer and closer and, finally, the most amazing place is revealed to me. Utopia doesn't even do it justice. Built entirely from gold and jade, the kingdom that time forgot is truly magnificent. Already there are people living here. Warriors patrol the walkways. The shop fronts are full of appealing objects. Everything is a far stretch from what it appeared from the outside.

"The Queen is waiting for you, Lieutenant Brandon. She says… 'You're late'." My stomach drops at the revelation, but Brandon laughs aloud, angering his wound once again.

While gripping my hand and panting with pain-filled exertion, he replies, "Tell our Royal Highness, better late than never."

Chapter Twenty-One

~ Soraya ~

The guard breaks into a wide smile and invites us into the hall. "The Queen will be with you shortly; she is receiving information about the Reverent Moon pack and your siblings at the moment." Brandon nods his acknowledgement; however, I grow more and more concerned about him as time moves on. It's obvious his wound is infected, and although the salve is working on extracting the wolfsbane, him not being able to rest or clean his wound properly isn't helping.

"Would Lieutenant Brandon be permitted to rest and have access to a shower and a healer please, sir." The guard, dressed in a uniform of green and red, smiles widely. His eyes glaze over to indicate that he is mindlinking someone.

After half a minute, he smiles at me again. "Of course, please follow me. You and your companions will be shown to your accommodations." Without waiting for us to agree, he begins to walk ahead. Two young boys step forward and take the horses from us, and I encourage Brandon to lean on me so he doesn't fall. As we walk through the gleaming gold and green pathway, curious faces look out at us. I'm not surprised; we must look like stinking tramps in disarray, muddying up their lovely paradise.

"Utopia is not yet completed, but as you can see, our settlement is full of beauty and riches. Befitting a Queen for sure." The short walkway opens into a courtyard. A high wall surrounds an extremely large tower, and the ivy and flowers that grow down it give it a whimsical feel, as though I have walked into a fairy tale. "That is Castle Point. From there you can see almost every aspect of our new kingdom. If you turn around, you can see the full effect of the castle. It is hidden from the outside by the mountains." As I turn around, the scene that opens up to me is jaw dropping gorgeous and surreal; a full castle seems to bulge out. I cannot see where it begins, but the side I can see is utterly overwhelming in it's sheer beauty.

"Is that jade?" I ask the guard, thunderstruck by the outstanding architecture of the building. The green is prominent, but it is made more prominent by the entwining gold. The guard smiles and nods, before he continues to walk on. There are birds singing, and a blowing wind rustles the leaves and the trees. I wonder at a place where precious stone and metal coexist in such harmony with the gentle little birds and the delicate flowers that grow in abundance. This is a place of virility, a sanctuary of plenty. This is Utopia.

We carry on walking through what I now know is the castle courtyard until we reach two sets of stairs that stand parallel with each other. "The Queen has allocated the west wing to you, Lieutenant Brandon. There are five chambers above for you and your contingent. When your siblings arrive, they will be allocated the northwest wing." Above the staircases are golden plaques with names upon; the west wing is on the left. "The healers will be with you shortly, and the kitchens are preparing you some food. Everything else you should need is in your new home. But if you need anything else, simply ring the bell." He bows to Brandon and me and leaves. Gerrard and Jude step forward to help me get Brandon up the stairs.

"I oversaw the planning for this wing. Soraya, you and I will take the end apartment," he tells us all while pointing to a wooden door that faces us. "Would you guys be okay with two to a room for now? Once Fallon and the boys arrive, there will be more space over in the northwest wing."

The guards nod. "Yes, Alpha. This is more than sufficient," one replies. Jude and Gerard continue to help us to our apartment, but I stop them at the door.

"Thank you. Thank you, all. You should rest while you can. I'll take care of Brandon from here." They nod to me, but I know they will never leave their Alpha without a guard, and though the other guards retreated into the hallway we have just walked down, taking the first watch, Jude and Gerard stand back-to-back outside our apartment door, never wavering in their duty.

Once the door closes behind us, Brandon allows the grimace he's been holding in to cross his face. He is burning up, and I'm terrified of the fever taking hold. Helping him cross to the bathroom, I slowly peel off his clothes that are dirty from our travels and troubles. Despite the dressing I tried to apply, Brandon's wound continues to weep, fouling his clothing. We haven't had access to hot water or a suitable place to bathe and clean. The bathroom has a toilet, sink and a bathtub with a shower over. It is compact and functional. The tiles are almost white with a border of jade. It is simple and elegant. I open the faucets and fill the tub, and once Brandon has finished taking off all his clothes, I turn to help him climb into the tub.

"Oi, eyes up here!" he says to me, a glint in his eye despite how bad he must be feeling. "No funny business; the healers will be here any minute now." My eyes widen in indignation. Does he think I am thinking about sex right now? I'm worried sick about him!

Then I realise Brandon is teasing me. He must be feeling a bit better after all. "My mate is irresistible though, and I do have needs."

He sighs in relief as he relaxes back in the hot water. The temperature obviously brings some reprieve from the pain. "Just you wait until the healers do their voodoo shit. You won't be able to walk for a week!" he declares, with his eyes closed. "Why don't you have a look around while I have a minute to rest here, Sweet. I'll shout to you if I need you." I kiss him on his forehead before I stand, eager to look around my new home.

Our new apartment is smaller than the one at the Alpha Quarters: two rooms, a bathroom and a kitchen. I love it. For all the opulence and beauty that welcomed us, our rooms are basic, functional. Safe. An overwhelming familiarity of both my homes, the one I had with Brandon and the childhood home, brings me feelings of nostalgia.

The whole place is mostly open plan with exception to the bedroom and bathroom. One room is a sitting room with chairs and a dining table, and separated only by a breakfast bar is a basic kitchen. It is sparse compared to the Alpha Quarters, but not as primitive as my childhood home. It's a blank canvas for us to make our own. The décor is white with accents of jade and gold and it's all very muted and understated. There is still a smell and feel of newness in the place.

The bedroom follows the same theme. The large bed looks comfortable enough, and there is a small, barred window letting some natural light in. Hanging in the wardrobe are some simple clothing and three uniforms, similar to the one the Guard was wearing, red and green but with black lapels that three gold stars gleam from.

The knocking at the front door disturbs my tour, but I don't mind as it is most likely the healers coming to help make Brandon well again.

~ Fallon ~

My whole life has turned on its axis. I am now a rogue with my two brothers in tow. Only the Goddess herself knows what would have happened to me without my brothers and best friend. It hurts that my mother turned back, and I fear for her safety and wellbeing now, just like I fear for my own, for Raya's and Alessia's too.

Alessia. Very soon I will see my sister again. I have been consumed by my thoughts of her and her safety for months now. Part of me can't actually believe she is alive; I had been convinced one of my brothers had murdered her. Bran says she is a Queen now and that she has changed, but I don't see how she could change so much.

Deacon, Euan and I have been walking for hours. We are taking a break from our wolf forms to not be so suspicious. Also, our mindlink has broken, and so it made communicating a pain in the ass. Deacon tells me that Brandon told him that the Crypts of Utopia are set into the mountain, and yet we have been here for an age and nothing has jumped out at us. Through wooded areas, down rivers and over hills, we continue walking. Euan uses the rest of the resources to make more of his horrid oatcakes, and I pray to the Goddess that we find a berry bush or something to take away the awfulness of them.

My brothers have become my guards. They are protective of me and considerate of my needs. After weeks of torture at the hands of Clayton, them caring for me and not being scared for my safety feels alien. Every now and again, they will look at me strangely until I remember that they aren't used to seeing me without my veil. "Last time I saw your face, you were cute. Now you're beautiful," Deacon tells me with a gentle smile. "You had no front teeth and your eyes seemed to take up all your face," he teases, and it's the first time I haven't felt self conscious since I discarded my veil. I once thought of it as my prison, but in real life, my veil had also become my comfort blanket, my shield. In relative terms, I suppose it's only fitting that I feel bare and exposed without it.

It was such a relief when Deacon and I met up with Euan. To know he is safe and to have another one of my brothers by my side is a comfort. The fact that I never thought to apologise to Euan before we left riddled me with overwhelming guilt. My brothers haven't been left unscathed by Clayton either, and it's only now that we all trust one another that we know the full extent of Clayton's abuse and betrayal.

We stopped in the cave that Euan found and took sanctuary there for a couple of hours. However, my howls of distress disturbed my brothers. Visions of attacking Clayton, blood and eyeballs haunt me, the memories of him assaulting me mingle with my attack on him. I don't think I'll ever find a moment's peace from now on. Deacon assures me that Clayton's rapid healing as a werewolf prevented him from dying, but he still chased me in ghost form when I closed my eyes to sleep.

Now we seem to be walking in circles, following Deacon's compass that I am sure must be bust, in pursuit of a place I'm not even sure exists. When it begins to darken again, I worry; I do not want my nightmares to visit me again this evening, and being outside and the radio silence of having no mindlink only seems to enhance my feeling of foreboding. Deacon taps his compass again, frowning in frustration as it directs us back the way we just came.

"Are you sure that thing works?" Euan asks him, and Deacon, having been so sure and focused up to now, shrugs and sighs wearily. "Deacon, can we sit down for a moment and talk. I need to tell you something." My head snaps to Euan, wondering what he has to tell Deacon and why he's doing it now. "Brandon and I should have told you before we left but everything happened so fast that we didn't get the chance."

"It's about Heidi, isn't it? I know something was said because father acted all shifty when I answered his call and then he didn't object when I told him I wanted to return to my prayers." Euan nods his head solemnly, and I tug on Deacon's hand, inviting him to sit down next to me while he receives this upsetting information.

"Yes, when we found out that father and Clayton had tortured Soraya, Brandon lost his shit. They tortured her for not getting pregnant and charged her with preventing an Alpha pregnancy. Brandon was furious and he asked father if that is what killed Heidi too." Euan looks uncomfortable, and I cover my mouth with my hand. We had been told stories about what had happened to Heidi, but nothing had ever been confirmed. "He confirmed they tortured her and that it resulted in her death."

Deacon seems to deflate like an old balloon, all his previous purpose extinguishes. "They always found a charge to put to her, and like an idiot, I would take her to him to answer the charges. The Elders constantly insisted on witnessing us mating so they could assure father that I was doing my duty." With tears running freely down his face, he stands up abruptly, kicking the leaves on the ground. "We had six months of being hounded and accused. Every time I defended her, father would remind me that I didn't know what Heidi was capable of doing in secret. It was t-torture. Absolutely horrific. I should have protected her better."

Rushing to my brother's side as he howls in pain, I have never been more sure of us leaving, of hurting Clayton. It also makes the next step much clearer. "We are going to make them pay, Deacon. They are going to pay for hurting us, for killing Heidi, torturing Raya and chasing Alessia from her home. We are going to take back the Reverent Moon pack and destroy all our enemies." Euan pulls Deacon into his embrace, and I wrap my arms around both of my brothers.

"We will avenge her. And everyone else they've ever hurt," Euan reiterates, and as we stand here hugging each other, it's the first time in a long time I have felt a part of something. I might have left my pack, but I got my family back in the process.

In the gathering darkness, a large light shines on us. "Our Queen is waiting for you. Please follow us to safety." Just ahead of us, I see a group of ten men all dressed in a red and green uniform. Some look vaguely familiar, while some I have never met before. "You've almost made it; it's just through here." He points to a gap in the mountainside that we must have passed a dozen times and missed.

"Lead the way!" Deacon says as we follow behind our escort, glad to finally be almost there.

We follow the soldiers through the mountain until we reach a crossing into what looks like a dark cave. I look back at my brothers. Is this safe? Can we trust these people? A few of the guards seem to look at me in surprise. Then I remember I am not wearing my veil and that might surprise some of the others. The moss and peat smells become stronger the further into the cavern we go, and just when I think I may suffocate, a magnificent column of green comes into view. As we step closer, the air becomes clearer, the overwhelming stench completely vanishing.

"Is that real Jade?" I ask the collective group with my voice full of wonder at the outstanding beauty that continues to reveal itself to us. "How did you keep this place hidden? We couldn't see it and we've been right outside for hours," I add as more and more of the castle and the realm of Utopia appear in front of me.

"The Queen had to grant permission to allow you in. She has been busy with your brother and his mate, and she had to wait for permission from the Moon Goddess." Brandon and Raya are already here! I had been hoping that we would reunite with them on the way here, I don't know how they managed to get here before us. "Your brother is very ill; he was wounded by your former pack. They are trying to save his wolf."

We didn't know they had been attacked. Who hurt Brandon and how did they manage to escape? Guilt swirls inside me as I think of all the reasons why we never went back to check on them. "What about Raya? Did she get hurt? Is she okay?" Euan tries to put a comforting hand on my shoulder, but I shrug him off. Clayton and his bloodied eye flash before my own, rendering me unable to step any further. I don't think random acts of kindness or displays of affection will ever be the same for me.

"Keep going, Fallon. The faster we move, the quicker we will be reunited with Alessia," Deacon coaxes, and almost robotically, I take another tentative step and then another.

"Lady Soraya seems to be in good health. Worried about her mate, as expected, but both her and her pup escaped unharmed." Is Raya pregnant?

We stop in a courtyard with the castle and the vast community of Utopia all in full view for us to see. "Welcome to the Crypts of Utopia. The Queen will see you now in the throne room." The soldiers move into a different formation, and walk in two single lines with my brothers and me in the centre of them. We follow their path until we reach gold and green steps leading to double doors manned by men in similar uniforms to our guards, only these ones wear hats. With their hats standing proudly on their heads, they stare ahead as they open the doors to us, never once looking at us or addressing anyone. Their behaviour intrigues me. I wonder if they are trained to act this way. What if they need to sneeze or laugh? I try with all my might to get a better look at them before we are shooed into the throne room; however, my brothers both tut in disapproval and push me along.

The throne room has a floor of solid, marbled jade. The cold, smooth surface almost feels treacherous to walk upon, like a floor of slippery ice. Columns of jade stand floor to ceiling, all decorated with finesse with gold detailing. There are seats and tables and a raised plinth with a golden throne in the centre, glittering and sparkling like something from a fairy tale. Frowning, I wonder why the throne is empty. We are meant to be seeing our sister, where is she?

"Her Grace will be with you shortly. Please take a seat and refreshments will be brought to you while you wait." Two of the guards remain with us, while one retreats for refreshments and another two head to a door at the side of the plinth that holds the throne. The rest leave through the doors in which we came.

"I didn't know Soraya was pregnant, did you guys?" Euan asks us. "I mean it was inevitable I suppose but don't you think they should have told us before we left."

"That must be why she couldn't shift. We should have stayed together," Deacon adds. "I hope Brandon isn't too badly injured. And how did they get here before us when we set off first, Soraya couldn't shift and Bran has been injured?"

"Lieutenant Brandon has been to visit me many times and so is familiar with the paths in and out of the realm." The eerie, faraway voice of our sister reaches us, and my head snaps so fast towards the throne that I almost crack my neck. Can this really be Alessia after all this time? "I'm happy to see you all arrived here relatively unscathed physically."

How can she sound so much like Alessia, but not at the same time. I stare in horror at the person sitting on the throne. She resembles Alessia, but she doesn't. Having glimpsed her a few times without her veil, I knew she had long, dark, braided hair, just like me. However, the Queen, as magical and beautiful as she is, has white hair that sits in dreadlocks under her gold and green crown. Her eyes are milky white and blank, and although she addresses us, she doesn't look at us. She is a mirage. A figment of my grief filled imagination. "Where is Alessia? I want to see my sister."

The Queen's head snaps towards me. "Lieutenant Brandon already explained to you, Alessia had to die so I could be reborn. Alessia has gone and I am here now." As the Queen's voice rises so do gentle mews of an infant. "However,

Alessia left you a gift before she... departed. One Alpha pup that I will raise to be my heir. This is Princess Jada, her daughter."

The guards carry a cradle towards us with a baby inside. "Alessia had a baby?" a shocked voice asks, as I peer into the casket at the doll-like baby girl with massive, beguiling green eyes. My heart melts, she is my kin. My final link to Alessia.

"Oh, Regina was insistent. It almost cost us everything," she says with a chuckle in her echoey voice. "However, this little one is very important. The future of our cause will rest on her shoulders. She needs us all to protect her and train her ready for the fight that will come."

"She's adorable. I love her. But why? I thought you were the Queen of Alphas? You are the Queen that was promised," I ask the Queen; she continues to glow and stare blankly.

"I am," she replies with surprising strength. "But, she is the Princess of Werewolves. I will unite the Alphas. She will lead you all."

Chapter Twenty Two

~ Euan ~

Brandon had told me that Alessia had changed, that she was now The Queen of Alphas, but I find her resemblance to my sister to be uncanny. Apart from the blank, staring eyes and white hair, she looks exactly like the last and only time I did see her before she disappeared.

Strictly speaking, I shouldn't even know what my own sister looks like. My father enforces the terms of the veil on the girls in our former pack far too harshly and with that, no one truly knew what Alessia looked like. As an unmated Lady of the Veil, Alessia had never officially been unveiled. However, one night, just before she completely disappeared, I had to drag my father off her. She had done yet another thing to displease him, and he physically attacked her, unveiling her. Brandon had been sent away on emergency Alpha business and Alessia had just finished yet another brutal heat that raged on for seven whole days. Her absence did not go unnoticed, especially by Clayton.

She used to look a lot like Fallon does now, with her long, dark hair in braids and her high cheekbones and flawless skin. The resemblance is still there, but Alessia or rather the Queen looks eerie, otherworldly like, surreal. She glows. Although where that glow comes from, I cannot decipher.

As the small child, apparently Alessia's baby, cries, I cannot help but feel spooked. "When was the child born?" I ask, realising I should have addressed the Queen and asked permission first. "Please, excuse me, my Grace. This has come as a shock. We didn't know Alessia… we didn't know she was carrying. We didn't know anything about this little one. If you please, I have some questions."

"I understand your curiosity. Alessia's child, conceived during one of her enforced heats by Regina, was born the night she died. Much of my power passed to her as well as her mother's wolf." She stops suddenly, before standing gracefully. "I am sorry, but there has been a development with your brother that I must attend to. I am leaving Princess Jada and her guard under your protection."

All at once, chaos breaks out around me. Deacon asks about Brandon and if he is okay. Fallon is objecting being left with a small defenceless child, stating she doesn't know what to do and doesn't want to break her, while I reel off a couple of questions in quick succession. Questions that are burning a hole inside me.

"Can you tell who a child's father is, my Queen. I need to know if I need to continue on this quest to retrieve a child that is mine?" The Queen's head snaps to me, and as menacing as it looked the first time she did it, I do not fear her when she does it again.

"There is no child, Euan," she tells me softly. "It was all part of the ruse to distract you. She was never with child. She never needed your help. She was tempted by the traitor to trap you so she would be freed from the ruins."

Sincerely, I thought I would be relieved, but rage and sadness consume me. The hatred of my brother knows no bounds. To allow me to believe that Esme needed me, that I was going to be a father and to consider taking her as my chosen mate based on all this is too much to bear. I mistrusted Clayton at one point and thought of him as an entitled jack-ass. After the past few days, I know he was complicit in the torture and death of Heidi, of sexually and physically abusing both my sisters and tearing our family apart from the inside out. Now, it is confirmed that he set me up too. Worryingly, I don't hate him. No, that is too good and decent for the likes of Clayton. No, I don't hate him, I despise him; a burning, deep rooted hatred that is raging like an inferno all around me, causing destruction and pain.

"Thank you for your candour, my Queen. Tell us how we can help our brother," I reply, trying my best to ignore the tearing sensation in my heart and soul. How will I ever trust another woman again? In spite of the circumstances, the thought of marking Esme, of us running away and being a family, had appealed to me. More than that, I had grown content with what my future was shaping to be. Now everything has been ripped away.

Deacon places his hands on my shoulders, and genuine empathy, a sincere feeling of knowing how broken he must feel, floods through me. He had loved his mate, and she died a painful, needless death. I can appreciate now how little my sympathy must have meant to him. He must be riddled with overwhelming emotion, of which I am experiencing a mere pinprick in comparison. Following the example that Deacon has set, I stand tall, braced for what is to come, ready to avenge.

"Unfortunately, Brandon has been injured and his wolf grows weak. His mate has tried to heal him, but his body has rejected the antidote. My healers are with him now, but they aren't hopeful of saving his wolf." The Queen adds. "I will try one last thing to save his wolf, it's the least I can do for him after everything he did for Alessia and, therefore, me. However, I cannot guarantee it will work; it's the first time I've tried to do it."

The heavy doors we entered through are dragged open by the guards, and the Queen floats through them as though she is gliding instead of walking. Without missing a beat, Fallon picks up the baby to bring her with us. Deacon picks up her bag, and I help Fallon wrap our niece in a green blanket. "She looks like a little flower poking out from the leaves," Fallon says as she holds on to the baby firmly. The little one, uncaring of what is happening around her, quickly falls straight back to sleep. "She's cute, isn't she?" she adds with an edge of awe in her voice.

"Yes. She looks like you when you were a baby," Deacon whispers tenderly. A war is happening in his eyes right now, love and hatred in equal measure, and I can only imagine what has happened to evoke such strong emotions in a benign person like my brother. "Who is the father?" he adds as we catch back up with the Queen, and as we walk through the green and gold corridor, people peer curiously out at the Queen and her entourage.

"It matters not. The child is here now. We need to concentrate on building her up. Her parentage is insignificant. It's her future we must focus on," the Queen retorts firmly, ensuring everyone knows there will be no further discussion on the matter. "This is your new home. I hope you will be comfortable here. This wing is Brandon's." She drifts faultlessly up the stairs, where we meet two guards, who I recognise from back home.

"How did you guys get here? How did you find us?" I ask the Holt brothers, who stand sentry outside the last door on the landing.

"We came to Alpha Brandon's aid when he was attacked. We have been committed to the cause for a few months now," Gerard answers stoically. "I'm afraid the healers are still inside. There has been no improvement in his presentation," he adds grimly.

"How long have they been in there?" Deacon asks the brothers, as the Queen opens the door to Brandon's new home. A blast of medical ointment and blood hits me, causing me to recoil. "Bran?" he shouts through the door, but Brandon doesn't reply.

Instead, the pale and tear-stained face of his mate greets us grimly. Worry and fear oozes out from every cell of her body. "Fallon? Oh, thank the Goddess you're all here. Brandon's hurt. He might lose his wolf, and I don't know what to do anymore." And with that she faints dead away, crumbling to the floor like a rag doll.

"Raya!" Fallon shouts as she rushes to her friend's side, checking her vitals, while our Queen turns and claps her hands. Out of nowhere, a large bird flies towards her, the plumage of gold and green just as beautiful and opulent as the rest of Utopia. The bird is unlike anything I have ever seen before. It's as large as an eagle but it's shaping is similar to a parrot. It flies directly to the Queen, landing on her outstretched arm, giving a loud screech when it does.

"This is Meadow, my companion. He is my gift from Diana, the Moon Goddess, in place of Regina. I can no longer shift, but I do have a counterpart." The bird bows to his Queen, nudging her head with his own in affection. On hearing the healer's struggles and Brandon's roar of pain, the Queen quickly moves back into action, gliding through the apartment with more purpose. "We don't have time, let me through. I am his last hope now," she declares to us, and obediently, we all step aside to let her through, following in her wake.

At Fallon's request, I stop beside her and help to lift Soraya from the floor, as Fallon is unable to as she still has the baby in her arms. The fragile mate of my brother feels like a broken sparrow in my arms, so small and slender, as light as a feather. Her head rolls back as I stand, and as instructed by my sister, I place her on the sofa. When Soraya finally begins to rouse, I follow Deacon into the bedroom to see my brother.

Brandon looks horrible. His complexion is deathly grey and with his shirt off, I can see the open wound on his once muscular rib cage. The wound has festered and smells rancid. It oozes angrily, and there are dark sinister lines radiating from the wound outwards across his body. Brandon is dying, and I don't know what the Queen can do to save him. The healers, at least half a dozen of them, rush around with medicines and apparatuses that only look vaguely familiar. The smell of the medicine is overwhelming here, along with the stench of Brandon's rotting wound; it suffocates and sickens me.

"Stand back!" she shouts to us in her echoing voice, and Deacon and I immediately do her bidding. She stands tall and strong, holding her gold and green staff with her bird now perched on her shoulder, and as she chants, the glow that emits surreally from her flows around the room, creating a gentle breeze that ruffles the sheets on Brandon's bed, and the curtains that were closed begin to bellow out as the breeze steadily becomes a gust.

"Goddess of the Moon, I implore you to hear my prayer. Lieutenant Brandon Ward is integral to my ascension to the Utopian throne. He is loyal, brave, and true, and was harmed by my mortal enemies in the pursuit of bringing his beloved mate and pup to safety. I plead for your help in healing him, ensuring the longevity of his wolf and his ability to lead the Utopian Wolf Pack as Alpha." The bird squawks and flaps its large wingspan, its green and gold feathers filling the room, and the gust of wind becomes an indoor tornado. "Diana, grant me this request. Meadow! Call her!" She stamps down her staff, and the bird responds to its name by opening its beak and singing. It is both a beautiful and frightening sound. Nothing else can be heard above the melodious tune it whirls out, not only across the bedroom but the entire kingdom, I would wage.

The floor rumbles and shakes, and I stumble unsteadily, trying to hold on to my brother and the wall to keep me standing. And then a light, similar to the glow that the Queen emits but stronger and brighter, emanates from the wound on Brandon's ribs. His eyes snap open and hold the same blank, milky orbs that the Queen has. His body contorts angrily, and flashes of his wolf's black fur, his paws and tail mingle with the hands and flesh of his human form, while the tell-tale noises of bones snapping confirm he is shifting in-between forms, and he alternates from groaning and roaring as he struggles in pain. We watch helplessly as the room spins around us and our brother floats on a plain between worlds, unsure of what will become of him.

The bedroom door swings open, and Soraya stands in the doorway, her eyes wide in shock and fear. Her golden hair flies out around her, as the storms continue to rage around the room. Her eyes grow wide as she observes her mate spasming in agony to the words of the Queen and the song of her bird.

Above all the noise that had been deafening until this point, I hear the tiny mate of my brother shout. "What's happening? Brandon? BRANDON?" she screams out as his body continues to float mid-air, convulsing and shifting involuntarily. Our Queen continues to chant incoherently, and the song of Meadow reverberates eerily off every surface in the once calm room. "Stop it, you're killing him. She's going to kill him. Please stop. I need him, I love him. BRANDON!"

With one last beam of light that blasts me from my feet, temporarily stealing my sight and ability to breathe, the Queen stops chanting and Meadow stops singing. The storm that had knocked us all off our feet diminishes, and green and gold feathers fall to the ground like a luxurious carpet. The Queen, having been so regal and graceful until now, stumbles backwards. Her eyes are closed, and if she didn't have hold of her staff, I believe she wouldn't still be standing. Her guards step forward and usher her out of the bedroom and back into the living room. The bird remains on her shoulder; its head under its wing.

On the bed is the large black wolf form of my brother. He continues to lie motionless. "Maverick?" Brandon's mate calls doubtfully. "Is that really you? Is he breathing?" she asks, as she rushes to their bed, eager to ensure her mate is still alive. Deacon recovers faster than me. Unsteadily, he stands and aids Soraya, checking the wolf that lies stricken on the bed.

"He's breathing. He's alive but he is completely out of it. A forced shift will do that!" Deacon assures the distraught mate of our brother, who climbs onto the bed to get closer to him. As the healers approach the bed, looking for permission to intervene, Deacon holds his hand out to Soraya, encouraging her to leave Maverick's side while the healers continue to check him over.

The soft cries of the baby remind me that both her and Fallon are still here. "What the fudge just happened, Euan?" Fallon questions me with a shocked expression.

"I honestly do not know. But I sure hope we find out." We all stand together and await the verdict from the healers. While we wait, I whisper to my little sister. "Fudge?"

Fallon shifts uncomfortably on the spot, avoiding eye contact. "Well, we'll all have to watch our language now, won't we?" she says as she affectionately strokes the head of our niece. A genuine smile, filled with love and hope, spreads across her face as she looks adoringly at the little girl we knew nothing about. "We can't have the Princess of Werewolves developing a potty mouth. No, we will raise her to be a proper little lady."

In the short span of a few minutes, Fallon has transformed before my very eyes from a petulant child to a doting pseudo-parent. It's a role that I swear she was born to have for never have I seen such a look of love and contentment before.

~ Soraya ~

The whole world is spinning out of control, and after all we've been through, it is beginning to feel overwhelming. My Brandon is dying, and if he does, then why the hell would I want to stay alive? No matter what I nor the healers do, he rapidly declines in health, and I worry for his mortality. My pup will grow without a home, a pack and, most importantly, a father if I lose him.

As Bran writhes in agony on our new bed, another treatment failing to heal him, I go to the building commotion just outside our apartment door. Waves of relief wash over me as I drink in the sight of Fallon and her brothers; they will help us, I'm no longer alone.

The next coherent thought I have is how on earth did I get back inside? And why am I lying down on the sofa? Bran is dying, damnit. I cannot lose my head right now. His gut-wrenching screams of pain spur me into action; he's in there alone and he needs me.

However, the door will not open. I push against it with all my might, and as soon as the door bursts open, a gust of wind almost knocks me off my feet, and a wall of gold and green swirls in front of me. It takes a few moments before I realise Brandon, or is it Maverick, are floating above the bed in what must be some black sorcery.

"What's happening? Brandon? BRANDON?" I look at the creature chanting as my mate floats in the air. Her eyes are blank, white orbs. She is going to kill him! I try to push against her to knock her off course or break her trance, but it's as though there is a forcefield around her. The woman looks vaguely familiar, but with her unusual white hair and empty eyes, I surely would have remembered her if I had met her before. "Stop it, you're killing him. She's going to kill him. Please stop. I need him, I love him. BRANDON!" I shout as I finally make it to the side of the bed that he floats precariously above, just as a robust and dazzling light, emanating from Brandon, blasts us all to the ground. Dazed and shaky, I crawl back to the bed and find Brandon in his wolf form. "Maverick? Is that really you?"

Relief washes over me, he hasn't lost his wolf after all, and when I check him over, he is breathing and his wound appears to have healed.

The healers ask for permission to approach Brandon once again, which I permit, but I keep a close eye on the newcomer, not knowing if I can trust her. Now that I have time to think, it crosses my mind that she could be the Queen, but if so, why does she look so strange? In comparison to Fallon, I can see a similarity apart from the odd features that seem so prominent. When I look at Fallon again, I realise she is holding a baby. A little girl it seems from the dress she wears, a cute little thing with golden brown skin and bright, captivating green eyes.

"Lieutenant Brandon is stable for now. As you can see, his wolf form has been restored. He will probably shift back once he wakes. He's been through a lot, and so we advise that you let him sleep for now." The healers begin to pack up their belongings, evidently happy with the recovery Brandon is making. "We have left the medicines he will need on the counter in the bathroom. If you need any further help, please summon us."

I thank them for their efforts, as I show them out, and when I return to my living room, I listen to the siblings of my mate as they talk amongst themselves.

"Why did the wolfsbane affect Bran like that?"

"How did you heal him?"

"What kind of creature is that bird?"

"How often do babies need changing?"

However, I have some long overdue questions I want to be answered too.

"Are you the Queen?" I ask outright. Fallon's eyes widen, and Deacon stands to allow me to sit down.

"She is the Queen. She was reborn from Alessia, and this is Alessia's daughter, Jada."

While I absorb the information, I coo at the child. She is so sweet and pure. "So she's Alessia then?"

"I am using Alessia's form as my vessel, as was always intended. I still have all her memories and recall; I still possess some of her physical features and attributes. But the spirit of Alessia is in the Promised Lands."

"And the child?" I ask. The poor little mite is an orphan.

"Will be raised as my daughter, the Princess of Werewolves, as thanks to Alessia for her sacrifice. However, she will need the rest of her family to raise and protect her. I will declare Brandon the Alpha of Utopia as of now, and you will, of course, be sworn in as his Luna. This is the humble beginnings of your new pack."

Brandon is Alpha after all, just not where he thought he would be, and now I will become the Luna of Utopia. What a daunting prospect.

"So our new pack will be what? Utopia?"

"You will become the Utopian Pack. You are the Utopian wolves now. That much has always been known. Before I go back to rest, I need to talk to you all about The Reverent Moon." The mood immediately lowers, and anxiety ebbs and flows between each person sitting in the room. "Clayton is now Alpha, and his number one priority is seeking revenge for his lost eye. Fallon, you are, of course, his main target. You do not leave Utopian grounds without permission. Do you understand?"

We all turn to look at Fallon, expecting her to object. However, she surprises us all with her easy acceptance of her ground rules. "I understand. I have to stay safe so I can look after Jada."

"That's right. Euan, Clayton is not finished with you. He is still seeking retribution for embarrassing him and assisting Brandon in bringing Alessia to safety. Deacon, he knows you helped Fallon escape. He has placed a bounty on your head, and you are wanted dead or alive. You have been expelled from the Bastion of Worship and no longer hold the position of Shaman."

Unable to hold back my outrage on behalf of Deacon, who has been nothing but pleasant and meek, I gasp and cover my mouth. However, Deacon smiles widely at the news. "Good. I wanted them to know it was me. I hope my deception hurts them. I haven't even started yet." His attitude takes me aback; he has always been so gently spoken and placid. It's a shock to hear him like this. "The way they hurt my mate will look like child's play when I am finished."

A shiver of dread runs through me. I obviously missed the memo on Deacon's mate being killed by the Alpha or Clayton. Perhaps she was tortured like me? My heart breaks for Deacon, for his mate and my anger at what they have taken away from him.

"Soraya, I wanted to wait for Brandon to be awake before I gave you this news. I'm afraid your family has been detained for questioning. As far as I know, they are being held in the dungeons, and the little ones have been sent to the orphanage."

My family. My poor, innocent family. I try my best to keep my composure, but with the extra hormones from my pregnancy already playing havoc with my emotions, I almost split apart at the seams with the hurt and guilt I feel inside. "Shhh, don't cry, Luna. You have to think of your baby too. We'll get them out, and we'll make my father and Clayton pay for what they've done." As Euan comforts me, I realise they all know about my pregnancy. "What about our mother? I couldn't get her to leave; she wouldn't come with me."

"I'm so sorry. Your mother died shortly after returning home. Your father took her throat for being a traitor. That is why Clayton is Alpha. Your father weakened himself in a moment of uncontrolled rage." It is now my turn to support them. Fallon openly cries and Deacon paces in rage. The baby, sensing Fallon's upset, wails too. Euan sits back in his seat, open-mouthed with shock.

"He killed her. He fucking killed her, and now I will take his throat. She deserved so much better than him. She wasn't even his. He took her because he could and did nothing but abuse and mistreat her all this time. I'm going to fucking destroy them!" As Deacon rages, barely containing his wolf, I take the baby from Fallon, while she and Euan lean on each other.

The baby looks at me curiously, grabbing on to my hair with a chubby hand. It's hard to believe that very soon Bran and I will have a baby of our own. Thinking of Brandon reminds me that this is his mother too; when he wakes, he is going to be heartbroken.

"What we need to do now is unite you all again. I am declaring Brandon the Alpha of the Utopian pack. He is already aware of my intention. Will you kneel before your brother and become the first members of his pack?" I nod my head immediately. Euan gets to his feet, and Deacon doesn't reply but simply walks to

Brandon's bedside, where we all follow him. "The sooner we form the pack, the stronger you'll be."

Deacon nods his head before adding stoically, "As long as vengeance is part of Brandon's plan, he'll always have my loyalty and support." Although the wolf form of my mate doesn't make a sound, he thumps his tail against the bed, making me believe that he has just agreed to his brother the only way he can.

Chapter Twenty Three

~ Soraya ~

The Queen, although she appears less sure and nowhere near as strong as she did the last time she was in this room, stands at the foot of the bed. Her bird obediently follows her, and one by one, the remaining Ward siblings file in behind her. Handing the baby back to Fallon, I sit on the edge of the bed and stroke Maverick as he sleeps. I miss Brandon desperately and pray he wakes soon; I need him and so does our child. We only have each other now. My mother and sisters are in prison, and Brandon's mother is dead at the hands of her own mate. It's all gruesome and scary, and I don't want to face it without him.

When the Queen requests us to kneel facing our Alpha, we all follow her instruction without hesitation. She mutters some words, some coherent and others not so much. "With the power that resides in this vessel, I form the Utopian Wolves Pack. I charge Alpha Brandon Ward with leading this pack. To pledge your allegiance to your new Alpha and pack, cut your palm and make your blood oath to Brandon now." One of the Queen's guards steps forward and makes a small incision on Maverick's paw. He passes the small knife to Deacon, who cuts across his palm before kneeling to Maverick and making his blood pledge. He smiles as a new mark appears on his forearm to show his status as a Utopian wolf. Euan goes next, repeating the process, and flexing his arm to show us all his new mark. The two brothers eagerly try out their new mindlink.

"It works. Goddess, I never knew how much I would miss you all prattling in my head!" Euan says good naturedly. "Hurry up, little sis. I miss you sassing me," he teases Fallon, who passes the baby for me to hold. I shiver as she slices across her palm, but Fallon hardly bats an eyelid. She kneels before Brandon, and a lump rises in my throat as she makes her oath to her brother. They've come full circle. Fallon would never pledge her loyalty unless she believed in the cause. The fact that up until a few days ago Fallon suspected her brother and refused to trust him made me doubt whether she would declare for Brandon. The ease at which she does it confirms that she now trusts her brother and we can move on.

Fallon shows me her new mark, displaying her forearm with pride, before lifting the baby back into her arms. As the final person in our circle, I pick up the knife and make a small incision along the crease in my palm, the blood draws immediately, oozing down my fingers and spilling onto the bedspread. I quickly drop to my knees and place my hand on Mavericks paw; his fur is now matted with everyone else's blood.

"I, Soraya Burke, the fated mate of Alpha Brandon Ward, pledge my loyalty to him and our pack, the Utopian Wolves. I will serve you, keep your secrets and protect your back. Our pack will be our family from now and until the end of time." As I finish giving my oath, a warmth spreads from the point where my cut and Mavericks connect. As though it is in our veins, our bond reignites, and the same mark the others got appears on my forearm too.

Welcome to the Utopian Wolves, Raya! Fallon murmurs inside my head, confirming that the mindlink between us all is restored.

Bran? Can you hear me? I ask as I try communicating with my sleeping mate. "Brandon? Maverick, wake up, please. I want to speak to Brandon." When he doesn't respond, panic builds up inside me, making my chest feel tight and constricted. *Brandon, please talk to me. Let me know you are okay,* I add desperately.

Sweet, I'm here. But I'm trapped. I can't shift back. In the pursuit of saving Brandon's wolf, we forgot to preserve his human side. And not knowing what the Queen's powers are capable of, I don't know if he'll ever be able to shift back. *Don't tell them yet please, Soraya. I couldn't bear to hear you worried and suffering. Let Maverick just sleep for now.*

I'm frightened. I need you, Brandon. How can you be the Alpha if you can't shift back?

Shhhhh, my sweet, sweet girl. Maybe, once Maverick has slept, I will be able to take back control.

Now we have all been inducted into the new pack, I crawl onto the bed next to Maverick. Exhaustion takes over. My body is changing because of my pregnancy, and the past few days have been challenging. I have no more capacity to endure. I just want to lie in my bed with my mate and forget everything else. The rest of the group must leave. They are probably exhausted too and filled with excitement to see their new home.

When I wake in the night, it upsets me that it's Maverick and not Brandon here. Maverick is wonderful in his own way, but I miss being held in Brandon's strong arms. I miss kissing him and making love to him. I miss us.

When I wake the following morning, I am groggy from too much sleep, and my body aches in places that have never ached before. Feeling across the bed, I notice for the first time that I am alone. Sitting up abruptly, I find Maverick waiting next to the bed.

"Can you shift back, yet?" I ask him, but Maverick simply tilts his head to the side, his ear flopping over as he does, making him look incredibly cute. "Maverick? Is Brandon there? Can I talk to Brandon?"

No. You can talk to me. As the voice of my mate's wolf fills my head, my eyes widen in confusion. Where is Brandon?

Maverick? Please tell me, where is Brandon?

Sick, healing, needs to rest. Let's go out and run! I want to scream in frustration as the wolf form of my mate drops a ball on my bed and then chases his own tail, laughing in my head as he does. He is huge, and his big bulky body sends my belongings crashing to the ground.

"Maverick, stop. Slow down!" I shout to him, but with his tongue lolling out, drooling, he pounces on the bed next to me, causing my whole body to bounce a couple of times before I can steady myself. "What are you doing?" I shout at him, holding on for dear life.

Let's mate, baby cakes. I've been dreaming about you. I jump off the bed in horror. What the hell has gotten into him?

"No. I can't shift; Pandora won't be around for a couple more months. I'm carrying a baby, remember?" I expected Maverick to be crestfallen, but he lies out on my bed, stretching his mammoth size until his head rolls backward.

I'm game if you are! Maverick adds, before lifting his head and looking at me.

"BAD DOG! Get down and get out of my room. If you want to act like a dog, I will treat you like one... There must be a leash around here somewhere!" I shout at him. I need him to see that while he is in wolf form, I am in charge.

No, no. Don't leash me. I'll be a good boy. I promise. As he jumps off the bed, his ball rolls off too, slowly at first, but after the initial bounce, it bounds off into the other room, and unable to resist, Maverick chases after it. *Mine, it's mine, my ball!*

I've temporarily lost my mate and gained an oversized, horny dog with the attention span of a gnat!

⟶⟩⟩·⟩·●·●·●·⟨·⟨⟨·⟵

It's a challenge to get Maverick to cooperate. He is over-excitable and easily distracted. His mind at the moment is very one dimensional. He wants to mate with me, and he wants to go for a run. Neither of which I can cater for, because I cannot shift into Pandora; it's too dangerous now that my baby is growing. Our basic kitchen has essential food, but I cannot calm Maverick for long enough to prepare myself something to eat. Eventually, I decide to accompany him on a walk around our new home.

Utopia is outstandingly beautiful, and with Brandon being ill when we arrived, we didn't get a chance to explore, but Maverick is the perfect companion for exploring with. After he sniffs and examines every stone in the courtyard, he gallops towards the open meadow that sits in the shade of the large tower. He cocks up his leg and pees up a large oak tree that seems to erupt from the ground very randomly. Upon closer inspection, I can see that the signature gold and jade from the rest of the kingdom runs like vines throughout the bark of the tree.

Maverick is completely oblivious to me at times. He chases the butterflies and the little gold and green birds that glow as they float and hum in the air above us. Other times, he doesn't leave my side, sticking to me like Velcro and almost tripping me up by sneaking up on me. He brings me dandelions in his mouth, the stems all serrated and snapped and the heads wilting, but the gesture is so sweet and heartfelt that it almost feels as though Maverick is channelling Brandon. The uncertainty weighing on me, I sit in the middle of the meadow while I contemplate a future with no Brandon. What if he's stuck as his wolf version forever. I love Maverick, of course I do, but I need Brandon too. I already miss him immensely, and the little reminders of his personality seem to impact the sense of loss even more.

Sensing my unhappiness, Maverick returns to me once more, nudging me with his nose and rubbing his cheek against my arm and leg. "I'm sorry, Maverick. I miss Brandon. I miss him so much, and I'm worried about what will happen if he doesn't return to me."

You have me. You are mine, too. I know the human can hold your hand and make you food. But I can look after you too. Almost on key, two guards begin to approach us, and Maverick makes his displeasure at their presence known. Baring his teeth, his hackles raise as he growls menacingly at the two men, who initially take no notice of him. However, Maverick stands in front of me, protective of both me and our pup, and within seconds, both men submit to him.

Tell them, I will kill them if they even look at you, Maverick tells me through our mindlink. *Tell them you are mine.* I giggle at him until he stares at me, and under his intense scrutiny, I not only stop, but I shudder in fear of what lengths he would go to so that he could ensure my safety.

Unsure of how to assure Maverick, I scratch behind his ears and kiss him on the tip of his nose. *I am yours because I choose to be. I couldn't care less if they look at me. I'm going home with you.* He closes his eyes and presses his head against mine. "How can we help you, gentlemen?" I say, addressing the guards at long last.

"The Queen has requested the Alpha and his Luna's presence in the throne room. The pack are ready to declare their allegiance to you both." My heart sinks when I realise everyone is going to expect Brandon to make an appearance, not Maverick.

Come on, baby cakes. You'll have to do the talking, though! Maverick tells me cheerfully as he tugs on my sleeve with his teeth. *Want to jump on and I'll carry you?* But with the memory of the last time I was on his back as we escaped our former pack still fresh in my memory, I decline, favouring to walk by his side instead.

We arrive at what I presume to be the throne room, and the soldiers open the doors. I recognise the uniforms as the same as the ones that are hanging in Brandon's wardrobe, only Brandon's has stars on the epaulettes. I get a shock as Maverick and I enter the throne room. Not only are we announced, but the rest of the pack turns to applaud us when we do.

"Alpha Brandon and Luna Soraya of the Utopian Wolves pack," the guard announces to the waiting pack. On the stage next to the Queen, Deacon, Euan, and Fallon stand proudly in their uniforms of red, green and black. Upon seeing Brandon and I, the siblings barrage us with mindlinked questions.

Why is he still in wolf form? Euan asks first.

However, Fallon is outraged and completely ignores Euan's question to put her own to us. *How come he gets to attend as a wolf, and I had to put this horrible uniform on?*

He looks strong, Deacon adds, relief evident in his stance. *Can we still do the ceremony if he's in wolf form?*

Overwhelmed by all the questions and commotion, I don't know who to answer first. I stall at the door and despite Maverick tugging on my sleeve, I don't budge an inch.

Baby cakes? Come on, they're waiting for us, Maverick encourages me but I shake my head. *What's the problem?*

As my chest tightens and my breathing labours, I contemplate running the hell out of here. *They aren't waiting for us, Maverick. They are waiting for Alpha Brandon and his Luna. I have no idea how to be a Luna, Maverick. I can't do this without Brandon.*

The last thing I want is to hurt Maverick. I love him, and he is awesome in his own way, but I need Brandon, too. The uncertainty of the future, a future where Brandon isn't present, is more than I can take. What if he never comes back? How can Maverick and I lead a pack with neither one of us knowing what to do.

Trust me. Please. Trust me. I'm an Alpha wolf and Brandon is coming back. He's getting stronger by the second. He pulls me along, and I take two steps further into the hall. Everything is completely silent, and you would hear a pin drop. *Brandon says to tell you he's never going to leave you, Sweet Soraya. You can do this. He knew it from the moment he saw you dishing out food down at the Huts. You were born to be a Luna. You have always been our Luna.*

I know they are Brandon's words, and that gives hope that he is still in there, healing, recovering, and resting just like Maverick told me. This gives me faith that he is coming back to me, and that I have to keep things going for him until he can return to me. With renewed purpose and optimism, I scratch behind Mavericks ears again before walking by his side towards the stage. I can do this, I repeat to myself. I have to do this for myself, my pup, my mate and for the pack and family who continue to live under a reign of terror.

This isn't an option, this is fate, destiny. I am and have always been Brandon's Luna, and I am not going to let him down today. When I reach the stage, I turn to face the crowd. The Queen stands and her voice reverberates around the hall.

"Bow and pledge your allegiance to your Alpha and Luna. In my name, join the Utopian Wolves pack."

In unison the pack all bow to us, and as each werewolf bares his or her neck to us, it forms an unbreakable bond until I am filled with the strength of my pack.

I look out at my pack, which is already two hundred warriors strong, and with my own child growing inside me, I know there are many more to join us. The Queen is no longer in hiding and has told me she has to unite the Alphas and that the Utopian Wolves will be instrumental in the freedom of the Reverent Moon Wolves. It is clear, as I accept my new reign as Luna, that the story is just beginning. My story is only just beginning.

Epilogue

~ Soraya ~

Time seems to move by quickly. There is always so much to do, and as a new Luna, I barely have time to think. Without Brandon's support, I feel all alone in Utopia, both with leading the pack and especially as my pregnancy progresses. He is missing everything, and I hate that I must do this alone. Well, not completely on my own. I do have Maverick, the great big oaf that he is.

Loving Maverick is hard work. He is messy, loud and erratic. I have thrown him out of our new apartment on several occasions. A couple of times, I've told him not to come back without Brandon being able to shift and then cried myself to sleep at my own callous and stubborn behaviour. I know it isn't Maverick's fault, he is being true to his nature. I just miss Brandon so much. Over time, Brandon's consciousness has become clearer, and we can now communicate through our mindlink for very short periods of time. He tells me that Maverick is channelling him in the same way he could channel Maverick when he was in human form. He uses the time to snuggle up to me, resting Maverick's chin on my tummy and watching in awe as our pup kicks and squirms inside me. We talk about mundane things, and he praises me for my work with our new pack and reminds me to rest and look after myself until he can return to me and do it himself.

Every time he fades away, I miss him even more. It breaks my heart that our child may never know its daddy, and it becomes a constant worry of mine of how I will have a newborn and Maverick in the same place. Maverick won't intentionally hurt our pup, but he doesn't seem to have any idea of how big and strong he is. How can I provide my pup with a safe and harmonious home when his daddy is stuck in his wolf form and likes to run about!

It just seems impossible.

This afternoon, my labour pains begin, and while everyone is at hand to help make this as easy as possible, I don't want anyone else. I want my mama and Brandon. My losses pile up around me, as I sweat and groan through my contractions. I barricade the door and damn the world for taking the people I love away from me. The pains overwhelm me, rendering me utterly helpless, and just when I think I can take no more, I hear his voice. I must be hallucinating; I'm sure I read in one of the textbooks that pain during labour can increase the likelihood of suffering hallucinations. This must be it.

"Sweet, please let me in. I don't know how much time I have. Let me help you," his voice calls to me, and it has been such a long time since I heard his voice, his proper voice, that I burst out into tears. How could the Goddess be so mean to torment me with the one thing I long for most of all. "Soraya, please open the door," he shouts again.

Realising that I cannot do this alone and without help, I crawl to the door and let in whoever is banging on it. When I see my mate staring back at me, I scream. "Bran?"

"I'm here, I'm here. Though I'm not sure for how long until I shift back. I can already feel myself weakening." He kisses me and then lifts me from the ground, just as another contraction ravages my body. I twist, spasm and groan in pain. When I feel the pressure building between my legs and in my back passage, just like the healers told me, I know it's time.

"Set me down. The baby is coming now," I tell him, and he dutifully listens to me, then quickly makes me comfortable. "I can't believe you're here, what happened?" I ask, as I stroke his face, partly because I miss how it feels and partly to ensure that he is real.

He captures my hand and kisses it. "I knew you needed me, and you locked everyone out. Eventually, I got mad enough to shift. I've missed you, Sweet. I miss us, and I'm so glad I'm not going to miss our child being born."

I groan as I bear down, pushing with all my might. "You're just in time, Brandon." It hurts, burns almost, and I swear I am splitting in two as I feel my baby's head crowning.

Brandon rushes between my knees and looks under my skirt. "I can see his head, oh my Goddess. Its real, a real baby's head." The idiot!

"Well, I've not been growing a cabbage, Brandon. Ow! It hurts. It hurts so much," I cry out. And through his laughter at my retort and his growing concern for me, he kisses my hands and looks at me with love and pride.

"Do you feel another pain? The healer said to push with the pain." I nod to him. The pain is almost constant now, but the waves of high and low let me know when the timing is right. "One more push and we'll have a baby, Soraya. Goddess, I love you so much."

Moaning as I push with all my remaining strength, I let my body lead me. Through all the pain and the uncertainty, my baby has been my one constant. My one reason to keep moving forward. As my baby leaves my body rather abruptly, I fall back in exhaustion.

"It's a boy. Sweet, look, we have a son. A perfect little boy." Brandon cradles our pup to his chest and weeps tears of happiness as he kisses both me and our little boy, who cries loudly. "He looks like me," he says, as he strokes the baby's black, curly hair. It's hard to see if he looks like Brandon. He certainly has similar hair, and his skin, although slightly lighter, is similar in shade too. Once Brandon hands my baby to me, I show him where the baby blankets are. He quickly fetches one and takes back our pup so he can wrap him up.

"He's perfect. Our perfect Alpha Heir," I remind Brandon, and he kisses me once more. "I don't have a name for him," I confess. With everything that has been happening, I haven't been able to concentrate or commit to anything. It all felt so wrong without Brandon's input.

"I've had a lot of time to think. I think we should call him Braydon. It's a mix of both our names." As he looks down at our boy, his face full of love and pride, I know it's the right name. With another kiss on our baby's head, he whispers I love you to his son, before handing him back to me.

"I love it. Alpha Heir Braydon Ward of the Utopian Wolves," I say, but our time is up; his wolf Maverick sits where he once was. This time I don't cry, for I know one day, one day soon, my mate will come back for me and our son. "Look Maverick, it's a boy," I tell him as I hold Braydon out for him to see.

My pup! he links excitedly. *I have a pup!* He licks Braydon's hand and rubs the side of his head against the blanket he is swaddled in, before licking my face and rubbing his whole body against my arm. *Well done, baby cakes. You whelped well. I'm so proud of you.*

The healers arrive, and Maverick growls at them. *Tell them to settle down; they will disturb my pup!* he links to me. I have a feeling this is going to be okay after all. Maverick's paternal instincts have taken over and now he is in full on father mode. I'm sure his playful, almost childlike, nature will come out every now and again, but with the way he looks at his pup and the protectiveness he is showing, I know both me and our boy have never been in safer hands, or rather paws.

^ *Two Years Later* ^

In the dark, basement room of the pack house, a single light flickers, as a female bears down, bringing forth life in this gloomiest of places. "One more push, Luna. One more big push and your baby will be here." As sweat beads on her head, the Luna bites on the rag between her teeth and pushes with all her might. Only her and the midwife are here; her Alpha mate forbade the presence of anyone else. He took the option of waiting outside, saying it is no place for a man to be. "That's it Luna, almost there," the midwife calls to her, and with a final whimper, the baby finally slithers out. "It's a girl, Luna," the midwife mumbles to her Luna, forewarning her of the trouble that will surely come.

The wails of the mother ring out alongside the gentle mews of the new-born, a perfect pink bundle with ten fingers and ten toes. "Not again!" she cries. "Not again." The Alpha hears the child's cries that heartily announce its arrival into the world and finally comes to see what he's been blessed with. "Please don't be mad at me! It's not my fault," the mother pleads with the Alpha. However, the Alpha is enraged.

He pulls open the towel that swaddles his child, looking between its legs. "Another girl? Another fucking girl?" he spits out at her in an uncontrolled rage.

"I'm sorry! I'm so sorry," the woman apologises profusely. "We can try again. I will give you your son, I promise. I won't let you down again," she cries out, while blood oozes from between her legs. The birth hadn't been easy and despite her werewolf healing powers and super strength, she will need time to fully recover.

Her young body has been ravaged by childbirth, but she will be given no sympathy from the Alpha, not when she has brought him yet another daughter. "You know the rules, Brianna," the Alpha replies. "Being the Luna does not excuse you from these rules. In fact, I depend on you to uphold the rules. You have let me and the pack down once again." Without casting his mate and child another glance, he storms from the room. Disappointment drips from his mere presence. All he has ever wanted is a son. Someone to carry on his legacy and his family's heritage, but the stupid bitch he is mated to has just delivered his second daughter.

Once he has returned to the main floor, his team remains assembled. His Beta wolf, Taylor, steps forward jovially, ready to congratulate his Alpha; however, a quick glance at the thunderous look on his Alpha's face confirms what they had all been dreading. The baby is another girl. "Congratulations on your daughter, Alpha. I'm sure she'll make a perfect Lady of the Veil," Taylor adds quickly, not wanting to further provoke his Alpha's toxic rage.

The Alpha addresses his men, making no mention of the babe, but dismissing them all, except his Beta. "Taylor, you know what to do. She must be punished for not doing her duty. Forty lashes should do it for now." Beta Taylor looks uncomfortable, for he does not relish the thought of punishing his delicate Luna. Nevertheless, he cannot deny the Alpha's command.

The Beta reluctantly trudges down the steps to the dungeon, wondering why the Alpha insisted on such a dank and dire place for his mate to deliver his child. She deserves so much more than this, her own comfortable bed with a team of skilled healers and her mother would be a start. He knocks and waits for permission to enter. Although he doesn't look directly at the women in the room, he can see the vestiges of her labours. The smell of blood and desperation are both strong here.

"Beta Taylor, did the Alpha send you?" the Luna asks him, fear and reluctance evident in her voice and expression. He hates that he is the face of her woe. If the Alpha wants his mate punished, he should do it himself.

"Come on, Luna Brianna," he whispers to her. "Give your baby to the nurse. She'll be well looked after here." He watches as the Luna hands the swaddled baby back to the nurse. "Did you give her a name yet?" he adds, trying to distract the distraught, tiny Luna.

"Arabelle. Her name is Arabelle."

"That's a beautiful name for the Alpha's daughter."

The Luna plasters a tight smile across her face in reply. Deep down, she knows until she gives the Alpha the son he desperately desires, her life is in danger and so is the life of her daughters. Only eight months ago, she delivered another fine, healthy pup. Another girl she called Bonnie, who quickly became the light of her life. Though she had been warned she would be punished if she didn't deliver a boy, she never really appreciated how dedicated her mate, his father and some of the Elders would be to the sentence. She was lashed continually until she was with child again. The dread of producing another daughter had all but taken the joy from her life. It was supposed to be a happy time, but the dread of possibly not producing a son for her mate all but stifled the delight she should have been feeling to be expecting again.

It has been less than two years since she found her fated mate. Despite her dreams of the future, the reality with the Alpha is so far removed from what she ever envisioned. He is cruel and unyielding. He is hell bent on revenge. He treats his mate without any compassion. It does not matter to him what she wants or what she needs. All that matters to him is that he has a son.

The little Luna follows Beta Taylor out of the dungeons. She pauses only once, grunting in agony as her afterbirth separates from her body. It falls to the floor with a splatter, but she does not stop for too long, knowing her mate will only make his Beta punish her much harder.

"My Luna, I'm so sorry for what I must do. I must follow my Alpha's command." The Luna nods her head in acceptance.

"I know, Taylor. I know. I promise next time I'll do all I can to ensure I give our Alpha a boy." Taylor knows she has no control over it and the Alpha's anger at her is misdirected and extreme.

"Yes, my Lady. Now please remove your gown and place your hands on the plinth in front of you." She follows his instructions, cringing that he must see her body at all, never mind straight after the birth of her child. "May the Moon Goddess forgive me for what I am about to do."

The Alpha returns to his office. His former Alpha father waits inside for his son to bring his news. "How is my grandson?" he asks pompously. He is already smoking a celebratory cigar and drinking whiskey from a crystal glass.

"Get out, father. I'm not in the mood!" His father sits back in his chair and sips at his whisky.

"Don't tell me it's another girl?" his father says in disgust, and the alpha nods his head grimly in reply.

"Another fucking girl. What the hell am I supposed to do with another girl?" he asks his father desperately.

"How many lashes did you give her?" his Father asks, hatred and anger rolling off him.

"Forty," the Alpha replies, as he takes a seat next to his father.

"Good boy," the Alpha's father praises proudly, "she needs to know her place. I will go and give her another forty lashes myself in the morning, and you should give her one lash for every pack member she has let down. She is a disappointment to us all. You cannot pass on this pack to a female; they're of little use to us."

The Alpha contemplates his father's words. "Would a bastard have a claim?" the Alpha muses, to his father's chagrin.

"No!" his father answers sternly. "No fucking bastard is taking over my pack. That useless girl will give you a son, or I'll fucking kill her and get you a mate that will. Even your brother has managed to produce a son and heir. The rumours say they're expecting a second."

The Alpha frowns in dissatisfaction. "I reckon they're not even his pups. His mate is a stuck up, little slut." His father laughs at his opinion, riling the Alpha. "Have you had any luck locating my brothers and sister?" the Alpha asks in annoyance.

His father shakes his head. "Not a Dickie Bird. The Trackers and the Scouts have been as far out as the Edge looking. No one is willing to talk to us." The Alpha slams down his glass, and it shatters, shards fly across the room.

"They can't just vanish! You are *trying* to find them, aren't you father?" The Alpha's father stands and faces his second born son menacingly.

"Of course, I'm trying to find them!" he shouts defensively. "For the past two years, I have served you loyally by trying to find the bastards. I brought our pack into disrepute. For two years I've been trying to clear your name after the vile insinuations your sister made about you. For the past two years, I've tried my best to give you justice for what was done to you. Back then we said we would do whatever it took to get revenge." The alpha nods back at his father, self-consciously touching his eye patch. A movement that doesn't go unmissed by his father. "We always said: an eye for an eye."

"I was just ensuring you haven't lost faith in our cause, that is all," the Alpha replies calmly, hiding how moved he feels by his fathers statement. Justice is taking a long time to be served, but he has always thought that revenge is best served cold. When his siblings least expect it, when they think the past is forgotten and the danger has passed, he will tear their world apart. Once he is finished, they will scream in agony and know deep in their bones, they should never have messed with Clayton Ward.

"I will never lose faith in our cause. I named you my heir; I have complete trust in you. Now do your duty and put a son in your mate. The Alpha grins and rubs his face once again, before removing an eye patch that he favours to wear.

"I am trying, father. She just keeps spitting out girls". He lifts his head and catches a glimpse of himself in a photo frame that hangs on the wall and sees what is under the patch. Even after all this time, it still comes as a shock when he catches a glimpse of his ruined face, a memento of the night he became Alpha. A hole where his eye once was and a twisted scar for company. His mangled face was the driving force, the physical evidence and incentive he needed to wage war on his siblings. Vanity raises its head more than he cares to admit, but there is nothing that can be done.

"I don't know why you bother to wear that patch. You know that the pack and your mate will respect you more once they see how menacing you really are." His father is the only person who would dare talk so nonchalantly about this sensitive subject. "The stupid bitch would spread her legs and bless you with a tribe of sons if you showed her how intimidating you can be. It makes them wet, you know."

The Alpha chuckles. "You mean scare a son into her?" the Alpha asks him curiously. The woman means nothing to him. He has refused to allow himself to be consumed by the Mate Bond and the sentimentality that had seen his brothers turn to dithering idiots. Yes, the tingles and sparks felt nice but so did fucking a Scarlet Woman. Brianna is weak and foolish. He only claimed her because she is the granddaughter of an Elder and she told everyone before he could stop her. Her presence is insufferable with her quietness and genteel ways. The Mating a mere means to an end. Although he did take great pleasure in taking her virginity in front of his father and Elders, and occasionally disrespecting her by commanding her to commit sexual acts in public places where they could be caught. While the thrill excited him, her moaning and outrage simply made him angry.

"Whatever it takes. She'll be healed in a week; I want another pup on the way with a Lunar Cycle. This time, no excuses. You need a son." It rankles that his father had the audacity to make commands on him, but he doesn't challenge him about it. Not when his position remains so tenuous still. But, he will. No one insults Clayton Ward. Not even his father.

The silence doesn't last long, being interrupted by a knock on the office door. "Alpha, come quickly, urgent news from the Trackers!"

-The End-

The Hidden Strength of a Luna

Declared the new Alpha and Luna of the Utopian Wolves Pack, Brandon and Soraya now have a million problems on their plate. Knowing it is only a matter of time before their kingdom is discovered, they must prepare their pack for war.

Maimed and betrayed by his brothers and sister, Clayton will stop at nothing to seek vengeance. Named the new Alpha of the Reverent Moon Pack, he has no qualms about upholding the pack's teachings and values, even when it means mistreating his newly found mate.

Tied to the most powerful and sinister man in the pack, Brianna faces a life of hardship and loneliness.

Will Clayton's siblings come to his mate's aid or will her association with him keep them away? After all, they know all about Clayton's desires for revenge. Or does Brianna have the strength to save herself?

Coming to Amazon 12th January 2024.

Pre order your eBook now: mybook.to/THSoaL

Ward Family

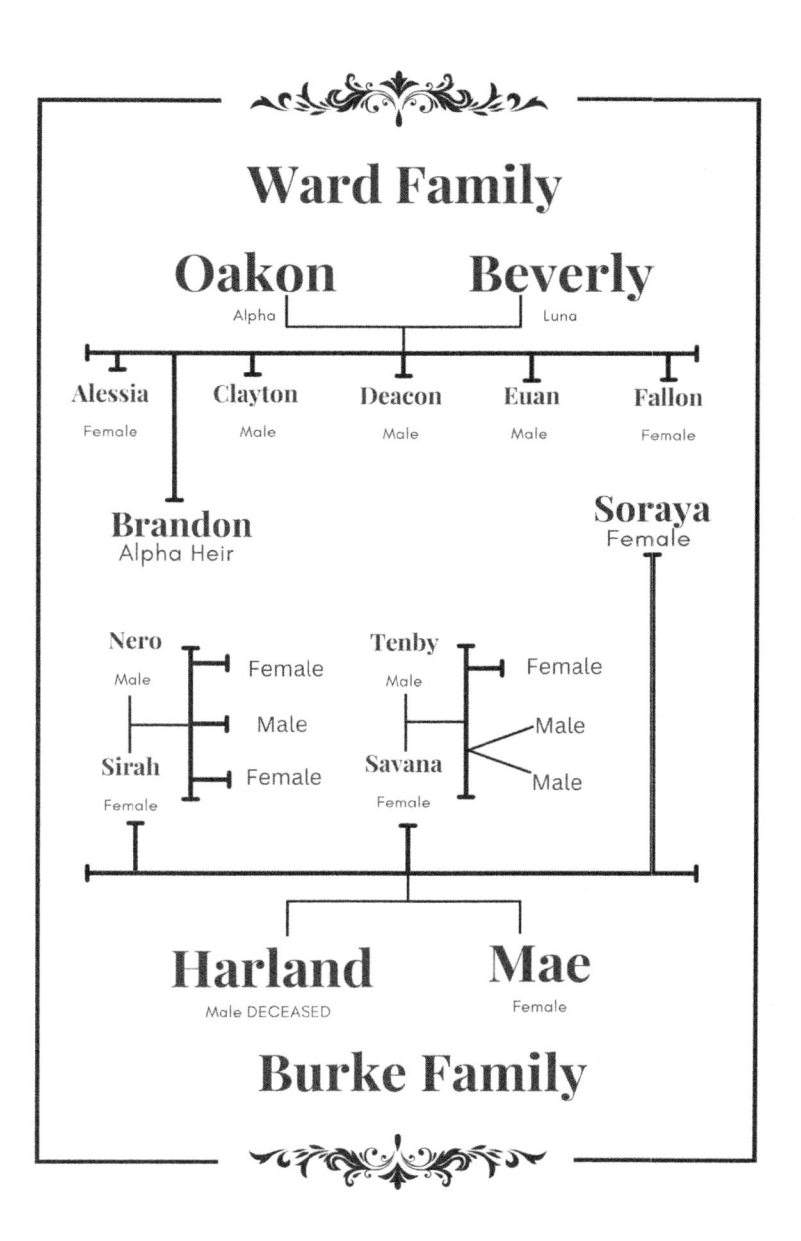

Oakon
Alpha

Beverly
Luna

Alessia
Female

Clayton
Male

Deacon
Male

Euan
Male

Fallon
Female

Brandon
Alpha Heir

Nero — Male
- Female
- Male
- Female

Sirah — Female

Tenby — Male
- Female
- Male
- Male

Savana — Female

Soraya — Female

Harland
Male DECEASED

Mae
Female

Burke Family

Acknowledgments

There are many people I would like to thank for supporting me. In the first instance, my husband and sons for putting up with me, for the copious amounts of tea and for always making me feel happy, loved and secure. You four are my world, My heart will always be yours.

To my castle castell friends. Thank you for keeping me sane and focused and for boosting me when I felt like giving up. Our trip to Chirk is what got this book back on track, and the wine helped too lol. When I felt like abandoning this book, you reminded me why I had to dust myself down and try again. Our joint venture didn't turn out quite as planned but we'll always have castle castell. Equally thank you to the rest of the Dirty Cows you're all awesome, even though you like frog spawn drinks and mouldy milk.

This book would be pointless without readers, and I have been fortunate enough to have plenty of readers who have positively challenged me and supported me in equal doses. A special call out to Ljiljana, Ngawang Chodron and Tiffani for always encouraging me.

To my ARC readers, you're the best! Thanks for reading and giving me feedback. I'll be forever in your debt.

To my friend, Melody, for reminding me of why I started writing.

Last but by no means least, to my amazing editor, Steph. I'm sorry for all the missing commas lol. You are absolutely fantastic and I cannot tell you how much I value you and your stellar red pen skills. Your input into this book, closing plot holes and pushing me to address the things I didn't want to is the reason it transformed from a story into a novel. My gratitude hardly seems enough, but its yours anyway. Thank you, thank you, Thank you from the bottom of my heart.

Many thanks to Chirk Castle for the inspiration and Gallo wine for the TLC oops.

About the Author

About the Author

Emma Lee-Johnson

A happily married mum of three, originally from Liverpool, UK. Now a self-published author of Paranormal, Contemporary and Mafia romances that are hot and sweet!

I am a hopeless romantic, with a gutter mind and a potty mouth, but I promise my heart is pure gold!

Books by this Author include:

- The Alpha's Property

- The Alpha's Heir

- Festive Flings

- More Than Just a Fling

- Festive Wedding

- The Hidden Queen of Alphas

- Substitution Clause

Also By

Emma Lee-Johnson

THE ALPHA'S PROPERTY

Eva: I used to dream about love at first sight and being swept off my feet. Instead, I have a husband who constantly humiliates me and puts me down, and has literally left me stranded at the side of the road. Life seems pretty grim until I walk into the car dealership and the most handsome man I've ever met tells me I belong to him.

Aiden: I've been waiting a long time to meet my mate, and I could never have imagined it would be someone like Eva. She's human, for a start, and she's already married. But dammit, the moment I laid eyes on her I knew I needed her. If there's even a chance for us to be together, I'll do whatever it takes to make her mine.

When Eva and Aiden's worlds collide, it's more than just their relationship at stake: there's Preston, Aiden's Beta, whose mate refuses to commit; Amber, Aiden's sister, whose trust issues prevent her from embracing the happiness her mate bond could bring; Salma, Eva's best friend and a Mafia princess who's being pushed into a marriage to keep her position; Alejandro, Salma's intended who wants a lot more from her than to share her throne; Melanie, whose eyes are gradually opened to the kind of man her lover is; and Ryan, Eva's husband who doesn't want her but doesn't want anyone else to have her too.

Lives intertwine and secrets are revealed as Eva comes to terms with Aiden's claim on her heart and soul: is she really ready to be The Alpha's Property?

Available now on Amazon on ebook, paperback and hardback.

Free to read on Kindle Unlimited.

mybook.to/thealphasproperty

FESTIVE FLINGS

Set in the festive weeks before Christmas and New Year, Festive Flings follows the intertwining romantic lives of 6 people at different stages in their lives and sexual experiences.

Recently dumped Jamie is ready to move on in time for the holidays, unaware that her boss has been secretly pining over her. Their colleague, Tim, meets the woman of his dreams, but her nightmare of a family has left her self-confidence in tatters. And Jamie's sister, Billie, is hoping for a Christmas miracle to rekindle the passion in her marriage, where kink has been replaced with kids.

Fun, fetishes and frolicking combine in an intertwining tale of spicy British romance in the weeks leading up to Christmas.

All you need for Christmas is... a festive fling!

This book is extremely hot and should be read with caution! Reported side effects reported include: involuntary Kegel and spontaneous pantie-wetting incidents. Read at your own risk... And pleasure!

Available now on Amazon

Emma Lee-Johnson

More Than **Just a Fling**

A FESTIVE FLINGS SPINOFF

Owen Matthews believes he is the luckiest man on this earth. He is young, successful, rich, good-looking and now he has landed the woman he has secretly been in love with for years. With Jamie right beside him, he is moving from London to New York City, after being promoted to a lucrative job with lots of perks.

Life couldn't get any better!

But as life often goes, when one thing falls into place, something else falls apart. Being in New York means being closer to his family in Ontario, and with that comes the baggage of the past. Is Owen really ready to commit to Jamie, or is there someone else lurking in the past who still shines a torch for him?

Owen's family is delighted that he is practically back on home soil; after all, New York isn't so far away. Will their expectations and plans for him match up to what his heart wants and needs?

Jamie loves her new life in New York, but she misses her family and friends... and then she starts to miss Owen too. What was the point in being here if she only sees him at work? She makes new friends and starts to find a life outside her relationship with Owen, making her wonder if this is even what she wants anymore?

With both being pulled in opposite directions... one question remains...

Is this More than just a Fling?

Coming soon:

AN ENGLISH ELITE FOOTBALL LEAGUE ROMANCE

SUBSTITUTION
Clause

EMMA LEE-JOHNSON

Leila Monrose has a life many would envy. In her prestigious career as an injury specialist in Elite English Football, she meets interesting people and travels the world. Beautiful and clever, she has a nice car, a stylish home and has made plenty of friends since she moved up north for her job. Sooner or later, someone will come along to share it all with her.

Could it be the younger footballer, Jack Cardal, who Leila helped regain form after a nasty injury? Handsome, rich and confident, Jack always wants what he can't have. When Leila declines his invitation to dinner, he sees it as a challenge.

Or maybe it will be his older brother, billionaire property and technology tycoon-turned-football club investor Nate Cardal, who is a perfect gentleman with a massive skeleton in his closet.

When one brother hurts her, the other helps her seek revenge, but with conditions attached.

In a world of high-stakes contracts, will Leila activate the Substitution Clause?

Kick off: Summer 2023

Emma Lee-Johnson

Romance Author

- https://viewauthor.at/emmaleejohnson
- patreon.com/emmaleejohnson
- instagram.com/author_emma_lee
- tiktok.com/@emmaleejohnson
- facebook.com/profile.php?id=100064632064511

Follow me on social media for exclusive content and updates.

Amazon: viewauthor.at/emmaleejohnson

Patreon.com/emmaleejohnson

Facebook Page: Emma Lee-Johnson

Facebook group: Emma's Angels with Attitude

facebook.com/groups/656345582368378

Instagram author_emma_lee

TikTok.com/@emmaleejohnson

Goodreads Emma Lee-Johnson

Ko-fi.com/emmaleejohnson

Emmalee-johnson.com

linktr.ee/emmaleejohnson

If you have enjoyed reading The Hidden Queen of Alphas, please leave a review.

Thank you for reading!

Copyright © [2023] by [Emma Lee-Johnson]

All rights reserved.

No portion of this book may be reproduced in any form without written permission from the publisher or author, except as permitted by U.S. copyright law.

Cover designed by GetCovers

Edited by Stephanie Cosgrove

Printed in Great Britain
by Amazon